TÏ

BLOOD MOON LEGACY

Blood Moon *(Blood Moon Legacy, #1)*
Wolf Moon *(Blood Moon Legacy, #2)*
Blue Moon *(Blood Moon Legacy, #3)*
Crescent Moon *(Blood Moon Legacy, #1.5)*
Hunter's Moon *(Blood Moon Legacy, #4)*
Snow Moon *(Blood Moon Legacy, #5) (Coming 2018)*

HORSE PLAY SERIES

Horse Play *(Horse Play, #1)*
Chompin' at the Bit *(Horse Play, #2)*
Breaking Rein *(Horse Play, #3)*
Foalin' Around *(Horse Play, #4) (Coming 2018)*
Back in the Saddle *(a Horse Play spinoff) (Coming 2018)*

STANDALONE NOVELS

Remember When
Just a Number
Rm w/a Vu
2 Have & 2 Hold *(A Rm w/a Vu Sequel)*

TANTALIZING TALES FROM GRIMM'S
(a collection of erotic short fairytales)

Snow's White Knight
Beauty & her Beast
No Strings Attached
Siren's Song
Gingerbread Kisses

Hunter's Moon

-A Standalone Blood Moon Legacy Novel-

A.D. RYAN

Ryan, A.D.
Hunter's Moon / A.D. Ryan

(Blood Moon Legacy; 04)

ISBN 978-1546319306

Text and Cover design by Angela Schmuhl
Cover Image: Deposit Photos, © Kantver

"Nothing is more sad than the death of an illusion."
                                    ~*Arthur Koestler*

CONTENTS

ACKNOWLEDGMENTS

As always, there are so many people I want to thank…

To everyone who read the original trilogy and BEGGED for more: this one is for you. I was positively overwhelmed (and honestly feeling the same way) by messages and questions about Jackson and whether or not I'd continue the series beyond the first three. I, myself, had questions about Jackson and needed to know more, so I'm glad readers pushed. You are the reason I am expanding this world (and also for my own peace of mind because this pack just won't leave me alone; Colby is a huge nag right now ;)), and I hope it all lives up to your expectations. I loved getting inside Jackson's head, even if sometimes it hurt my heart.

My rock, my soul mate, my husband, I thank you for being unwaveringly supportive in this crazy dream I had. This last year has been … insane, to say the least, but you never stopped believing in me. I can't begin to tell you just how much that means to me.

I also have some of the best cheerleaders in my children. While my younger two are far too young to read my work, they're way too quick to tell their teachers and any other grown-ups they encounter what their mom does, and it has brought me new readers. ~~They're basically pimps at eight and ten~~ … They're so excited to share my work with others at eight and ten ;)

Sandy and Caroline, I want you to know how truly appreciative I am of all you do, and for always keeping it real when it comes to my books. You're two of my closest friends (though we've never met face-to-face — yet), and I value your opinions, and love you for taking time out of your busy lives to help these books be the best they can be for the rest of the world. No one wants to be told their baby is ugly, but sometimes, I need to be told when something is truly awful or doesn't fit in the storyline, and you're both so good at it.

And lastly, to the rest of my advanced reader team: Thank you for signing up to basically be the test market for my work. I know not everything will be your cup of tea, but your reviews and honest feedback are what drive me to better myself and my craft. You're all so invaluable to me.

Cheers,
    Angela

PROLOGUE | STALKING

The humid summer air clings to everything. A thunderstorm is immanent. Rain hangs overhead, clouds moving around the full moon — the second of the month.

As if one isn't bad enough.

There's been an increase in Lycan activity in the area over the last few months. No one knows the exact reason they're here, which is exactly why it's causing panic. All anyone knows is that people are being attacked and turned.

Normally, werewolves wandering around isn't a big deal. Most of them typically stick to hunting animals, but sometimes, select individuals — usually purebloods — hunt humans. Some innocents die for the Lycan's sport, while others are merely bitten. Those bitten will usually turn by the next full moon. Turning humans, while frowned upon, isn't exactly against their laws. What's most concerning is the sheer number of attacks.

At several wolf bites a week, this is a blatant attempt to increase their numbers, and it has become more obvious that whoever is behind it is building their own pack...or an army. With this many new wolves automatically comes the increased risk of human casualties since new Lycans are a lot more hostile and unpredictable. They have yet to understand what's happening to them or how to control it, and they haven't yet been taught to live amongst humans.

From the shadows, a couple approaches. The woman looks terrified, staring around the park as she sidles up to the man. She's seen the news, read the papers. The man only laughs, the sound carrying toward the trees.

"You're too paranoid," he tells her. "There hasn't been an attack in weeks."

"That's not the point, Nate."

He stops walking, taking her by the hand and pulling her to him. "Ellie, baby," he says, his hands falling to her hips. "I wouldn't let anything happen to you."

She rolls her eyes, but smirks when her gaze collides with his. Soon, his lips are on hers, and she gives in, stepping up onto her toes and wrapping her arms around his neck. Nothing about them seems threatening — they're mind-numbingly human — but before moving on, a low growl rips through the night.

A quick scan of the park turns up nothing. The couple remains completely unaware of the potential risk, tugging at each other like a couple of horny teenagers, but soon the glowing yellow eyes of the newly turned werewolf appear in the distance.

It looks at the couple, lost in a private moment on a hot summer night, eyeing them for what they are to it: prey.

Crouching low, the hunter grips the cold hilt

of the sword and unsheathes it. She watches the wolf advance, taking one stalking step at a time. Its flaxen coat gleams beneath the blue moon, but it doesn't seem to sense the threat that's been waiting for it in the shadows all night. White teeth gleam as it pulls its lips back, and the muscles in its shoulders tense right before it leaps.

Sword in hand, the silver blade shines in the moonlight as the blonde woman steps from the darkness, running full-tilt across the park until she collides with the massive beast.

CHAPTER 1 | INVESTIGATION

Red and blue lights flashed against the backdrop of a dark sky. Cop cars were everywhere. I didn't make it on time to stop this from happening, and that pissed me off. Brooke had been counting on me to stop another attack from happening, and I had failed.

I walked on the outskirts of the park, staying close to all the other people who were trying to catch a glimpse of what was going on. I could smell the blood, even though I was too far away to see much.

"I bet it was another animal attack," a short woman with dark hair said to one of her friends. I could smell the alcohol on them and would hazard a guess they were fresh from one of the many nightclubs Calgary had to offer.

"But there hasn't been one in weeks," one of her friends slurred in response.

They weren't wrong. It had been weeks since the last attack. The Pack had been monitoring them for months. Whoever was in charge was covering their tracks, which only further told us that it was someone who knew our Alpha had been murdered, and a new one had taken his place.

Brooke was still new to our world, but she was a quick study. She might have been reluctant to accept what she had become, but any of us who'd been bitten had been.

Myself included.

My own initiation, like Brooke's, wasn't exactly something I had anticipated, nor was it something I wanted. What had started out as a fun family night out quickly turned into a real-life horror movie. I could still hear the screams of my wife and seven-year-old son as Gianna's newborns fed from them before breaking their necks. It was so vivid, I swore I relived it every single time.

At first, I didn't really understand what was happening. One minute, I was fixing a flat tire, and the next, windows were being shattered and my family murdered. But instead of weapons, these savages were using their teeth. Obviously they were vampires, but I didn't even know such things existed back then, so I was stunned by what I was seeing.

I fought to get to my wife and son, but as soon as I realized they were already gone, I gave up. I stopped struggling and accepted that I would soon join them when three large wolves came out of nowhere.

The vampires and wolves fought. Honestly, everything happened so quickly, that I don't even remember the moment I'd been bitten by one of the wolves.

With several of the vamps dead, their dust blowing on the wind, the rest fled. I found my way to where my wife and son's bodies lay, their flaxen hair soaked with their blood, and I cradled them to my chest, praying for my own death so I could be with them.

A warm hand on my shoulder drew my focus to a man with long black hair. His eyes were kind, remorseful, and there was a tiny trickle of blood in the corner of his mouth.

"Are you okay?" he'd asked me. It was probably the most idiotic question I'd ever heard, given the circumstances, and he was quick to amend himself. He started rambling about werewolves and vampires, which seemed like a load of bullshit at the time. It wasn't until I noticed that he was naked and kneeling in the snow with five wolves surrounding us that I questioned the validity of his statement.

I closed my eyes and tried to force the memory of that night from my mind. It wasn't often I thought about Ashley and Tyson like that, but when I did, it took everything I had to not fall down the rabbit hole.

And I couldn't afford for that to happen; there was work to be done. Wolves to be found.

When I found an opening in the crowd, I slipped through. Sticking to the shadows, I snuck through the park, hoping to get a good view of what happened earlier. The cops were so busy dealing with the crime scene that they didn't even notice me sniffing around—literally.

While I conducted my own investigation for the Pack, I noticed a man and woman sitting on the ground. Both of them were covered in dirt, but beneath that, I could see the scratches and smell the blood. The woman was shaking, tears leaving tracks through the dirt on her cheeks.

"It came out of nowhere," she sobbed, and her boyfriend pulled her closer, kissing the top of her forehead. Her pale blonde hair fell over her face, and she reached up to push it back. The boyfriend did his best to comfort her by putting on a brave face, but I could smell his fear; it was thicker than the girl's, which I contributed to being afraid of losing her as well as for himself.

I lingered nearby as the cops asked them all sorts of questions: what were they doing? Where were they coming from? Why were they going through the park after all the reports of animal attacks? What did they see?

That last question piqued my curiosity—or more accurately, the answer did.

"I-it all happened so fast," the man said. "One minute, we were kissing, and the next, we were thrown to the ground."

"By what?" the cop asked. Upon really looking at this cop, I recognized him from somewhere, though I couldn't exactly put my finger on it. He stood about six-foot with a thin build, but probably fit. Judging by his greying dark hair and the deep creases in his forehead and around his eyes, I'd put him around fifty.

I moved in to get a closer look and maybe catch his scent. Scent usually registered with me over appearance, anyway. As I walked and listened, I kept my eyes on the shadows, trying to see if something was still out there.

"There was a dog—a wolf, I think. It came out of nowhere and moved so fast. The ground that thing covered in only seconds..." the girl said, her eyebrows pulling together as she remembered the attack. "It was on us before we even realized what was happening. Nate managed to push me out of the way, but not before it nipped my hand."

My head whipped toward the couple again just as she held out her hand for the cop to look at. "It's just a scratch, but it still hurt."

Even from where I stood, I could see that the animal had broken skin. She'd shift on the night of the next full moon. I was going to have to track them home and find out who she was so I could keep an eye on her before the one who made her came back to claim her.

"I managed to push it off of her," the man said, "and I was helping her up so we could run when a woman came out of nowhere."

The original wolf that made the one who attacked? I thought to myself.

"She went after the wolf with a sword."

So not *the one who made the wolf,* I deduced before wondering who this mystery woman might be.

"Can you describe her?" the cop asked, glancing around before noticing me a few yards away. He didn't say anything to me, but he did narrow his eyes like he was trying to figure out who I was.

"Um, she was taller than me," the girl said. "About five-six, I think? Looked to be in her thirties, maybe, with long blonde hair, and she was really in shape."

"Anything else?" the cop asked, turning his attention back to the victims.

"Not that I can think of," the man said again. "She came out, got the wolf's attention, and they took off that way." He pointed a finger toward the southeast quadrant of the park, and I wasted no time heading in that direction.

I knew I should have stayed with the victims so I could track the girl home, but I had a responsibility to my pack to find this stray and deal with it in whatever way necessary.

The copper notes of blood stung my nostrils, telling me I was where I needed to be. There had to be a lot spilled in order for it to hit me this hard, so I closed my eyes and prepared myself for carnage. New werewolves were often far more volatile because they had no clue what they were doing and wouldn't remember it the next day. The animal was in full control in those early months.

Resolving myself to accept that there was no way the woman those two kids had seen walked away from this, I pressed forward. I was stunned to find the body of a wolf, its throat slit and a pool of blood around it. How was it possible?

"Guess this means the woman got away," a deep voice said from behind me.

Instinctively, my muscles tensed, hands balling into fists, and I spun around, coming face-to-face with the cop who'd been questioning the couple. Now that I was right in front of him, I recognized him as the detective who'd investigated my previous Alpha, Marcus, and his wife, Miranda's murders earlier in the year.

Their deaths were still so recent, the Pack continued to feel their loss like a black hole. None of us saw it coming, which was the worst part. We had just returned to the manor after I'd been rescued from Gianna's coven to find them slaughtered in our library. To make matters worse, those responsible called the cops, involving humans in otherworldly affairs.

"Detective," I greeted, relaxing my posture

when I realized he wasn't a threat.

He continued to stare at me a moment before realization sparked in him. "Jackson Devereux, right?"

"That's right," I replied with as nod. "You're...Detective Matthews. You investigated my friends' murders a few months back." He only nodded.

"You know this is an active investigation, right?"

My head bobbed once more. "I do. It's why I kept my distance earlier. Just another curious by-stander who's desperate to know what's going on in my city." I looked down at the slaughtered an-imal, then back at the detective. Decided to take a walk and stumbled upon this." Even though I al-ready knew the answer, I asked, "Think it's the wolf that attacked that young couple?"

"Seems likely," the detective said, kneeling next to the animal and investigating the wound. "Is it me or does the laceration seem cauterized?"

I hadn't been with the body long enough to look too closely, so I knelt next to the detective and got a closer look. Sure enough, the wound was partially burned. Without thinking, I reached out and touched the wound, pulling back when the tingle of silver singed my skin. "A silver blade," I muttered.

"Pardon me?"

Mentally chastising myself, I cleared my throat and stood. "Oh, uh...nothing. It's weird, right?"

"Indeed," Matthews agrees, pushing to his feet, also.

Looking past the detective's shoulders, I noticed the couple being questioned by another cop before being excused. My window of opportunity to track them was running out.

Forcing a smile to my face, I shrugged. "I should probably let you get back to your investigation. I didn't mean to intrude, Detective."

He watched me as I walked toward him, and I sensed his eyes on me while I walked away. If we weren't careful while looking into the stray situation, this detective might put the pieces together, endangering the Pack. And maybe himself.

"Have a good night, Mr. Devereux."

"You, too, Detective," I replied, raising my hand and waving before sauntering through the park.

Trying to be discreet, I watched as the couple walked toward a cop car, where they got in the back seat. I quickly climbed onto my bike and followed a safe distance behind.

We drove for about forty minutes before the cop car rolled to a stop outside a downtown highrise apartment building. I drove past the cruiser, parking a few cars ahead and watching the couple get out of the car through my side mirror.

"You'll stay with me tonight, Nate?" the girl asked softly.

Nate took her injured hand in his and kissed the bandages. "Of course, Ellie."

As soon as they entered the building, the police cruiser pulled away from the curb and drove away. As soon as it was gone, I climbed off my bike and headed for the entrance. Nate and this Ellie girl were already gone, so I slipped in the main entrance in order to find out her last name from the tenant listing on the buzzer system.

I ran my finger down the list until I found an "Elizabeth King," and she lived in unit 603. With this information, I could get Brooke to use her detective prowess to hopefully find out more information on this girl. Knowing as much as possible would help me in tracking her before the next full moon when she would change for the first time.

As I exited the building, a breeze picked up, bringing with it a unique scent. I couldn't place it, but it niggled at something that must have been buried deep in my memory. As if that wasn't unsettling enough, I caught traces of the wolf's blood from the park.

Almost as quickly as it had caught my attention, it disappeared, though the feeling that I was being watched lingered as I hopped back on my bike and headed back to the manor.

CHAPTER 2 | HISTORY

"What did you find out?" Brooke asked, descending the stairs with her newborn child asleep in her arms.

Even with her fiery red hair piled on top of her head, she looked absolutely jubilant. Though the darkening circles beneath her eyes told the truth of how exhausted she was. And who could blame her? She'd only just given birth earlier that afternoon, not to mention the weeks leading up to the birth were stressful, and she wasn't sleeping well. The stray problem definitely didn't help, either.

I closed the front door softly so as not to wake the baby. "There was another attack in the city," I told her, running my hand through my hair.

"Shit."

The baby stirred in Brooke's arms, but was soon quieted by her mother as she nodded me toward the kitchen.

"Why aren't you sleeping?"

Brooke laughs. "You're starting to sound like Nick."

"Well, he's got a point."

With a smirk, Brooke glanced back at me over her shoulder. "Did that hurt?"

"More than I'd care to admit," I quipped.

It was no secret that Nick and I never really got along. He seemed like a good guy, but I think our dominant personalities just clashed. Of course, it didn't help that Marcus took him under his wing shortly after being turned, while I'd been pushed to the side. I hated to admit it, but I harbored a lot of jealousy over that.

Looking back, it made sense why Marcus would rely on him; he and that vampire scum, Bobby, had a history before either one of them had been turned. Nick was able to help track them, and for whatever reason, he was able to anticipate that the coven would go after Brooke.

"So, why are you up?" I asked, sitting at the island while Brooke opened the fridge. "You gave birth a few hours ago. You should be in bed."

Smiling, Brooke looked down at Azura. My heart clenched and my stomach rolled when I recognized the love and adoration that only a mother could bestow upon their child.

"I'm too wired to sleep." She placed a kiss to the baby's head. "Besides, Nick snores."

Brooke grabbed a bowl of leftovers and placed it on the counter before she turned to grab a plate. She just started to stretch her one free arm when I shot up and rounded the island to help her.

"Go sit down," I ordered.

"Don't be ridiculous."

All it took was a stern look, and she conceded. I grabbed a couple of plates, suddenly feeling a little hungry myself. I opened the dish to find the roast we'd had earlier.

"Sandwiches?" I offered, and Brooke nodded. "Sounds great."

While I prepared a couple of sandwiches, I continued to glance up at Brooke as she stared at her newborn daughter. Several emotions warred inside me. There was love as I remembered the way Ashley looked at our son, sadness because I miss them both so much, and finally, anger for having them taken from me so violently and far too soon.

"You okay?" Brooke asked, looking up at me.

I was about to lie to her, sliding her sandwich across the counter, when I realized she could always tell when I was acting off. Normally, that wouldn't matter, but Brooke and I had formed a bond since she joined us last year. Maybe it was that she'd felt alone and confused about what was happening, or maybe it was because I could relate to her having lost her brother to vampires the way I'd lost my family.

It felt like a bit of both.

"Just...thinking about my family."

Her face instantly transformed, and I picked up on her remorse. "Oh, God. Jax... I'm so sorry."

I shook off her apology. "You have nothing to apologize for, kiddo," I assured her, passing one of the plates to her.

Digging into my own sandwich, I watched Brooke struggle for a minute. She held Azura close, but couldn't get a decent hold on her sandwich.

I wiped my hands together over my plate. "Here. Let me have her. You eat."

Brooke glanced between her daughter and me. "You're sure?"

"Yes." I laughed, rounding the island and taking the baby. She stirred, but quickly settled into my arms. "You need to eat."

While Brooke dug into her sandwich, I watched Azura sleep. Her lips moved as she inhaled a shuddering breath. Holding her reminded me of when Tyson was this small. It felt like a lifetime ago.

"Why haven't you found a mate?"

Surprised, I looked up, my heart beating faster in response to the unexpected question. "What?"

"I'm sorry. My filter isn't working. New baby, little sleep…" Brooke took a deep breath, but then asked the question again. "I just mean, you must have thought about it."

"Every day since they were taken from me."

"You deserve to be happy, Jax."

"I am."

Brooke exhaled heavily. "No. I know that. It's just—"

"What?" I replied with a laugh, startling the sleeping baby in my arms briefly before she settled again. "It's not that I've closed myself off to the possibility. I've been involved with women since then…"

"Roxy?" Brooke suspected with a knowing smirk.

I smiled. "For one. We didn't have anything meaningful. We were just…filling the void in our lives."

Brooke dropped her eyes to the remainder of her sandwich. "I get that."

It wasn't very long ago that Brooke suffered the same loss I had all those years ago. Her partner and boyfriend had walked in on her being attacked by a vampire. The filthy bloodsucker was there to collect her for Gianna, the vampire queen who had plans of creating a hybrid species of vampire and werewolf. David died that night in his efforts to keep the woman he loved safe, and Brooke still held onto a lot of guilt about that night. A werewolf's enhanced sense of hearing made us aware of everything that happened in the manor; Brooke's nightmares happened less and less as the months passed by, but every once in a while, her screams would wake us all. Now that she was our Alpha, we often found ourselves in the hall, ready to defend her, until we realized exactly what was happening.

I may not have known her for very long, but I empathized with what she'd gone through.

"I'm not closing myself off to the possibility of finding my mate, but I'm content in my life here, so I don't plan to go out of my way to make it happen. Not when there are more important things to deal with."

Heavy footsteps and a throat clearing from the doorway granted me a reprieve from the conversation. I knew Brooke didn't mean anything by it; she just wanted me to be happy.

"You're back." Nick entered the kitchen, rubbing his hand over his stubbled face. He looked exhausted. His blue eyes moved between Brooke and me before they settled on Azura in my arms. It was brief, but his eyes narrowed.

"Brooke was hungry, so I offered to hold the squirt until she finished eating," I explained, preparing to hand the baby over. He took her, smiling when she released a tiny whimper, but then he looked panicked the second it escalated to a wail.

It was a dick move, but I smirked. He always excelled at everything, pushing his way to the head of the Pack, so it was comical to see him struggle at this.

He swayed from side to side, trying to soothe her back to sleep. It was no use, and her cries continued to grow.

Brooke finished the last bite of her sandwich and stood up. "She's probably hungry. Here." She extended her arms, and Nick transferred Azura into them. Within seconds, Brooke had the baby nursing.

"You find anything tonight?" Nick asked, flopping onto one of the stools.

"Oh, yeah," Brooke interjected. "You said there was an attack?"

They both waited for me to deliver my findings, and listened raptly as I told them about the young couple, how the girl had admitted to the detective that she'd been bitten, and about the dead wolf I'd tracked down.

"Dead?"

"Throat slit," I explained. "Looked like whoever killed it used a silver blade. The wolf bled out, but some of the wound at the surface had been cauterized."

Brooke sat next to Nick, her expression telling me she wasn't quite sure what to make of what I'd told her. "So whoever it was knew what it was. Knew how to kill it." She gave her head a small shake, as though she were coming to her senses. "Did you see who'd done it...pick up on anything?"

I thought back to the park and shook my head. "Aside from the scent of the wolf, there wasn't much I picked up on."

"And the girl?" Brooke asked, adjusting Azura and her top discreetly. Nick took the baby and started patting her back.

"I followed her and her boyfriend back to her apartment," I began. "Her name is Elizabeth King. I thought maybe you could dig up some info on her. Give me something to work with so I can figure out how to make a connection."

Brooke nodded along. "You bet. I'll get started on it first thing in the morning."

"Good," I said. "I think it's important we make a connection."

"It's possible she's being watched by whoever targeted her, so stay alert at all times," Nick warned. "Strays don't play by our rules."

He wasn't wrong. I'd been a part of this pack long enough to have seen how strays act—hell, we had one in our pack up until he attacked one of our own. Any loyalty this pack had toward Karl dissolved the second he tried to have his way with Brooke.

Marcus had taken Karl in when he was younger, but he was never able to shake the stray mentality. Having always been with a pack, I didn't understand it, but I could imagine it would be difficult to give up the freedom to do whatever you want...within reason. If a stray got a little too out of control—which most of them do—it was up to the packs to take care of the issue. Karl had trouble with authority. He often targeted those weaker than him, those unsure of what they were.

Brooke had been on the receiving end of his sick games, and it got him killed.

"Nick's right. We need to try and get some of

the newly turned on our side, but I'd also like to know who's behind the attacks." Brooke stood up from her seat to put our plates in the sink as I tidied the mess. "If they're putting together an army to take my Pack down, I want to make sure we're prepared."

"Of course," I agreed before making a suggestion of my own. As Brooke's right hand, she valued my input almost as much as Nick's. "I think we should meet with the rest of the Pack and get a team together."

"That's a good idea," Nick quickly agreed. We'd been getting along much better lately, but it still felt a little strange to have him back me up. His new position at the head of the Pack with Brooke, and mine at their right hand could explain that. "If there's something out there taking wolves out, we need to make sure we're not going out alone. Our Pack can't survive if our numbers continue to dwindle."

"Okay. Let's meet in the library after breakfast," Brooke said. "There has to be something in the dossiers to help us figure out who our suspects might be. Marcus kept pretty detailed records from what I've seen over the months."

"Sounds good."

Brooke yawned. "I think that's my cue to get some sleep."

Holding a sleeping Azura to his chest, Nick walked with Brooke toward the doorway. They both turned their heads as Nick asked, "You turning in?"

I tilted my neck to the left, cracking it loudly. "I'm wired. I'm going to head out for a run. I won't be long."

Brooke looked at Nick, then me. Her expression screamed anxious, but when Nick shook his head, she acquiesced to whatever they'd silently communicated. "Stay close to the manor," she ordered firmly. I nodded, heading for the patio door before she added, "Be careful."

"I will, kid." Warmth spread under my skin as I began to anticipate my run. "You guys get that beautiful baby girl to bed. Get some sleep."

I waited until Brooke and Nick headed upstairs before slipping off my clothes. I folded them and left them on the chair closest to the patio door, and then headed outside. The mid-summer temperature was quite warm, but there was a breeze coming off the mountains that made it tolerable.

I stepped off the patio and crouched down, digging my fingers into the ground as I let the fire of the change consume me. In the beginning, the change was excruciating...not that it was much better now, fifteen years later. I guess we just grew used to it.

My spine cracked first, then my ribs as they realigned, and fire burned through my veins like lava. Clenching my eyes shut, I grunted through the pain and clawed the grass and soil as sweat dripped from my body and my temperature rose. Thankfully, the change was quick, and soon I stood on all four legs, shaking my body to settle into this version of myself.

Once ready, I sniffed the air until I caught the scent of a rabbit. I followed the scent into a clearing, being careful to stay back until the moment to strike was perfect. The rabbit remained unaware of my presence as I watched and waited. The rabbit's head lifted, looking around, its ears twitching as it listened for any signs of danger. Appeased for the moment, he resumed his foraging.

Muscles tight, I crouched down low, my hind quarters shifting in anticipation. Saliva pooled in my mouth, and my heart raced as I sprang from my hiding spot.

The rabbit was quick to react, skittering off to safety. I followed it, my massive strides allowing me to close the gap between us. It wasn't long before the rabbit was in my mouth, it's hind legs kicking furiously at my face in a last attempt to survive. One final clench of my jaw, and the animal fell limp.

I let it fall to the ground and was just starting to eat when the wind shifted, bringing with it a familiar smell. It triggered something in the recess of my brain, but I couldn't pinpoint what it was. I stood over my kill, staring off into the distance and inhaling deeply.

Subtle notes of tuberose and jasmine hit me first, followed by sweat and blood. It was the blood I recognized first—from earlier this evening. There wasn't much, just mere traces, but it was there, and I knew without a doubt that it belonged to the wolf I'd found in the park.

I abandoned the rabbit, ignoring my Alpha's orders to be careful and stay close to the manor. The wolf in me struggled with that, but only briefly. Normally, an Alpha's orders were difficult to bypass; never impossible, but one definitely struggled to act if it went against what was instructed.

But something made it possible. Whatever was out there was a threat to us, and it was up to me to protect the Pack. My obligation and loyalty to them was what pushed me forward. Not my outward defiance.

The scent grew stronger the further west I travelled. My muscles started to ache and burn, exhaustion setting in, but I pushed myself to keep going. I needed to figure out what we were up against. It was bad enough that there was a group of strays out there, rallying to usurp our new Alpha and take over our territory, but to have something else out there with the knowledge and skill to hunt us was an even bigger obstacle.

I was so caught up in the chase, that I hadn't even realized how much ground I'd covered until I hit the edge of the lake and lost the trail completely.

Whatever was out there was gone now, but I had the scent now. If it was watching out for the attacks and tracking me back here, it was bound to show itself again. I would just have to figure out a way to draw it out.

My lips curled back into a snarl, warning whatever was out there that I would find it.

CHAPTER 3 | PLANNING

"I think we're almost all here." Brooke looked around the large library, taking note of who was missing.

Layla and Vince sat on the bottom step of the stairs that led to the second level with their three-month-old baby boy in their arms, while Roxy and Alistair sat a couple steps above them. Nick had perched himself on the windowsill behind the desk that Brooke stood behind with Azura cradled in her arms. Corbin was off to the side, leafing through one of the many dossiers we kept on strays and other potential threats, and Zach was next to him. They, as well as the rest of us had been spending a lot of time going through our files to try and narrow down which strays might serve the biggest threat to Brooke and the Pack.

"I think we're just waiting for Colby," Nick pointed out.

"I'm here," a small voice called from the hall. A tiny hand appeared about a foot from the ground, waving up and down to prove her presence.

Brooke sighed, her face twisting with pain.

Ever since the bodies of Colby and Corbin's parents—Marcus and Miranda—had been found in the library, she hadn't been able to step through the door. And who could blame her? The scene was horrific. Something straight out of a horror movie. Of course, it probably didn't help matters much that it was her estranged younger sister who was responsible for their deaths.

"Colby, honey, why don't you come join us?" Brooke tried. She always tried, but had yet to succeed.

At Brooke's silent behest, Zach sauntered over to the door and crouched to where she sat, likely propped against the one closed library door. "Babe, come inside."

"I can't." There was a quiver in her voice that cut through each and every one of us like a serrated blade.

Brooke knew of Colby's aversion to this room—we all did—but she continued to hold our pack meetings here in hopes Colby would come around. It wasn't that easy. I still had trouble driving past the spot my family was attacked, and I was willing to bet Brooke would suffer a relapse in if she ever had to go back to her home where David had died. She was on the right path with Colby, though, it would just take time. It always took time.

Brooke looked down at the desk, defeated, and Nick placed a hand on her shoulder in support. "It'll happen. Let's just get started."

"Colby? Can you hear us okay?"

"Yup."

Brooke looked to me and nodded.

"I hit up Glenmore last night when I went

out," I started. "There was another wolf attack."

"Was anyone hurt?" Layla asked, soothing Samuel when he fussed.

"A couple was walking through when the wolf got to them. The man wasn't hurt, but the girl claimed to have been bitten."

"Shit," Roxy muttered.

"Her name is Elizabeth King. I followed her to her apartment building last night. I plan to keep tabs on her so I can catch her before she shifts for the first time. However, there's always a possibility whoever is calling the shots will be doing the same, so I'm going to have to win her trust fast.

"There's more, though." The Pack all turned to me. "I found the wolf that attacked her."

"Good," Corbin stated through clenched teeth.

I shook my head. "Dead…"

"Even better."

"…and not by my hand."

"So who?" Vince inquired.

"No clue. She was gone before I got there."

"She?" Layla interjected.

"That's what the victims said," I continued. "They said a wolf came out of nowhere, and then a blonde woman chased it off. When I came across the body, I found it's throat had been slit. With a silver blade, based on how the wound had been cauterized."

Silence fell over the Pack as they all processed the information.

"So someone knew what they were doing," Vince finally spoke. "Vamps?"

"My guess is they wouldn't rely on blades," Nick pointed out.

Brooke scoffed, startling Azura. "My experience might be limited, but based on my time with them, they aren't opposed to using weapons."

Nick's expression soured with remorse. It had been just over six months since Brooke had been lured away from the manor and taken by Gianna's coven. They tortured and performed multiple tests on her to learn more about us physically and mentally, and they had plans to use her to merge the bloodlines. Gianna and her mate, Bobby—who also happened to be Brooke's dead twin brother—wanted to test the theory that if the two original hosts shared the same genetics, that the two species wouldn't reject each other when infected. Turned out it wasn't really a test, though. They'd already had a successful run with one of Gianna's descendants that had been born a wolf: Cordelia, Marcus and Miranda's youngest daughter who'd been taken by Bobby when she was six.

Brooke was just a vendetta that Gianna and Bobby had against Nick for destroying one of their nests.

"You're right. I'm sorry, babe."

"No need to be," Brooke assured him. "I do agree. I don't think this was vampires. They'd make a bigger show of it. They'd want the credit. Keeps them relevant to the human world for their own sick amusement."

Brooke wasn't wrong. Vamps were attention whores by nature. Look at the media. They were glamorized in books and movies and television. Werewolves were there, too, but in smaller doses, and we were often portrayed as volatile creatures with no self-control.

Okay, so that part was pretty factual.

One of the biggest differences between us was that wolves preferred to keep to the shadows. We didn't like humans to know about us. Vamps? They were all too willing to put themselves out there and get noticed. Hell, there was a whole life-style dedicated to blood-letting amongst humans who thought they were vampires.

"Okay, so it's probably not vamps," Roxy said, running her fingers through her newly-dark brown hair. "Then what? Humans? I find it hard to believe a wolf—especially a new one—would let a human that close without some major car-nage."

"The Order." It was Alistair who spoke this time.

Everyone looked at him. Even Colby's head peered around the door for a brief second before she realized what she was doing.

"The Order?" Brooke asked, confused. She looked to Nick, who shrugged. "What the hell is that?"

"It's a very private sect—so private, that even The Circle thought they might be a myth."

"That's not exactly helpful," Roxy pointed out.

"Sorry," he apologized with a soft chuckle. "I don't know much, just what the legends say." Alistair pushed his glasses up his nose. "From what I can recall, they're thought to be a group who trains hunters of otherworldly creatures—vampires, warlocks, demons…" He paused to take a look around the room. "Werewolves."

"I've seen that show. Cute little blonde girl chosen to kick demon ass. Original," Brooke said with a laugh. Alistair's silence cut her off abruptly.

"What? Seriously?"

"You exist," Alistair pointed out, curbing Brooke's skepticism immediately. "Everything the media portrays about the supernatural world is rooted in some truth. Why not these hunters?"

"So they hunt us?" Corbin interrupted. "Why have we never seen or heard of them before?"

Alistair shrugged. "Maybe because, over the centuries, packs have formed and have been policing their own territory against each other and other creatures. They probably haven't felt the need. The recent uprising in Lycan activity must have forced them into action."

"Awesome," Brooke said, exasperated. "So, not only do we have to worry about an ever-growing army of strays looking to usurp my new Alpha status, but now a super-secret organization of…demon hunters is after us. This is just perfect."

"Brooke," I spoke up. "It'll be okay. We just have to be careful. If we come across this hunter, we'll reason with her."

"Until she slits one of our throats with her silver knife," she argued.

I snickered. "You're so pessimistic."

"With my track record, can you blame me?" she demanded. Azura fussed in her arms, the soft sounds quickly escalating to a demanding wail.

Nick stepped in to take the baby. "I'll go see if she needs to be changed."

"Thanks. I'll come up in a bit to feed her." She turned back to me. "Jax? I found a little more on Elizabeth King. Along with knowing where she lives, I've discovered she works as a paralegal downtown in Calgary and boards a horse just outside the city. Chances are she'll be in one of those three places. We need you to get to her before an-yone else."

"That'll be hard unless I need legal help."

Brooke smiled. "Let's keep you *out* of trouble, Jax. No need to get the legal system involved if we plan to keep our existence under wraps." She paused and picked up some papers she'd printed earlier. "Based on the address you gave, there's a vacancy in her building. Let's see if we can get you approved for an apartment. You can get to know her routines and hopefully get close to her."

"Sounds potentially expensive, not to mention I'm not much of a people person."

"It'll only be until the next full moon. Every-one else has their orders on how we can find the rest of the strays and hopefully their victims."

Even though she hadn't been our Alpha for very long, Brooke spoke with authority and cer-tainty. She really was perfect for the role. Marcus chose his successor well.

"Okay," I agreed. "Let's get me an apart-ment."

The idea of living apart from the Pack created a tornado of conflict within me. On the one hand, a lot of people lived in the manor. It wasn't easy to find a peaceful place to think. Then there was the reality that they were my pack. My family. After so many years, there was a loyalty there. It made me nervous to leave them — my Alpha — alone. Es-pecially after what happened the last time I was away for a stretch.

"I'll make a few calls," Brooke said before she was distracted by another shriek from Azura up-stairs. She looked at me, slightly panicked. "Can you finish up here?"

"You bet. Go check on her."

Once Brooke was out of the room, all the focus was on me. I had no trouble barking orders before reminding everyone in the room that, depending on how old some of these strays were, or if they were being taken in and taught, they wouldn't need the full moon to shift. The attacks had definitely slowed as of late, but that didn't mean they were done. They probably just wanted to draw less attention to themselves. The first couple of months, they were anything but discreet.

By the end of the day, Brooke had set up a time for me to view the vacant apartment. I wasn't expecting anything to happen right away, so I was surprised to be on my way into the city by sunset.

I parked my bike in a visitor parking spot and headed inside the building, looking around and honing my senses for the presence I felt the night before. The feeling I experienced the night before was gone, though; I felt certain that no one was watching me.

The apartment manager met me in the updated lobby, a huge smile on her face. She was attractive, standing about five-eight and wearing a knee-length skirt and a tight blouse that did wonders for her curves. She wasn't skin and bones like a lot of women nowadays.

"Mr. Devereux? I'm Jade." She held her hand out and looked me right in the eye. Her big blue eyes sparkled beneath the lights, and her dark hair was pulled back off her face, accentuating her high cheekbones.

"It's nice to meet you."

"So, your...wife?...tells me you're looking for a place?"

I laughed at her poor attempt at fishing for my relationship status. "Brooke? She's not my wife. She's more like a sister."

"Oh." Hope simmered in her eyes, but I didn't let it come to a boil. While she was attractive, the simple fact remained that I just wasn't interested. I might never be.

"What is it you do for a living, Mr. Devereux?" Jade asked, leading me through the lobby. Our footsteps on the tile echoed in the empty lobby.

"I'm a mechanic," I replied as we stepped into the elevator. "And please, call me Jackson." I watched Jade select the sixth floor and appreciated the happy coincidence since my intended target lived on the sixth floor.

"You been doing it long?"

"Since high school," I told her honestly. I dabbled a little when I was younger, but I didn't make a career out of it until I was in my early twenties. Working on vehicles was an escape for me, and I held onto it from my past life like it could keep me grounded there in some way. Plus, it allowed me to escape to the garage when the manor got a little too active.

The elevator dinged when we reached our floor, and I allowed Jade to exit first so she could lead me to the available unit. "We offer your standard six- and twelve-month leases," she explained as she slipped the key into the lock of unit 605. I noticed 603 was right next door, and when I inhaled deeply, I picked up Elizabeth's scent. It had changed a little in the last twenty-four hours, but that was to be expected as she transitioned.

I looked down at her and smiled. "Any way to

rent on a month-to-month basis? I'm kind of a free spirit and never know where life might take me."

Jade seemed a little uncertain, but then she nodded. "I can't guarantee your rent won't fluctuate, but I'm sure we could work something out." Jade pushed the door open. "This is the available unit."

We stepped inside and she showed me around the small apartment. While being alone definitely held some appeal, living in a small apartment in the city with no room to run was a huge disadvantage.

"The kitchen comes with all three appliances. Electric, heat, and water are included in the rental price."

I nodded along as she led me through the small living area. Manor living spoiled me. I couldn't imagine being cooped up in here longer than necessary.

"This is the bathroom."

It was smaller than I expected, too. My private ensuite at the manor was bigger. Hell, the *shower* in my private ensuite was larger than this entire room. I didn't let on how claustrophobic I felt, though, because I knew how important this was to the mission.

"It's available immediately."

"That's perfect."

We discussed the specifics a while longer before Jade suggested we head down to the rental office. Just as we were exiting the apartment, the door next to the unit opened, and Elizabeth stepped out. Something in me twisted the second I laid eyes on her before slowly morphing into a pleasant quiver that worked its way under my skin.

Seeing her up close, I realized just how beautiful she was. She couldn't have been older than her mid-twenties. Even though her skin appeared flawless, it was alarmingly pale, her cheeks were flushed, and she looked almost lethargic. I could tell just by looking at her that the fever had set in. This usually lasted two to four days after being marked. Soon, the fever would break, and she would feel stronger as the wolf took over. Cravings, excess energy, and strength were common side effects as the wolf gained momentum closer to the full moon. It was all just part of the process.

"Miss King," Jade greeted sweetly.

There was a pheromone spike in the air when Elizabeth's eyes met mine. I recognized it wasn't necessarily *her*, but her wolf recognizing mine in the same way I could sense hers, though it was still buried deep for a few more weeks.

Elizabeth smoothed her pale blonde hair back and smiled. "Hi."

"Hello," I replied with a nod and a friendly smile. I made sure the smile was wide enough to show off my dimples. I was told they made me more approachable.

"Moving in?"

"Hoping to." I decided to kick it up a notch and flirt, hopefully breaking through a little more. "Possibly more now that I see how pretty my neighbor is." Hearing it back, I wondered if I sounded more creepy than seductive. I definitely *felt* creepier. I was out of practice with the whole charisma thing.

Much to my surprise, Elizabeth smiled and held out her hand. "I'm Ellie."

"Jax," I supplied, clasping her clammy hand in mine.

She looked apologetic as she pulled her hand away and wiped it on her sweater. "Sorry. I'm a little under the weather. I hope I didn't just give you whatever this is."

I laughed softly, knowing it wasn't possible since I already had what was affecting her. "I have a pretty good immune system."

She nodded. "Me too, usually. I have no idea what this is. I was fine yesterday, and I just woke up feeling like junk." She rolled her eyes, slapping her left hand to her forehead. "I'm sorry. You don't need my life story. I tend to ramble when I'm delirious. Welcome to the building."

Still wanting to make small talk in an effort to get off on the right foot and be friends with her, scrambled for something to talk about. Until I noticed the bandage that was still (and likely unnecessarily) on her hand. "What happened?"

"Huh? Oh, my hand. I was attacked in the park last night."

"Dear lord," Jade gasped.

"It was a wild dog or a wolf or something. It's barely a scratch."

"I'm so sorry to hear that," I told her.

Ellie smiled, holding my gaze and biting her lip demurely. "Thanks. I'm fine, really...aside from this flu bug, I mean."

Jade cleared her throat. "We should head down to the office, Mr. Devereux. I'd hate for someone else to snatch up this apartment."

"Oh, right." I offered Ellie one more smile. "It was a pleasure meeting you. I guess I'll be seeing you around... Neighbor."

Her smile widened, and I noticed the dimple in her left cheek. It was adorable. "Can't wait."

I felt confident that I'd gotten off on the right foot with Ellie. Befriending her before the full moon and convincing her of what was about to happen should be easy enough.

CHAPTER 4 | MOVING

Boxes were scattered all over my room. I didn't pack everything, but I figured I should have enough to make my living there believable. I went through my dresser, tossing clothes toward my bed. Some made it, others didn't. When I reached the bottom of my shirt drawer, I touched the edge of the picture frame I kept hidden there.

I pulled it out slowly, swallowing the lump that formed in my throat when I saw the smiling faces of my wife and son. There was a time that this photo lived on my night stand, but the constant reminder of how I failed to keep them safe made me pack it away.

I ran a finger over Ashley's face, smiling as I recalled the way she laughed. A tightness spread through my chest when my gaze shifted to Tyson's toothless grin. He'd have been twenty-two next week. Fifteen years had passed since they'd been taken from me.

I was nineteen when I met Ashley. She was only seventeen and had fallen on hard times, having just run away from her abusive family. She never went into detail about what they'd done to her, but based on how anxious and timid she was in the first few weeks that I'd gotten to know her, I could tell it wasn't good.

The first time I'd seen her was in the supermarket in Calgary, where I worked as a cashier when I was nineteen. My shift was almost over, and I had been helping another employee stock the produce section when I spotted her.

Her blonde hair was pulled on top of her head, and the army green jacket she wore to guard her against the winter wind hung heavy at the pockets. I noticed her big blue eyes darting around the busy store nervously, so I continued to watch her, knowing what she was up to. She appeared thin, her complexion sallow, and her cheeks were sunken in from malnourishment. I could see the desperation in her eyes, so I decided to just let it go.

That was when I saw my manager notice her slip a peach into her jacket pocket.

I excused myself and went to her, making it to her before my manager did.

"We have baskets," I'd informed her.

Her breathing had picked up, and she met my eyes timidly. "I-I'm sorry?"

"For the food weighing your jacket down. We have baskets."

She inhaled sharply, knowing she'd been busted. "I-I... Um..."

She made a move to bolt, when I placed a hand on her lower back. I smiled at her, hoping to set her mind at ease. "My manager has been watching you," I ex-

plained. "Let me buy you some food."

"What?" She seemed shocked at my offer. "No, I couldn't possibly…"

I shrugged. "It beats you stealing it and getting arrested," I reasoned. "You don't want that. I don't mind."

I glanced over her shoulder to find my manager glaring at us, his arms crossed. Her head turned toward him also, then back to me and she nodded. "Okay. Thank you."

We walked through the store together, and I told her to pick out a few things. She tried to fight me on it, but I told her if she didn't pick, I would, and I would much rather purchase things she'd eat over stuff she might just toss.

After paying for her food, I walked her outside. We stood there awkwardly for a minute before she tucked a stray strand of golden hair behind her ear.

"Thank you, again," she murmured. "For not letting me get caught." She shrugged, making the plastic bags rustle. "And for buying me food."

"Where's your car?"

She bit her lip nervously. "Oh, I don't have one."

"How are you getting home?"

Her eyes fell to the ground. "I…don't have a home."

"So…" I said, trying to process what she was telling me. "Are you staying with friends?"

She shook her head, then started to look around nervously. "I don't…have any friends in the city. I'm not exactly from around here"

"Where are you staying then?"

Still unable to meet my gaze, she shrugged her right shoulder. "I don't know. Bus station?"

My stomach flipped. I felt sorry for this poor girl.

"Where are you from if not the city?"

"F-far from here," she replied, eyes darting around the dark parking lot as though something might jump out and grab her. "Look, thanks again. Really. I should go."

"Wait!" I cried out as she took a step away from me. "What's your name?"

Her blue eyes met mine finally, and she swallowed thickly. "Ashley."

I smiled, holding out a hand for her. "I'm Jackson."

The corners of her lips slowly lifted and she timidly reached for my hand. "It's nice to meet you." A loud crash spooked her. "Look, I really should be going. Thanks again, Jackson."

"Ashley, wait!" I called after her. "I don't feel right about you living on the street. It's cold."

She stopped, posture rigid as she slowly turned her head. She wasn't looking at me, but I could see the profile of her face in the streetlight.

"It's not much, but you could come stay at my place. Electricity, heat, food…"

Nothing else was said between us, but she slowly turned around, eyes trained on me, sizing me up. I imagined she gauging whether or not I was a threat to her.

"I know you don't know me," I tried to reason with her, "but you also don't know the hundreds of other people you'll run into out there." I took another step forward. "You can trust me."

"O-okay," she stammered, understandably still hesitant. "Thank you."

Relieved, I smiled. "Cool. Okay, I'm going to go and clock off. Why don't you come wait inside, and I'll be just a minute."

As promised, I ran to the back, clocked off and grabbed my belongings. I tried to hurry because she seemed like a bit of a flight risk, and, even though I'd only just met her, I really was worried for her safety.

Thankfully, she was still right where I left her.

"My car is this way," I said, leading her toward my 1982 rust bucket. It was embarrassing, but it also got me from point A to point B, and the insurance didn't rob me blind.

We reached my shitty apartment within twenty minutes. The hinges on the front door creaked when I opened it and held it for her.

"Thank you," she said quietly before allowing me to lead her up to the second floor.

I slipped the key into my door, suddenly wondering how messy the place was. I lived there alone, and I wasn't exactly the best housekeeper between my two jobs. In addition to working at the supermarket, I apprenticed at a local mechanic shop, but it didn't quite pay enough, so I picked up a second job with flexible hours. I didn't love it, but it helped pay the bills.

"I'm going to apologize now for whatever mess might be behind the door," I warned. "I don't usually get a lot of company."

"I'm sure it'll be fine."

Sure enough, there was shit everywhere. Dirty dishes filled my sink, and there were clothes scattered down the hall from my stripping and dropping them wherever as I headed to my room after a late nights at work.

Ashley was more than accepting, telling me this was still better than her previous plans. I led her inside, locking the door behind us, and then gave her a quick tour, picking up my clothes as we went.

When we reached the living room, I looked at the old, third-hand couch my mom had given me when I moved out. "I'd offer my bed, but the bedding isn't clean."

Ashley shrugged out of her jacket. "Jackson, this is perfect. Thank you."

I ran to the hall closet and grabbed the one spare blanket I had. I gave it a sniff to make sure it wasn't too musty, and brought it out to her. She had made herself comfortable on the couch and was eating the peach she'd tried to steal.

I grabbed her plastic bags and took them to the kitchen, offering to put the stuff away so none of it went bad. When I returned to the living room, I found her standing up and fixing a make-shift bed out of the blanket. Even through her T-shirt, I could see how thin she was. I found myself wondering how long she'd been on her own.

I cleared my throat, letting her know I was there. "Do you have a change of clothes?"

Her nose scrunched up in this adorable little way, and she shook her head. "No. This is all I have."

I nodded, excusing myself. I ran to my room and grabbed a pair of sweats and another T-shirt. "Here," I said, holding them out to her. "They'll probably be too big, but this way we can wash the ones you have."

Ashley accepted the clothes with a smile and then headed to the bathroom to change. When she emerged, her hair was down, and she wore a shy smile. She looked at the bare walls around her and lifted her left hand to push her waist-length hair back over her shoulder. I noticed the black ink on the inside of her wrist.

"Nice ink," I said, trying to make out the design. "What does it mean?"

She inhaled sharply and slapped her right hand over it. "Oh... Just an old family sigil," she replied shakily. Something in the way she reacted made me recognize this was a sore spot with her, so I dropped it, and *we hung around in awkward silence for another moment before she yawned.*

"Okay. I should let you get some sleep." I had just turned to walk down the hall when I suddenly realized something. "Will you still be here in the morning?"

She remained silent before clearing her throat. "Would that be okay?"

I smiled, my back still to her so she couldn't see. "Absolutely. I can even make you breakfast."

That was the first night. She actually never left. I recommended her for a job at the grocery store, and while my manager was a little leery at first, he agreed once I explained the circumstances. Weeks passed, and Ashley and I had become pretty good friends. She was still reluctant to open up about her family or where she was from, and I didn't push. She'd tell me when she was ready. All I could do was continue to be there for her in whatever way I could.

One night, after a particularly bad day for her for whatever reason (she wouldn't say), we were hanging out on the couch and drinking a couple of beers. I was hoping to help take her mind off whatever was troubling her, and one thing led to another, she wound up sharing my bed.

Two months later, we found out she was pregnant.

"She's beautiful," a soft voice said from behind me, startling me and making me almost drop the frame.

"Shit!" I cursed, turning around to find Brooke peering around me at the picture. She was smiling brightly as I stalked over to my bed and shoved the frame in a box. "You need to stop sneaking up on people like that."

Brooke only laughed. "I knocked and called your name before I came in," she tried to reason.

I ran my fingers through my hair. "Sorry. I was caught up in…"

"The memories?" she interjected. "I get that. I often think about David and how things might have been different if…" She turned away, looking ashamed for even voicing the thought. "You almost packed?"

The change in topic was exactly what we both needed. I nodded. "Yeah, but are you sure this is a good idea? I don't like the idea of being away from the Pack."

"We'll be fine. Do what you can to get Elizabeth to believe you and bring her here so we can work with her. Watch her, gain her trust before the full moon. Make her understand. Vince and Layla are moving back in to back us up if we run into trouble, and you're only a phone call away. Alistair can get you here quickly if we need you."

She was right. Having a shaman in the house was definitely a perk. His transportation casts were convenient if we had to be somewhere quickly. His powers seemed to be increasing now that he was free to cast at his leisure and practice without the fear of The Circle punishing him for breaking their rules. I didn't know much about them, but from the way Alistair told it, The Circle had very strict rules on the types of casts they could use, limiting them in their powers. Dark casts were strictly forbidden due to how addictive they were.

I began folding clothes as Brooke sat on the edge of the bed and picked up the photo. I fought the urge to rip it from her hands. I was very protective over my past.

Brooke smiled as she looked at it. "He looks like you."

"Looked," I corrected through clenched teeth.

"Jax…" I raised my eyes to hers and was met with her remorse. "I didn't mean anything by it."

I sighed heavily. "I know. I just… It's hard to talk about it."

Brooke nodded. "I get that." She paused. "Have you ever talked to anyone about it?" I shook my head. "You know you can trust me, right?"

"It was fifteen years ago. There's not much sense in reliving it."

"Except the closure."

"I got closure when you killed that miserable bitch back in Scottsdale," I said, reminding her of when she took out Gianna.

Brooke reached out with her right hand and placed it on my forearm. "Jax, you once told me that the hurt never goes away, but you need to remember the good times."

I laughed dryly. "I did? Was I drunk?"

Brooke smirked. "Probably. Will you tell me about her?"

I couldn't be sure if it was because my Alpha was requesting or if it was because I had this deep bond with Brooke that I gave in, but I did. I told her how we met, sitting next to her and taking the photo. Even if I didn't want to.

"We'd only known each other a couple months before we got pregnant."

"Did she ever reconnect with her folks?" Brooke inquired.

I shook my head. "Nah. She said they were abusive, and I wasn't going to press the issue. Probably for the best given what happened to her almost a decade later."

"Right," she replied. "I guess that makes sense."

I looked at Tyson's toothless grin again, remembering how he'd lost the top two teeth a couple days before the photo was taken. "He was a lot like me," I told Brooke. "So full of energy and easy-going."

Brooke laughed, shoving me gently. "Easygoing?" she challenged.

I rolled my eyes. "I was a very different man back then," I explained. "I was a good dad. A good husband."

Brooke leaned over and rested her head on my shoulder. "I can see that. Every time you hold Azura, she instantly calms. I think it drives Nick a little crazy."

I snickered. "Does it make me a dick to say I feel a little pleasure when that happens?"

With a laugh, Brooke shook her head against me. "Yes, it does, but I won't tell him if you don't."

"Deal."

Tightness spread through my chest as my grief started to take over. My eyes stung with tears, so I cleared my throat and blinked them away. "Okay," I said, slapping my hands on my thighs and standing up, disrupting Brooke's headrest. "I should finish packing so I can get moved in as soon as possible."

I could tell Brooke wanted to know more about my past, but that was all I was willing to share. "Do you need a hand? Nick and Azura are napping downstairs, so I could—"

I shook my head. "No, thanks. I'm just going to pack my clothes and then turn in for the night. Thanks, though." I looked into her eyes, my brows pulling together. "For everything."

Brooke forced a smile and stood up. She crossed the room and stood on her toes to wrap her arms around me. "Thank you for letting me in. It means a lot."

I returned her embrace. "I wouldn't have told you any of that if you hadn't asked," I admitted honestly.

"Then I'm glad I did," she quipped, kissing my cheek. "Have a good sleep. I'm sure the guys would be happy to help get you moved this week while I take care of a few things around here."

"Sounds good. I'll see you in the morning. Go snuggle that baby of yours and get some sleep," I ordered. "We've got a long few weeks ahead of us as we prepare for the next phase."

"Goodnight, Jax."

With that, Brooke left me alone so I could finish packing. Truthfully, there wasn't much left to pack, I just needed to be alone before my heart shattered.

CHAPTER 5 | FOUNDATION

A week had passed since I signed the rental agreement and started packing, and I was finally moving in. Brooke was hoping I could take possession sooner, but unfortunately that wasn't possible. Because I was being forced to wait, different members of the Pack took turns watching over Ellie. We had a pretty good idea about her regular routine now, so I was hoping it might help me find a way to get to know her.

As I brought the last of my boxes into my new apartment, Nick and Vince were both looking around. They weren't doing it to be nosy, they were just getting to know the new territory. It was just one of those things we had to do. It was how we made sure everything was safe before we claimed the territory as ours. Sometimes we didn't even realize we were doing it.

"Thanks for helping out," I said, setting the box marked "bedroom" onto the short stack in the hall. "I can take it from here."

"You don't want a hand unpacking?" Vince offered, looking around at the boxes and random pieces of furniture.

I shook my head. "Nah. I don't have much to set up."

Nick nodded. "Okay. Make sure you call us if you need anything."

"I will. Thanks for the help."

"No problem. Good luck with the neighbor." Nick smirked, and I knew he was implying that maybe I'd get to know the potential werewolf next door a little better than just a pack mate.

I showed them out, and once I was alone, I started opening a couple boxes before taking my suitcase to the bedroom. I set it on the end of my bed and stood there, looking out the window above my bed.

The muscles in my back tightened as the claustrophobia started to set in. For whatever reason, whenever the wolf felt closed in, it wanted out more than ever. The last time I felt like this, I'd been caged, collared, and used as a decoy while my previous Alpha and his wife were slain.

I closed my eyes and clenched my fists at my sides, telling myself that I had to wait until nightfall before I could find somewhere quiet to shift. Maybe I could track the hunter that had killed the stray last week while alleviating my claustrophobia. That would be ideal.

A knock at the door jarred my focus. Shaking off the tremor that had started in my hands, I stalked from my room and toward the front door. I was about three feet away when Ellie's scent hit me, and I inhaled her sweet scent until it threatened to consume me. Now a week into her transition, the wolf was stronger in her, which meant everything was heightening at an exponential rate.

Another knock forced my hand to the knob,

and I opened the door. A smile stretched across Ellie's face. She was even more beautiful than the day we met. I wasn't sure why this surprised me so much. Maybe it was because the first night I saw her, she was so rattled from the attack, and the second time, she'd been in the first few days of the transition, which were always rough.

It felt like it was something else, though. I just didn't know what. Just being around her for those few minutes last week made everything just a little bit…brighter? It seemed ridiculous and a little too sappy. I'd never admit it to anyone. Not even if I was being tortured.

"Hi," she said brightly, pushing her blonde hair back over her shoulder. The color had returned to her cheeks now, making her pale blonde hair a striking contrast to her skin as opposed to washing her out further. "Jax, right?"

I nodded. "Hey."

"I was just wondering if maybe you needed a hand with anything? Unpacking? Organizing?"

I laughed. "Thanks, but I think—" I cut myself off, remembering I was here to build a friendship and her trust in me. "You know what? Sure. Come on in." I stepped to the side and allowed her to come in, noticing she held a bottle of wine in her left hand. "Can I take that for you?"

"Oh, duh!" she replied with a laugh. "I brought it for you. Kind of a 'welcome to the building' gesture. Do you drink wine?"

"On occasion." I took the bottle and set it on my kitchen counter.

I watched Ellie walk around my bare apartment, inspecting the labeled boxes. Like the guys earlier, she wasn't being nosy, the wolf was exploring, making sure it was safe. She just didn't realize it. The human side never understood the wolf at first, even in the first few months after their first shift. Unless they had proper guidance from the start, which is what I was hoping to accomplish here.

"Do you know where you want everything to go?"

"Hadn't really given it much thought beyond the couch in living room, table in kitchen, and bed in bedroom."

Looking at me, her deep brown eyes locking with mine, she bit her lower lip. My wolf reacted, recognizing her subtle attempt at flirtation. He was definitely a little more sensitive to everything thanks to being cooped up.

"Where do you want to start?" she asked coyly. I felt there might have been an underlying implication to her words, but it was possible she wasn't even aware of it.

"Living room, I suppose?"

Ellie gathered her hair behind her and tied an elastic around it. "Cool. Do you have an idea where you want your..." She paused, looking around. "No TV?"

I smiled. "I'm not really a TV person."

"How is that even possible?"

"I'm a very busy guy."

She watched me for a moment — sizing me up, maybe? Wondering if I was insane? Maybe I should get a TV in order to look less suspicious.

"Besides," I said finally, hoping to ease her into thinking I'm normal, "I have access to the internet on my phone like everyone else. If I'm in the mood for something to watch, I'll go online."

That didn't seem to work. This only made her right eyebrow arch and her smirk reappear. She thought I meant porn. That was just great. Exactly what I was going for. Now I was the weirdo neighbor with no TV who watched porn on his phone.

I knew assigning me to this mission was a mistake. I was so socially awkward. How did Brooke think I was perfect for this assignment again? Maybe she was more overtired than we all realized.

I felt like I was sinking fast, so I tried to change the topic. "Wine?"

"Sure."

I went back into the kitchen, allowing myself a minute to come up with a plan. I opened a couple boxes before noticing I didn't have any wine glasses. Coffee mugs would have to do.

I poured the wine and decided to just start over with Ellie. If I thought about it, my awkwardness hadn't pushed her away yet. Perhaps she found it endearing in a strange way.

"Sorry, I don't have any wine glasses, I hope this is—" Upon entering the living room, the sun from the balcony window had bathed the room in light. Ellie was turned away from me, hands on her hips and looking as though she was trying to decide something. Just seeing her there, standing like that took me back to when Ashley and I moved into our first home together and she was trying to decide where everything should go.

"I don't think we have enough stuff, Jax."

I stepped forward and wrapped my arms around her middle, resting my hand flat on the swell of her stomach. "We have plenty of stuff, Ash."

She placed her hands over mine and turned her face toward me, her nose pushing against my cheek. "We still need to buy furniture for the nursery. How are we going to afford that? We spent our savings on the down payment for this place."

I shook my head. "My parents are buying us the furniture." I paused, taking a deep breath before making my next suggestion. "If you're so worried, though, maybe we could reach out — "

With a disapproving sigh, Ashley shrugged out of my arms. "Jackson, please," she pleaded, hugging herself and looking anywhere but at me. "I've told you — "

"Nothing," I interrupted, growing frustrated. "You tell me **nothing**. I've never even met them!" My voice grew the deeper into the fight we got. I wished I could say it was the first one, but the truth was, we had this argument more often as our relationship progressed.

"They're not…good people, Jax." Tears glistened in her eyes when she looked at me finally. "Where I come from…you wouldn't understand."

"How do you know that?" I demanded. "You can't just assume I wouldn't get it."

"But you wouldn't! she shouted. "You grew up in a normal house, doing normal things. I…" She let the thought trail off, biting her lip. "Didn't. The things I went through. The things I've seen?"

I took three giant steps across the room and grabbed her upper arms gently, locking eyes with her. "What things? Why are you so reluctant to talk about it?"

The tears won the battle and fell down over her cheeks. "You know I can't." Her chin quivered and her eyes danced back and forth between mine. "Please, don't press this."

My hands slid down her arms until they reached hers. I gathered them up and brought them to my lips, kissing her knuckles. I let my eyes drift down, and I caught sight of the tattoo on her left wrist. She noticed immediately and pulled her long sleeve back down over it, then locked her hand around it as she turned away and walked to the big bay window. She was always so protective over it. I didn't understand it, and she never tried to help me.

"Look, Ash," I started. "I'm sorry.

She exhaled a shaky breath, looking down and turning around. Her hands moved softly over her stomach. "I'm sorry , too. It's just…they can't know where I am…that I'm pregnant. They'd come for us, and you'd never see us again."

"They can't do that, baby," I assured her, going to her and wrapping her in my arms.

"That's where you're wrong," she mumbled. "They can and they will."

Her body shook with sobs as she clung to me. I'd had my suspicions about her upbringing, but hearing her tell me her family would take her and our child away and I'd never see them? It made me wonder if she was raised in one of those cult compounds in the middle of nowhere.

I ran my hand over her head and made soft, soothing sounds. "It'll be okay. I won't let them take you from me."

In a very uncharacteristic move, one of the mugs slipped from my hand and fell to the light carpet. The burgundy liquid spread quickly and started to soak in before I could even move.

"Shit," I muttered. "So much for that damage deposit. Day fucking one, Jax…"

Ellie turned around, the illusion of my dead wife shattered. "Oh no!" She rushed over quickly as I set the other mug down on the empty coffee table nearby. I ran to the kitchen and literally ripped another box apart in my search for something to use to clean the spill. The contents of the box spilled out all over the floor, but I didn't care as I grabbed a handful of dishtowels and ran back to the living room.

Ellie was on her knees in front of the stain already. I joined her and handed her a couple towels before I started scrubbing.

"Stop! Oh, my God! What are you doing?" Ellie sounded both horrified and amused. It was very confusing.

I looked at her, shocked by her reaction. "Trying to clean this shit up?"

Instead of freaking out again, she laughed. "Dab at it, Jax. If you scrub it, you'll just push it around and make the stain worse." She started blotting at the stain, turning the dishtowel a dark shade of red.

I hoped Brooke hadn't paid too much for these. They were going to be ruined.

"Damn it," Ellie muttered. "Do you have any dish soap and hydrogen peroxide?"

"I don't have anything."

"You're adorably unprepared," she replied

with a shake of her head. "I have some in my apartment. Peroxide will be in my bathroom and the dish soap by the kitchen sink. The door's unlocked. Why don't you go grab it while I try to blot as much of this out as I can. I'm not sure I can trust you enough to leave you alone with it."

I could tell she was teasing me, but I didn't argue, I just got up and headed to her place. The door was unlocked, just as she said it would be, and once inside, I was surrounded by Ellie's scent—both old and new. Her old scent was soft and feminine with subtle floral notes, while her new scent—the wolf—was deeper and a little more wild.

As I made my way through Ellie's apartment, my desire to look around grew. I knew it would be an invasion of her privacy, and since I was on a mission to gain her trust, I decided to just grab what I came here for. I could look around another day.

The front door opened as I was grabbing the peroxide from the medicine cabinet, and I laughed. "You can trust me to not snoop through your personal belongings, you know," I quipped, stepping out of the bathroom.

The scent hit me before I saw who it was, and I stopped abruptly in my tracks when I recognized the man who'd been in the park with Ellie the night of the attack. Nate.

Chapter 6 | intuition

His confusion and rage infused the air as his dark eyes burned into mine. The hairs on the back of my neck stood on end, and the wolf crouched just below the surface, readying for the attack. I held it back, knowing a human held no real threat.

"Who the hell are you?" he demanded angrily, his eyes moving over me as though sizing me up for a fight.

It was ridiculous. Not only was I twice his size with several inches on him, I was stronger than him thanks to the wolf.

Even though it went against my nature, I pushed my defensiveness aside and held out my empty right hand. "Jackson Devereux," I introduced. "I just moved in next door. Ellie came over to welcome me to the building."

Nate crossed his arms over his chest, eyes skeptical as he tried to decipher if I was telling the truth or not. "Doesn't explain why you're here, bub."

I had to bite the inside of my cheek to keep from laughing at his attempt at alpha-maling me. "You're absolutely right. I spilled wine on my carpet and haven't had a chance to go and buy any cleaning supplies." I held up the peroxide. "Ellie sent me over here to grab peroxide and dish soap while she tried to sop the wine up from my carpet. Apparently I can't be trusted to be alone with it."

Nate opened his mouth to say something when the front door opened again and Ellie came bursting in. "Jax, what's taking you do lo—?" She stopped talking when he saw what was holding me up. "Nate. What are you doing here?"

He looked confused. "I thought we had plans?"

Oddly enough, my stomach churned upon hearing this. I didn't like this guy, and I most certainly didn't want Ellie to go off with him. It actually felt a little like...jealousy.

She looked at her watch. "Oh, wow. I didn't realize how late it was." Raising her eyes to me, then Nate she smiled. "Why don't you just...wait here, Nate. I'm going to go and help Jackson clean up the stain on his carpet. It'll just take a few minutes."

"You know what?" I interjected. "Just tell me what to do, and I'm sure I can figure it out."

Ellie smiled. "It's fine. I'll just come help. It won't take very long."

Nate was obviously reluctant, but Ellie didn't seem like the type to roll over and submit. And if she used to be, the wolf wouldn't allow for it anymore.

After grabbing the dish soap, Ellie closed her door behind us, sweeping a stray strand of hair back off her face. "Sorry about that."

I waved it off. "Nah. I get it. Strange guy in your apartment when the boyfriend comes home…"

Ellie giggled as I opened my apartment door. "He doesn't live with me. In fact, I'm not sure he's really my boyfriend. We've only been seeing each other a little while, and, if I'm being completely honest, I'm not sure I want to continue the relationship."

She led me to the sink, pausing when she reached it, and laughed. "I…don't know why I'm telling you all this. I hardly know you."

I shrugged, leaning against the counter next to her. "I'm told I'm easy to open up to."

Ellie looked up at me with an arched, disbelieving brow. "Really?" I shrugged, and she turned the faucet on. "Do you have a large bowl, or something?"

I looked at the boxes in the kitchen before finding the contents from the one I ripped open a little while ago all over the floor. There was an overturned mixing bowl. I grabbed it and gave it to Ellie. She filled it with warm water before adding some dish soap and peroxide. She took it back to the living room where the stain remained, but was slightly less noticeable.

Kneeling down, Ellie grabbed one of the unused towels and dipped it into the solution before blotting at the stain again. I watched in amazement as the stain lifted bit by bit.

"So, why are you thinking of ending things?" I asked, trying to keep the conversation going to and see just how much she would tell me. She seemed to trust me, but I wasn't sure if that was just because part of her sensed something familiar.

She shrugged. "I don't know. Things were good in the beginning, and then this past week,

I've just been feeling...different. Like I need, I don't know, more?"

That was the wolf. It was insatiable during the transition. Food, sex... Most humans couldn't handle or understand it.

"Well, it's probably for the best, then." She looked up at me a little strangely. "Better to let him off easy before someone gets hurt."

I meant that in more ways than one. In a normal relationship, humans were always getting hurt, but when a relationship involved both a human and a newly-turned werewolf, the human almost never walked away from that.

Getting rid of Nate was probably the wolf recognizing this, and it really was for the best. Without him hanging around, I would be better able to talk to Ellie and help her understand what was going to happen to her in a few short weeks.

"Okay," Ellie announced, standing up and looking at the carpet with her hands on her hips. "It's not perfect, but it's definitely less noticeable."

I glanced down to see she was right. "Wow. Thanks so much."

"No problem." An awkward silence hung between us before she laughed. "Well, I guess I should get going. Sorry I didn't help out more today."

"Don't even worry about it. I'm sure I'll manage on my own," I assured her, that weird pang in my gut returning.

Ellie looked up at me with a coy smile and a spike in pheromones. I tried not to read too much into it, because it was just the wolf wanting to play. If I was being honest, I found myself feeling a little aroused, too. Ellie bit the inside of her cheek. "Well, I could maybe stop by tomorrow morning?"

Smiling, I countered, "I'm not really a morning person." Disappointment flashed in her eyes, so I quickly tacked on, "How about lunch?"

"Yeah. Sure. I can maybe stop by around one?"

"Perfect. I'll run out tonight for some groceries."

Ellie said goodbye a couple more times before leaving me alone in my apartment. As I stood there, surrounded by her scent, I felt the need to run even more than before — to clear this odd sensation from my head. I glanced at my watch and frowned; I still had a couple more hours until sundown.

I woke up just a little before noon after a particularly restless sleep. I'd been hoping that my late-night run would exhaust me enough, but for whatever reason, I couldn't stop thinking about Ellie. The only thing that set my mind at ease was when I returned to the apartment and picked up her scent, indicating she was already home.

Energized by the fact that she'd be coming over soon, I hopped out of bed and decided to wander down to the nearest store for a few things. I had meant to get up earlier, but I was out later than I anticipated the night before.

Suspecting that Ellie was probably craving meat over anything else, I grabbed eggs, bacon, steak, and then a few other essentials just in case things like fruit and vegetables didn't turn her off.

I headed back to the apartment and set everything up to start cooking before realizing I still hadn't unpacked anything else. Because I needed tools to cook, I decided to start in the kitchen. I picked up the stuff off the floor, placing it on the table until I could put it all away, and then I started organizing a few things. There was a light knock on the door before I heard it creak open.

"Jax?"

"In here, Ellie."

"What the hell are you doing?" she asked with a laugh.

I looked at her, freezing from putting a pot in the cupboard above the stove-side counter. "What?"

"Don't put your pots *there*," she instructed, taking it from me. "Put them down here. Keep your coffee, spices, sugar, and stuff there." She opened the cupboard below the counter and put the pots in there.

Watching as she took charge took me back to when Ashley first moved in with me. She completely changed The Order of my kitchen. Sure, it made more sense, but it wasn't like I ever really cooked anyway.

The two of us worked together to get the kitchen organized before I started on lunch. Ellie stood nearby, watching as I cooked the steaks. Her chest heaved with heavy breaths, and I noticed her pupils dilate, tiny flecks of amber beginning to shine in her dark irises. The wolf was famished. Was she not giving into her cravings?

"How do you like your steak?"

Ellie blinked a few times, her pupils retracting

as she focused on the question. "Usually medium, but for some reason, I'm thinking rare today."

"Sounds good," I said, suppressing a smirk. "I'm going to make a steak sandwich with mine. Would you like the same?"

She looked like she was seriously debating her options before she decided on just the steak. I steamed some vegetables to round out the meal, and when everything was ready, Ellie and I sat at the table and ate together.

"How was your date last night?" I asked.

"It was all right," she said, cutting into her steak and licking her lips when she saw how pink it was in the middle. She took a bite and closed her eyes and hummed as she chewed. "This is really good."

"Thank you. Normally, I'd cook them on the barbeque, but I don't have one yet."

"Oh, no. This is perfectly fine. It's good."

"So, last night was only all right? Does that mean you ended things?"

Ellie's cheeks turned pink, and she smirked as she cut another slice off her steak. "Yes…?"

I laughed before taking another bite of my sandwich. "You don't sound so sure."

"No, I did. But not until after we…"

She didn't have to let her sentence hang for very long before I understood. "You gave him a pity lay."

Instead of looking ashamed, she looked kind of proud. "I didn't intend to, but I just felt like…like I needed *something*."

"Hey, you don't have to explain yourself to me," I told her. "I'm a guy, I get it."

Something I couldn't recognize flashed across

her face before her eyes went really wide. "Oh, my God! Again, I hardly know you; why am I telling you all this?"

I smiled, hoping to assure her that she wasn't overstepping any boundaries. If she were to join our pack, it wasn't like her sex life would be a big secret. Not only was our hearing heightened, but so was our sense of smell. We all had desires and needs that needed to be met, and often times, we couldn't help but submit when the air was infused with it.

"It's fine, Ellie. Honestly. I'd like for us to be friends."

This seemed to put her at ease, but it also awakened the wolf. I could smell it, and see it in her eyes. The inner circle of her brown eyes glowed amber. A sure sign that the wolf was close to the surface. She was transitioning quickly, probably embracing her change in behavior when others often fought and questioned it like Brooke had.

"I think I would like to be friends with you." There was an inflection in her voice that both excited and frightened me. It had been years since I'd been in any kind of relationship—serious or casual. While I knew I wasn't ready for anything serious, I found myself quickly warming to the possibility.

Ellie finished her steak before she started pushing the vegetables around her plate with a scowl. I suspected she might not find them too appealing—it was rare any of us did in those first few months—but I wasn't going to assume as much. I didn't want to make her suspicious.

I chuckled under my breath. "You have something against broccoli and carrots?"

"Not usually," she replied, sounding confused by her own preferences now. "But for some reason..."

"Well, don't force yourself on my account. Obviously your body doesn't require it if you don't find it appealing."

"I just don't want to offend you."

I stood and grabbed our plates, taking them toward the sink. "I assure you, I'm not offended, I go through something similar every so often."

Ellie shrugged. "Maybe my iron is still a little low from the attack last week."

She wasn't wrong. The attacks often depleted our iron levels. It was partially why we craved a lot of red meat in the weeks before our first change. Marcus explained it to me when I struggled with the idea of eating meat after almost two decades as a vegetarian.

"I'm sure it'll all level itself out."

Ellie and I moved into the living room where we moved my couch and unpacked a few boxes. I hadn't realized it yesterday when the guys had helped me unload everything, but one of my bedroom boxes had been placed in the living room instead. Ellie opened it without reading it and reached inside.

"Who's this?" she asked sweetly, drawing my attention to the frame in her hand.

Recognizing it immediately, I rushed across the room and snatched it from her before tossing it back in the box. "Nobody."

Ellie's dark eyes watched me, her forehead creased with concern and confusion. "Jax?"

I inhaled deeply and closed the box. "I don't

want to talk about it." I picked up the box and took it to my room. I had to give myself a minute to calm my racing heart before I could go back out there. I knew I needed to learn to let go of what happened, but it was difficult.

"Fuck," I muttered under my breath, realizing I probably just took three giant steps back with Ellie.

"Jackson?" Her voice was soft, remorseful. "I'm sorry."

I sighed with defeat, turning and sinking onto the end of my unmade bed. "No, Ellie. I'm the one who should be sorry."

Hesitant, she took a few steps into the room and sat next to me. She didn't say anything, she just sat there with me. Waiting patiently for... something.

"I've been having weird dreams," Ellie finally said. I was confused at first, because it had nothing to do with what just happened, but then she continued. "Ever since the attack."

That was normal. When we were asleep, the wolf was awake, trying to show you subconsciously what you were becoming. I was told it was supposed to help when the first shift happened, but I was starting to think only full-bloods retained that conscious control.

"I bet nightmares are to be expected after a traumatic event," I tried to explain.

Ellie nodded, looking blankly ahead. "Yeah. That's what I thought...at first."

"And now?"

Her head turned, her deep brown eyes looking straight into mine. "I don't know. Now they feel...natural. It's like *that's* who I'm supposed to be."

I'd been a wolf for the past fifteen years, and I'd never heard a half-blood speak this way. It gave me hope that convincing her would be easier than any of us had thought. "And who's that?"

She pressed her lips together, almost like she was afraid to tell me. I already knew what dreams she was having; we'd all had them. The dreams were always about the wolf running free, hunting, playing.

"Ellie, you can tell me. I promise, nothing you can say will sound stupid to me."

With a laugh, she tucked her blonde hair behind her ear. "Somehow I doubt that."

Without thinking, I placed a hand on her knee. She glanced down at the same time I did, and there was a moment where the wolves were pleased and oddly content by the connection.

Ellie inhaled deeply, steeling herself for her confession. "Ever since the attack, I've been dreaming of wolves. Or…one wolf." She gauged my reaction before continuing. "In the dreams, the wolf is running through the woods. Sometimes it feels urgent, like it's hunting, other times it feels… fun. What's even more strange, I think the wolf is supposed to be…me."

I smiled, nodding along. Maybe telling her would be easier than I'd thought.

"So they don't feel like nightmares, which I fully expected them to after what I went through, you know?"

"I think I can imagine."

"Along with these strange dreams, I've been acting kind of peculiar."

"How so?"

"Well, there's the food thing. I'm normally a huge fruit and vegetable fan, but lately, it's just such a turn off. Even chocolate, and that's something I indulge in daily. Now, it makes me sick if I eat even the tiniest amount."

"That does sound unfortun—."

"Sex."

Stunned, I stared at her, my eyes going wide and my palms beginning to sweat. "Excuse me?"

Ellie turned to face me fully on the bed, bending a knee and bringing it up onto the bed. Her eyes were bright, the amber center flaring, and her heart was beating excitedly, pushing her obvious excitement through her veins. "I don't know what's going on, but I just can't seem to get enough of it."

My stoic reaction must have made her think this was a huge over-share, because she quickly dropped her eyes to the floor. Her pulse slowed, but only slightly, and lust still radiated off of her in waves. "Again, we just met and I'm talking as though we've known each other forever. I'm so sorry."

"Don't apologize." I gave her leg a gentle squeeze. "We're all human and have...itches that need scratching."

There was another beat of silence that hung around us before her eyes found mine again, her irises glowing in the middle again as the wolf emerged. "I don't know why, but I'm drawn to you, Jax. I barely know you, and I can't wait to be around you. When I first saw you a week ago... I could barely sleep all week. And yesterday? I waited until your friends left before coming over."

"Ellie..."

"I know it sounds...insane, but even when I was with Nate, all I wanted was to be with you. Even if it was just to help you unpack. Why do I feel this way?"

I wanted to tell her everything, but even though she seemed to accept her dreams for what they were, I was still at risk of spooking her. I needed to wait, make her understand what was happening to her.

Moreover, I needed to understand what was happening to me; everything she'd said resonated with me. It was like she was inside my head.

"I think this has been a tough week," I said, swallowing a lump in my throat. "First the attack, then the breakup. It's bound to take its toll on a person.

Ellie nodded along. "Yeah, you're probably right. I mean, what other possible explanation could there be?" We both laughed at the same time before she shook her head. "I mean, it's not like werewolves even exist."

CHAPTER 7 | CLOSER

"How was work today?" I asked as I closed the door behind Ellie.

I'd been living in the building for a week now, and Ellie and I were getting along really well and, I hoped, on our way to growing closer. In an effort to avoid coming across too desperate, I made sure to "accidentally" run into Ellie in the hall a few times before inviting her over for dinner. She seemed really receptive to the idea of hanging out and getting to know each other better, but I wasn't sure if that was her or the wolf...though, it could very well have been both. I found myself wanting to be around her more and more, and whenever we were apart—even if not very far since I was watching her every move—I craved her.

It was...different.

She set the bottle of wine down on the kitchen counter and turned to me. "It was pretty good. How was your day?"

I'd forgotten how nice it was to be around a woman who wanted to hear about your day, and I about theirs. Brooke and Layla didn't count, because they were more like sisters to me, Colby was

young and we didn't have much to talk about beyond Pack business, and Roxy and I were purely
physical; our conversations never ran too deep.
There was a desire to know how Ellie spent her
day that ran deep—so deep, I wondered if it was
hardwired into me.

"Busy," I replied, though it wasn't really. Ellie
thought I worked as a mechanic, though I hadn't
held a job for years beyond a few odd jobs for old
acquaintances when they needed mechanical work
done to their vehicles. Living at the manor, we
didn't have a lot of extra expenses. Over the years,
Marcus had made some pretty good investments,
so money was never a problem. When he and Miranda died earlier in the year, Corbin and Colby
had inherited everything, but it was stipulated in
his will that the money be used to secure the future of the Pack.

"So," Ellie said, looking around the kitchen,
"what's for dinner?"

"I was thinking we'd order in? I couldn't decide on any one thing, and I wasn't sure what
you'd be in the mood for." Truthfully, I just wasn't
a great cook. I could cook a few things, but my cul-
inary skills were seriously lacking in a lot of areas.

"Cool. What are our choices?"

"Pizza, Chinese, Indian... You pick. I'll eat
just about anything," I told her.

It didn't take Ellie long to decide on Vietnam-
ese food from a new restaurant she'd heard about
through a co-worker. Once the food was ordered, I
opened the bottle of wine and was about to pour it
into a couple of mugs when Ellie stopped me with
a laugh.

"Not that your coffee mugs aren't lovely, but

please let me go grab a couple glasses from my place."

While I didn't really care how I drank my wine, I nodded. She was only gone for a couple minutes before she came back with two wine glasses. After I filled them, we headed to the living room and sat on my couch.

"You know," she started, looking around at the room she'd help me set up. "I kind of like that you don't have a TV."

"Oh?"

"Yeah. It allows for actual conversation." Ellie took a sip of her wine and smiled. "The first thing Nate would do when he came over was turn on the TV, then we'd spend hours watching it and hardly speaking."

I nodded along, suddenly worried I wouldn't be able to hold a decent conversation. Maybe it was the perfect time to ease her into what was going to happen to her over the next couple weeks.

"How've you been feeling?" I asked. "Sleeping okay?"

Ellie's head bobbed. "I sleep great. Still having those weird dreams, but I wake up feeling rested and energized. I go to the gym early to work out, otherwise I feel almost antsy."

"That's good, right? I mean, it helps?"

"It really does. Though, I've beat some personal bests when it comes to free weights. Actually 'smashed' might be a little more accurate." Shifting next to me and pulling her legs up onto the couch, she leaned in. It was like she was going to tell me a secret in a room full of people, even though we were completely alone. "Before the attack, I was lifting light, but recently it just didn't feel like enough, so I increased it by a couple pounds. I was easily benching fifty pounds more on that first day. Now? I'm benching double my body weight."

Her news wasn't surprising; increased strength usually happened within the first couple weeks. Sometimes sooner. "Interesting."

"I think you mean 'weird.'"

I laughed just as my phone rang. When I answered it and saw it was the delivery guy, I buzzed him in and grabbed cash from my wallet to pay and tip him. While I collected the food at the door, Ellie grabbed some plates and cutlery, and we met in the living room again where we dished up.

We remained silent for a few minutes before Ellie finally spoke. "So, I'm just going to come out and ask you something."

I swallowed thickly, caught a little off guard. "Shoot," I replied nervously.

"I've got this work thing next Wednesday. It's a formal fundraising dinner-gala thing. Nate was originally going to go with me, but...well, you know, so I was wondering..."

"You want me to go with you?" I concluded after she trailed off. She only nodded, having a bite of her dinner. "When you say 'formal,' you're talking suit and tie?" Another nod. I hated suits more than I hated fucking vamps, but I forced a smile to my face, hoping it came across as genuine. I knew that refusing to go might send the wrong message and could push her away, and I couldn't do that. Besides, I felt like this might be a good opportunity to get to know her even better. And, much to my surprise, I wanted that. It was a feeling I hadn't experienced in almost two decades. I'd grown quite fond of her. "That sounds fun. I'd love to go."

The smile that formed on Ellie's face was radiant. "Really? That's great."

We spent the rest of dinner talking about the gala before cleaning up the dishes together and pouring another glass of wine. As the alcohol flowed, I felt myself loosening up, and I didn't really notice just how close we were sitting together on the couch. And, to be honest, I didn't hate it. The more I got to know her, the more comfortable I became around her. I felt like maybe I could finally move on after losing my wife and child all those years ago.

Ellie laid her head back on the couch and looked up at me with glassy eyes. "Tell me about yourself. I feel like all we ever do is talk about me." There was a pause as I thought about what to say.

"What do you want to know?"

Ellie bit her lip and shrugged. I could tell by her expression where the conversation was headed. "Where are you from?" she began.

"Calgary. Born and raised. You?"

Ellie grinned. "Born up north in Grande Prairie, but my mom moved us to Edmonton before I was one when my dad bailed without giving her a reason. I moved here a few years ago for a job opportunity."

"Holy shit, Ellie. I'm so sorry."

"Don't be." Ellie shrugged and took a sip of her wine. "I'm not."

"Are you and your mom at least close?"

She dropped her gaze to her lap. "We were."

While there was a certain amount of relief that came from hearing she wouldn't have to cut ties with her mother until she could control her gifts, there was something sad in her tone. I found it cut through me until her grief became my grief. It was unsettling.

"She died a couple of years ago. Home invasion. Whoever broke in strangled her."

To look at Ellie—so cheerful and vibrant and full of life—one would never think that she'd had such a difficult upbringing. I wanted to pull her in my arms and comfort her. Take away all the pain she still carried with her and tell her she could and would rise above it.

"After her death, I thought about tracking my dad down. My mom always told me that he was a free spirit and that his leaving had nothing to do with me, but after her death, I came across her journals." Ellie sighed, a sad smile slowly creeping across her face. "In one of the entries, she wrote about the day he left and how he told her I wasn't what he expected. There was some other stuff about their relationship that led me to believe they were just toxic for each other, but it doesn't really matter. I'll never know him, and that's probably for the best."

"Jesus, Ellie…"

Clenching her eyes, Ellie laughed it off and shook her head. "It's fine, really. I've had a lot of years to process it and accept that I'm just not meant to have him in my life. How old are you?"

She barely even gave me time to react before she asked the next question. I wanted to inquire further, but I got the feeling her past was a sore spot with her, so I dropped it. "Forty-three. You?"

"Twenty-five." Her eyebrows pulled together. "You look younger...except your eyes. Your eyes are filled with experience. Ever been married?"

My stomach flipped, and it felt like a knife had been plunged into my heart. It was no secret I didn't like to talk about my life before being turned. I knew it wasn't healthy, but Ash and Tyson were taken from me so violently that it was difficult for me to talk about. "I was," I finally answered.

"The woman in the photo?"

"My wife. Ashley."

"And the boy?"

The knife in my chest twisted. "My son."

Ellie picked her head up off the back of the couch, looking at me with curiosity. "Do you not see him anymore?"

"They, uh...they died fifteen years ago."

I could see the instant Ellie regretted bringing it up. Her expression changed in a flash, like she'd been struck. "Jax, I'm sorry. I didn't know..."

I shook my head and stood up, suddenly feeling too confined. I needed to get out and run. "It's fine. Happened a long time ago."

Ellie set her glass down and stood up. "It's not okay. I'm an asshole. I shouldn't have pried."

Awkward silence filled my living room. Both of us were unsure where to take the conversation from here as I stood five feet away from Ellie while she fidgeted with her hands.

It made me wish I had a fucking TV.

While I wanted to run away from the topic entirely, I also felt this need to be close to her. I *wanted* to share things with her.

"I should...I should go," Ellie stammered,

making a move for the front door.

"We got a flat on our way home from the movies one night," I blurted out. "There was…" I paused, not sure how to continue without her thinking I was insane, so I chose to omit a few facts until she was ready to know more. "A group of people attacked us. Killed my wife and son."

Ellie's hands flew to her mouth and her eyes widened with shock. "Jesus, Jax. I'm so sorry."

With a slight smile, I shrugged a shoulder. "It's not your fault."

"Did the cops find who did it?"

I dropped her gaze and looked out the balcony window before walking over and opening it. I breathed in the fresh air in hopes it would calm me a little. It only made the urge to shift and run stronger. "The killers were caught, yes."

Ellie crossed the room in three giant steps, placing her hands on my back in an act of support. Much to my surprise, her touch calmed me more than the cool air. "I had no idea."

"It's not something I advertise," I confessed, turning to her. "It's not the easiest thing to talk about. Had she just taken him and left, I could probably talk about that more openly. Call her all sorts of nasty names, or otherwise unhealthy coping mechanisms. But we were madly in love, and they were taken in the most violent way. Right in front of me." Without thinking, I reached out and ran my hand through the length of her blonde hair, twisting the ends of it between my fingers. "You remind me a little of her."

"Oh? How so?"

"You look a little like her. Same hair, same tenacious attitude."

Ellie smiled, looking deep into my eyes as her hands came to rest on my hips. I dropped the length of hair, trailing my fingers up and down her back. Her eyes fluttered slightly, fingers curling into my shirt. I could smell the spike in her pheromones, and it travelled straight through me. My skin rippled as I grew aroused, and before I could weigh the pros and cons, I placed my other hand along her jaw and tilted her face to mine, pressing a kiss to her lips.

It didn't take long before Ellie's hands tightened into my shirt, pulling me closer until our bodies were pressed firmly against each other. I'd like to say the wolf took over and was navigating this entire experience, but that would be a lie. If anything, my human side wanted this even more than the wolf.

My hands moved down her body until they were splayed wide across her back. Ellie moaned into the kiss before pulling back, her cheeks filled with color as she released a breathless laugh.

"That was…unexpected."

"Sorry," I whispered, pushing a strand of hair off her face for her. Even though our conversation had gotten a little awkward, this—being with Ellie—felt right. Finally.

"That wasn't me complaining," Ellie quickly assured me. "I've imagined doing that for days."

It was my turn to chuckle. "I hope I lived up to your imagination."

"You surpassed it."

I glanced back toward the couch. "You want another glass of wine? We could talk a little more."

Ellie smiled sheepishly. "That would be nice."

I was just tightening the tie around my neck when there was a knock at my door. "It's open," I called down the hall, before it opened and Ellie's scent hit me.

I heard her shuffling down the hall before she stepped into my room. "Wow," she said approvingly. "You clean up nice."

I turned around, knot securely in place and strangling me, and the sight of Ellie in a knee-length purple dress took my breath away. It fit her body like a glove, hugging every curve. Her hair was pulled up, and the neckline of the dress was high, running just below her collar bone and accentuating it and her shoulders beautifully.

"You look incredible," I told her.

She stepped further into the room and up onto her toes to kiss me lightly. "Thank you.

The last five days since Ellie and I kissed, there'd been progress. Personally. I was still worried about how to tell her what was happening to her. Some days, based on the things she'd say, I felt like she'd be open and accepting to the news, but other days, I feared she'd think I was insane and get a restraining order out against me. I was finally starting to see how Nick had such a difficult time telling Brooke.

How did Marcus do this so many times?

"You ready?" Ellie asked. "I've got a cab waiting downstairs."

"Lead the way," I said, holding an arm out like a gentleman. However, as she walked down the hall, I appreciated the tight-fitting dress even more. There was nothing gentlemanly about the way I ogled her ass. It was purely selfish on my part.

Ten minutes into the thirty-minute cab ride, Ellie reached over and placed a hand over mine. While I half-expected it to feel odd, it didn't. If anything, it felt as natural as breathing. Smiling, I turned my hand over and returned the gesture before bringing hers to my lips and kissing it.

When we arrived at the hotel the gala was being held at, I paid the driver and held a hand out to help Ellie out of the car. Once she was finished fixing the skirt of her dress, I tucked her hand into the crook of my elbow and led her inside.

The banquet hall was busy, music from the live band filling the room and setting the atmosphere. There were several servers wandering around, so I gladly accepted two glasses of champagne from one as Ellie led me through the crowd and toward some of her colleagues where she introduced me.

The night was a bit of a whirlwind, filled with new faces and laughter. It had been a really long time since I'd willingly hung around this many humans, and I was actually enjoying myself. When dinner was announced, Ellie led me to our assigned table where we waited to be served. The dinner was elegantly served, and tasted even better than it looked, and afterward, people danced to their hearts content.

I had never been much of a dancer, but, like Ashley, Ellie had been able to coax me into a few. While the band played a slow song, I pulled Ellie close, my left arm wrapped around her body, and my right hand holding her left against my chest. We swayed to the music as we laughed, and when she laid her head against my chest comfortably, I inhaled deeply, wanting to take in everything about this moment.

But instead of just getting Ellie's sweet scent, I picked up something else. Not only did I recognize the tuberose and jasmine from the night of Ellie's attack, but there was a very strong wolf scent that accosted and worried me. My posture went rigid, and I stopped moving, eyes darting around the room for the source.

"Jax?" Ellie lifted her head. "What's wrong?"

Not wanting to worry her, I smiled and looked down at her. "Nothing. You want to get out of here?"

A smile tugged at the corners of Ellie's mouth as she nodded. "Yeah."

Keeping an arm around Ellie at all times, I remained aware of my surroundings so I was ready for any attack that might come at us as I led her toward the exit. Thankfully, we didn't have to wait long for a cab, and were on our way back to the apartment building before anything could go wrong. When we stepped out of the cab, I took a look around, inhaling deeply to see if we'd been followed, or if maybe there was someone else waiting for us.

There wasn't.

"That was fun," Ellie exclaimed as we made our way upstairs. I walked her to her door like a gentleman and waited for her to unlock it before I headed next door, but instead of saying good-night, she looked up at me with those expressive brown eyes. "You want to come in for a drink?"

With the threat gone for the moment, I smiled, allowing myself to enjoy her company again. "Sure."

Inside, Ellie kicked her shoes off and released her hair from the twisty-thing it was in. I watched as it cascaded down over her back while following her into the kitchen where she grabbed a bottle of white wine from the fridge and was standing on her tip toes to reach two glasses from the cupboard when I came up behind her to help.

My fingers brushed hers, a jolt of electricity moving beneath my skin upon contact, and she sighed, tipping her head to the right. A fog of lust rolled in around us, seeping into every part of me. Desire shot through me until kissing her was all I could think about.

But I had to control myself. I couldn't just force myself on her like some kind of animal. Even though it went against everything my body was screaming for, I set the glasses on the counter next to her as Ellie turned around, her body pinned between mine and the counter. Our new position did little to keep my mind out of the gutter, or my groin from straining against the front of my pants.

Neither of us moved, but I opened the bottle of wine and poured two glasses before handing her one. Our eyes remained locked in some kind of battle for dominance and submission, and the room continued to grow heady with the ever-thickening desire between us.

"Thanks," she said breathlessly, pulling her pillowy bottom lip between her teeth before taking a sip.

I took a drink before setting the glass down and caressing her cheek with my fingertips. It didn't take long before the wine was forgotten, and soon my hand was behind her neck, tilting her face up to mine so I could kiss her.

She whimpered when my lips gently pressed against hers, and I could taste the wine on them. The wine only added to the combination of her natural sweetness, and soon, I was prying her glass from her hand and setting it down behind her.

"Jax," she breathed, letting her head fall back as I trailed my lips down the column of her throat.

I pressed my tongue against her carotid artery, feeling it pulse excitedly, as my hands travelled to the zipper of her dress and lingered there. I looked into her lust-filled gaze for her consent, and when she nodded once, I slowly lowered it until the dress fell slack around her body. My hands moved over the bare flesh of her back, feeling her temperature rise even more.

With a frustrated moan, Ellie brought her hands to the side of my face and pulled me in for another scorching kiss, tracing my lips with her tongue and deepening it. We kissed like a couple of horny teenagers in her kitchen for the better part of ten minutes, letting our hands explore each other's bodies over our clothes.

At some point, Ellie had pulled my tie loose and tossed it on the floor, and was working to undo my shirt when she looked up at me. "Should we take this to the bedroom?"

I smirked wickedly. "Lead the way."

CHAPTER 8 | UNANTICIPATED

We'd been home from the gala for several hours now. It was four in the morning, and Ellie had drifted off about an hour ago with a blissful smile on her face and a rosy glow in her cheeks after we'd slept together. Ellie moaned softly as she rolled over, the blanket slipping from her and exposing her as she relaxed onto her stomach.

Smiling, I reached down and pulled the grey comforter up over her bare back to keep her from catching a chill, kissing her shoulder and inhaling the lingering scent of sex on her skin. I sat there and continued to watch her sleep, allowing a feeling of contentment to wash over me. It was the first time in a long while that I'd felt anything like this. And I liked it.

Being with Ellie, even over such a short period of time, had been incredibly freeing. For years, I'd been resistant to let anyone else in, mostly for fear of having them taken from me the way my wife and child had been. I'd put up a wall, letting very few people see the real me, and in a matter of days, Ellie had been able to penetrate that wall and bring it down brick by brick. I felt comfortable with her and found myself wanting a future with someone for the first time since I lost my wife.

Ellie stirred next to me again, and while I knew I should also try to get some sleep, I was feeling a little hungry. I got up and wandered down the hall to Ellie's kitchen, hoping she wouldn't mind if I grabbed something to eat. Sadly, Ellie didn't have much, and I knew my fridge was even more bare. Knowing Ellie would probably sleep straight through the night since the wolf within was still building its strength, I decided to slip out and go for a quick hunt.

I slipped back into the bedroom for my shirt and pants, kissed Ellie softly on the forehead, and closed her front door behind me. After grabbing the keys for my bike from my apartment, I did a quick check of the building to make sure there weren't any strays or the hunter hanging around, waiting for the opportunity to get to Ellie. Once I felt confident that she was safe, I hopped on my bike and drove to the outskirts of the city. After all the attacks within the city limits, it was definitely safer to hunt as far away from civilians as possible.

Once I was a safe distance from the city, I trekked out into the woods, found a secluded area with a decent cover of trees, and I shifted. It had been a few days since I'd run, so it felt good to release the tension that had been slowly building. Especially after almost coming face-to-face with other wolves and the hunter that was currently stalking my kind. That only added to the unease I'd been feeling.

As I wandered through the woods, trying to track down something to hunt, I wondered why Ellie and I hadn't been followed back to the apartment. It would've been easy enough, yet there was no sign of any danger. Even as I left, everything was fine. Regardless, I wasn't going to stay out here too long; Brooke would skin me alive if I let anything happen to Ellie.

The sky began to lighten as I finished eating the rabbit I'd managed to hunt, and I could smell the warmth of the sunrise as it heated the air. I didn't think I'd been gone that long, but it would seem it had been about an hour. After shifting back and getting dressed, I headed back to the city, deciding to stop and pick up a couple cups of coffee and some bagels for breakfast to surprise Ellie.

I parked my bike in front of the apartment and then walked down the block to the little coffee shop that was there. Not knowing what Ellie liked, I bought several different flavors of bagels, and then I went back to our building. When I approached Ellie's door, a wave of panic hit me and seeped in until dread churned in my gut.

I threw the door open, afraid of what I might find, but also ready to take down whatever threat was waiting. Instead of finding a life-threatening situation, I was met with Ellie throwing her arms around me.

"Where were you?" she asked, fingers curling into my shirt desperately. I instantly feared the worst, thinking maybe something happened while I was gone to warrant her fear. Had someone shown up and threatened her?

I inhaled deeply, unable to pick anything unusual up, and grew more confused by the emotions that continued to roll off her. I was finally comforted when relief seemed to override it all.

While I didn't want to discount her feelings, I knew I needed to diffuse the situation with levity.

Pulling back, I offered her a smile and held up the offering of morning coffee and bagels. "Breakfast."

Ellie's cheeks turned a deep shade of pink, and she looked at her bare feet while she tugged at the hemline of the oversized T-shirt she was wearing. "Oh."

"Where did you think I'd gone?" I followed Ellie into the kitchen and set everything down on the table before turning to her and pulling her into my arms.

"I...wasn't sure." She wrapped her arms around my waist and shrugged.

I picked up on the tremble of uncertainty in her voice and eyed her suspiciously. "Ellie?"

"When I woke up and you were gone, I thought maybe you...left." There was a pause as she exhaled heavily. "Like maybe you'd gotten what you wanted and had no reason to be here."

Her confession stung, but I could understand it in a world as sexually liberated as ours had become over the years. One night stands and casual sex were considered the norm, and while I'd indulged in both over the years, I'd never left a woman in the middle of the night never to be heard from again. I wasn't wired that way.

Placing my hands on either side of her face and urging her eyes to mine, I asked, "Do you really think that little of me?"

"I barely know you, and most guys—"

I pressed my lips to hers to silence her. "I'm not most guys, Ellie. After you fell asleep, I got a little hungry. Neither of us had anything, so I went out to go grab something." I wasn't sure just how honest I should be; part of me wanted to tell her everything, but in her current state, I wasn't sure she'd react positively. "I lost track of time as I walked around, and before I knew it, the sun was coming up, so I stopped for breakfast, thinking you'd still be sleeping and I could surprise you."

Ellie's eyes danced between mine, possibly gauging whether or not I was being honest. When I still saw uncertainty in her expression, I sighed heavily.

"Ellie, it's been a long time since I allowed myself to feel anything for another woman. I've been involved with others casually, but I feel very drawn to you in a way I haven't felt since Ashley." I saw the first crack in her hesitation, and I smiled. "I'm sorry if I frightened you. I should have left a note, but you just looked so peaceful. I really didn't think you'd be awake before I came back."

Slowly, Ellie started to come around, bringing her hands up to cover mine as she leaned into my touch. "I'm sorry for being so damn insecure," she whispered. "It's not who I am…I'm just feeling…"

"Out of sorts," I concluded for her, kissing her forehead and inhaling deeply. Her panic had dissipated. "I get it. You'll feel like yourself soon enough." I pulled away from her and gestured toward the table. "We should eat, then maybe we could head back to bed. I'm finally feeling like I could sleep."

Ellie looked almost disappointed as she grabbed an everything bagel from the bag and tore into it, so I reached across and pulled her chair to mine. She released a little squeal. Slowly, I ran my hands up the outside of her thighs until I reached her hips, then I pulled her forward so she was straddling me on the chair.

"What's with the pout?" I teased, brushing my lips over hers.

Ellie groaned when I refused to let her kiss me. "You're a tease," she accused breathlessly.

"Am I?" I tightened my hold on her hips and pulled her against me. She moaned again, narrowing her eyes at me as she tossed her breakfast on the table. She ran her fingers through my hair, tugging on it until I looked up at her. Amber flashed in her eyes, and I recognized the wolf's hunger as it ignited my own. We stared each other down for a minute before I finally asked, "What are you going to do?"

I reveled in the predatory look in her eyes as she grinned. One of Ellie's hands slid down over my shoulder, her fingers dancing down over the planes of my chest. "I have to tell you, Jax... I feel so alive whenever we're together. You have this pull over me, and I've tried to ignore it, but I can't." Her eyes flitted to mine. "Don't tell me you haven't felt it."

I couldn't deny the attraction I felt toward her. It was all I could think about most days. While a large part of me suspected it was nothing more than our wolves craving each other, I had to wonder if it could be more. Could Ellie be the one I've been waiting for? Could she be my mate?

Asserting her dominance over me once more, Ellie pressed her lips to mine. My body reacted positively when she shifted her hips above me, my hands leaving her hips and travelling up her shirt until I was palming her breasts. She moaned into my mouth before throwing her head back, and I quickly removed her shirt before gripping her back and pressing my lips to the hollow of her throat.

Her hips moved again, and my fingers curled into her warm flesh before dragging them down her back. My lips travelled down to her chest while her nimble fingers made quick work of the button up shirt I'd pulled back on before leaving the house. She pushed it open, dragging her nails down the planes of my chest until she reached my belt. She pulled her body back far enough to break my contact with her as she focused on freeing me from my pants. Once she had them undone, we maneuvered our bodies enough until they were out of the way, and then Ellie slowly lowered herself onto me.

We both moaned through the sensation of me entering her, and I had to draw my focus away from it momentarily before it all came to an abrupt end. Soon, Ellie started moving above me, setting a slow and steady pace. She draped her arms over my shoulders, threaded her fingers into my hair, and leaned forward to kiss a trail along my jaw until she reached my neck. She inhaled deeply when I thrust my hips upward, and growled before biting down on my shoulder as we increased our pace. The sting travelled beneath my skin until it spread out like tendrils of pleasure. Her behavior this morning was a little more primal—a little more possessive. And it only spurred me on more.

Ellie dropped one of her hands to the high back of the chair and gripped it for leverage. The wood creaked, and we groaned. Ellie's skin grew hot against mine as her cries escalated and became more intense. Seconds later, we reached the summit together, welcoming that body-numbing sensation of free-falling, when all of a sudden we were literally crashing to the ground.

The chair splintered and shattered beneath us, and we landed in a heap on the kitchen floor. Ellie started giggling as she raised her head, and I soon joined in.

"Whoops," I said, still trying to catch my breath.

"Yeah." Ellie pushed herself up, looking around the kitchen floor at the chair's remains. When her eyes travelled back to me, they widened with shock and remorse, her fingers flying to the tender skin of my shoulder. "Oh God, Jax…"

I craned my neck to find the bite mark on my shoulder. Droplets of blood were present, but the puncture marks were already starting to heal. "Ellie, it's fine."

"Jax, no. I broke skin." A blast of cool air covered my lower half when Ellie stood abruptly, running to the sink for a cloth. She ran it under water and came back to me as I sat up. She knelt next to me and gently pressed the cold cloth to my skin, then her eyebrows furrowed with confusion.

I looked down to see the bite was barely visible now that the blood had been cleared away. I offered her a smile. "See? It's not so bad."

"But…you were bleeding. How is this possible?"

Taking the cloth from her, I gathered her hands in mine and brought them to my lips. "Ellie, it's not serious, and I'm not hurt."

"Yeah, but…"

"Come on," I urged. "Let's get this cleaned up and finish our breakfast so we can go grab a little more sleep."

Ellie still seemed confused, but she helped me clean up the splintered remains of her dining room chair while we drank our almost-cold coffee and ate some breakfast. Once everything was squared away, I led Ellie back to her bedroom and we curled up beneath the covers and fell asleep for a few hours.

CHAPTER 9 | REPERCUSSIONS

With every passing day, Ellie grew stronger in order to survive her first shift in six days. She seemed to embrace the changes her body was going through better than anyone I'd ever known. Unfortunately, even with all the hours I'd put in to building a friendship with her, I was still no closer to telling her that her dreams, and the feelings she had about them, were her new reality. I knew it had to happen, but I needed help on how to broach the subject with her in a way that she'd believe me. Why did I ever think this would be easy?

A knock on my door reminded me of the time, and I pulled it open with a smile when I saw Brooke standing there, Azura in her arms. I hugged her and invited her in.

"I'll be honest," she said, setting the diaper bag down near the door, "I didn't think I'd miss you this much. The house is too cheerful without your personal brand of…charm."

"Well, I can't say I'm too surprised," I quipped, taking Azura and smiling down at her. I couldn't believe how much she'd changed already. "What are you feeding this kid? She's growing so fast."

Brooke laughed. "You think?"

I shrugged. "Maybe I've just been gone too long."

Brooke sat on the couch and rested her head back. "How's it going here? Have you told her yet?"

I shook my head, standing up and rocking the baby gently. "I can't figure out how."

"Nick's approach was successful."

"As I recall it, you tried to run out of the house screaming."

"But I didn't."

"Pretty sure that's because you were naked."

Brooke glared at me. "If you weren't holding my baby, I'd kick your ass."

"You'd try." I looked down at Azura, who opened her eyes and focused on me. "Your mommy thinks she's so tough."

"Her mommy is tough," Brooke corrected. "Seriously, though. We've got six days until she'll be forced to shift with the next full moon. It might be risky to wait until the day of to tell her."

"Telling her early will only freak her out. She could run."

"You're sure?"

I sighed heavily, glancing up at the ceiling. "I've gotten close to her."

The springs in the couch groaned as Brooke shifted. "Oh?" I heard the curiosity in her voice before I saw the intrigue in her eyes.

I rolled my eyes. "You know the great thing about living on your own?" I asked. "My business remains mine."

Brooke flopped back on the couch with a

heavy sigh. "I just want you to find someone. You deserve that. Most of the time. When you're not being an asshole."

I laughed. "So, three days a year?"

"At least."

I relaxed next to Brooke, still chuckling. "She's getting stronger, her senses heightened."

"Is she questioning it?"

"She was," I admitted.

"And now she's not?"

"I don't know. She seems to have accepted it all so far. She even told me how her dreams feel like something more."

"How I don't miss those," Brooke muttered. "So she seems like she might be okay with the news?"

"I can't be sure. Her comments could be those of acceptance, but they could also just be her way of making light of it because she has no idea what awaits her in six days."

"So what's the plan?"

"I don't know," I confessed. "I've never had to do this before. Marcus always talked to the bitten before they changed. You were the first one brought into the pack he didn't get to ahead of time, and Nick wasn't sure how to bring it up without pissing you off. I actually gave him a pretty hard time about it."

Brooke snickered, but something told me she still didn't find it very funny. She sat up and looked up at me. "Well, what did Marcus say to you?"

"To be honest, it was hard for me to deny what he told me because I was there when he shifted back into a man."

"Well, Nick convinced me by shifting. It was also successful when we brought my parents in on the secret," she reminded me.

I considered trying that for a moment. It might work. It might also make her run screaming into the halls, alerting our neighbors...

"If Nick had shown you before your first full moon, would you have believed him?"

"What do you mean?"

"Would it have been easier for you to accept had you not woken up, confused and covered in dirt after a night of hunting?"

She pulled her eyebrows together as she sat forward, folding her hands. "I'm not sure. I guess it might have been a little harder to swallow."

"I just worry that shifting in front of her will freak her the hell out, and we can't have that. Whoever targeted her has been watching her. I've picked up their scent, but I've been unable to track them down. Whoever they are, they're good. I imagine they haven't made a move, because they can smell me, too. If I scare her and she runs...?"

"They'll grab her. Yeah, you're right. Okay, maybe wait until the day of. Make plans, and when the change starts, talk her through it. Nick did that for me. It might be the best way in this situation, too."

"What should I plan?"

Brooke shrugged. "I don't know. Ask her out? Take her for a walk somewhere secluded?"

I laughed, disrupting Azura. "In the middle of the city? With someone currently hunting our kind and the cops looking for wild animals ?"

"Hmmm. Good point. We'll keep thinking." She paused. "Are you okay with her for a sec? I think all the coffee I drank this morning is catching up with me."

"You bet. Down the hall on the right."

While Brooke was in the bathroom, there was another knock at the door. One deep breath, and I knew it was Ellie. I opened the door to her bright smile...which faded when her dark eyes shifted to the baby in my arms.

"Jax, I thought...?" She lifted her gaze. "What's going on?"

"Good lord, Jackson," Brooke said, coming out of the bathroom. "That bathroom is smaller than your shower back at the manor."

I glanced back to see that her head was down as she adjusted the rings on her right hand. She should have smelled Ellie's presence as immediately as I had, but sometimes she forgot to channel the wolf side of her. It was something she said she was working on.

"I'm sorry," Ellie said, "I didn't realize you had...company." I picked up on the surge of jealousy and the desire she felt to claim territory.

Brooke must have, too, because she slapped on a huge smile and stepped forward. "You must be Elizabeth."

"E-Ellie," she replied, a little shocked.

"Well, Jackson has had nothing but nice things to say about his new neighbor." Brooke was really laying it on thick. Ellie seemed to be buying it, but I could still sense her hesitation. "I'm Brooke, Jackson's friend." She reached for Azura. "And this precious little bundle is Azura."

Ellie inspected the baby as Brooke took her, then looked at me. "Is she...?"

"Jackson's?" Brooke finished at the same time

I said, "Mine?"

Brooke laughed. "No. Her dad is my...well, I guess he's kind of my boyfriend again. Or is that a juvenile term now? I mean, we're almost thirty..."

"Brooke, you're rambling," I interjected.

"Sorry. Lack of sleep." Brooke reached for the diaper bag, and I helped her adjust it on her shoulder while she held the baby. "Thanks." Her eyes met mine. "You'll call if you need anything, right?"

"You know I will," I assured her.

Brooke turned to Ellie again, and her eyes went wide with realization. "Jax, why don't you invite Ellie to dinner at the manor on Saturday?"

I shook my head. "I don't know if that's a good idea. Saturday at the manor is sure to be...hectic."

"Probably less than you think. It would be perfect, and just what you were hoping for."

I thought about it for a moment before realizing Brooke might be right. It was far enough out of the city we weren't at risk of being seen. "I think Ellie and I should discuss it, and I'll get back to you."

Brooke smiled triumphantly. "Perfect." She stepped up and gave me a one-armed hug. "Take care." Turning toward Ellie, she held out a free hand, which Ellie accepted. "It was nice meeting you."

"You too, Brooke."

I closed the door after ushering Ellie inside and turned to her. "I'm so sorry. Brooke can be a little—" Before I could finish, Ellie's arms were around my neck, and her lips were on mine, moving eagerly.

"Ellie," I mumbled, forcing her lips from mine. "What are you doing?"

Breathless, she smiled up at me. "Kissing you."

I smirked. "Well, yeah, I can see that. But why?"

Amber flashed in her eyes, the wolf's dominance returning. "Because you're mine."

CHAPTER 10 | SHIFT

We pulled up to the manor at five. With sunset at about eight-thirty, Brooke wanted to be sure we had enough time to eat and for me to talk to her privately before everything started. After talking to the Pack, Brooke felt like this might be our best option, so I waited. It wasn't hard considering how much I enjoyed procrastinating over the last few weeks.

Some of the Pack would be shifting tonight, but they'd agreed to wait until Ellie's forced shift was complete, to give her space while I helped her through it. The rest of them had been shifting regularly while they tracked other new strays and investigated the ones who were so clearly building their army against us.

When Brooke told me that the rest of the Pack was still out investigating the stray problem, I felt a little guilty. She assured me that what I was doing was just as important—if not more-so—because Ellie was probably still being watched. She wasn't wrong, either. There were several instances where I picked up the scent of a few different wolves tracking her. They must have smelled me, too, though, because none of them ever made a move to get close to her. Even when I was following her at a distance to keep an eye on her.

"Wow," Ellie said, hopping off the back of my bike and removing her helmet. "This place is incredible."

"It can feel pretty crowded some days," I confessed, setting the helmets on the bike and placing a hand on Ellie's lower back. "Come on."

We walked into the manor to find it quiet versus bustling with activity like usual. I would have to thank Brooke for that. I could tell Ellie was on edge today more than usual because of the moon. I didn't want to overwhelm her.

"Holy shit," Ellie mumbled when we stepped inside.

"Oh, good. You two made it," Brooke said, coming from the dining room to our right. Nick was flanking her.

"Where's the little one?" I asked, noticing neither of them had the baby.

"Napping upstairs while we cook dinner," Brooke said before turning to our guest. "Ellie, this is Nick. Nick, Ellie."

Nick held out a hand, eyes evaluating her. "It's nice to meet you."

"You, too." Her eyes wandered around the foyer again, oblivious to Nick's analytical stare. "Your home is beautiful."

Brooke looped an arm through Ellie's and led her for the dining room so we could make our way to the kitchen. "This is just the foyer. There's plenty more house to be seen."

The kitchen was also empty, as was the sitting

room right next to it. I could smell the roast cooking in the oven, and my mouth watered for a home-cooked meal. Since living on my own again, I found myself missing our big family dinners. Plus, while I was capable enough in the kitchen, Brooke was a far better cook than I ever had been.

"Where is everyone?" I asked, sitting at the kitchen island as Brooke offered us all a glass of wine.

"Vince and Layla are at home with Sammy tonight," Nick began. "Colby and Zach went for a run a while ago, Corbin is in the library, and Roxy and Alistair are in the city. Date night." The look he shot my way told me this "date" was likely recon.

Ellie's eyes widened with the knowledge of just how many people lived here, but Brooke just winked at her. "We figured a quiet dinner might be a little less intimidating than forcing the entire family on you all at once."

"Family?"

"We're all very close," I explained, nodding to the seat next to me.

Ellie smiled and accepted, reaching across the counter for the wine Brooke had poured for her. "Thank you."

I tried not to focus on the fact that Ellie seemed agitated. She was constantly shifting in her seat, cracking her knuckles, and looking around. Brooke noticed it too and had trouble hiding the sympathy from her expression. It wasn't too long ago that she'd experienced the same unease whenever the moon as full. Soon enough, Ellie's tension would be relieved. I just hoped to make it as easy on her as possible.

Brooke and Nick worked together to finish dinner. Watching them was a kick in the nuts, but it also filled me with hope. It hurt, because I used to have that, but it also gave me hope that I could again. With Ellie. Brooke had been able to find happiness after tragedy, proving it wasn't impossible or scary. Was she over David? Her still-frequent night terrors told us she continued to struggle.

"So, how long have the two of you been together?"

Brooke glanced at Nick and smirked as she picked up a knife to cut the carrots. "We reconnected about nine months ago."

Ellie stopped moving, and when I looked at her, I noticed a confused look on her face. She looked as though she were trying to work something out. It wasn't until she asked her next question that I realized where her confusion rested.

"So the baby…?

"Shit!" Brooke hissed, setting the knife down, quickly and moving to the sink. Droplets of blood fell to the floor, and I noticed Ellie's nostrils flare as she picked up the scent. Her brow furrowed, and she shook her head before standing up to offer her help.

Nick was at Brooke's side first with bandages. "I've got it, but thanks, Ellie." He took Brooke's hand after she was done cleaning the cut and bandaged the finger, even though I knew the cut had already closed. We healed rapidly, unless silver was involved. "It's not even that deep."

"Are you sure?" Ellie asked. "That was a lot of blood."

Brooke turned to us with a smile. "Yup. Nothing a Band-Aid won't fix." Brooke cleaned up the blood and washed up again while Nick pulled the roast out of the oven and carved it.

Once everything was ready, we migrated to the kitchen table to eat. Since it was just the four of us, there was no need to move everything to the formal dining room, and this would hopefully make Ellie feel a little more comfortable.

While we dished up, Brooke and Nick asked Ellie about her job, and listened with interest when she told them about her work at the law firm. I wondered if it was a line of work she might continue on after she learned the truth about what she had become. Some of us continued to work when we could to busy our minds. Being idle too long often led to the wolf getting restless.

Ellie was the first to finish eating, and looked at the remaining food as though she hadn't had enough. Brooke noticed and smiled. "Help yourself to seconds, Ellie. There's plenty."

I could tell she was hesitant, so in an effort to make her feel better, I helped myself to seconds, even though I was satisfied. "Brooke's a great cook. I wouldn't be surprised if you wanted seconds. I can't get enough." I was happy when she took more food, because her body was just trying to fuel up for the change in a couple hours.

After dinner, Brooke cleared the table and put a pot of coffee on to brew. Just as it started percolating, the baby woke up, so Nick excused himself to go get her.

Brooke continued to glance at the sky above the mountains as we all sat around the table with our coffee. It was a magnificent combination of oranges, pinks, and purples as the sun began to set. While the rest of us could feel the pull of the moon, we'd grown used to the feeling and could suppress the urge. Ellie, however, only grew more and more restless, and I suspected she might shift early.

Brooke must have gathered the same thing. "Jax, why don't you take Ellie on a tour of the grounds. It's so beautiful out tonight. We won't have the nice weather for much longer."

I looked to Ellie, noticing the amber ring in her eyes was brighter than ever. She was teetering on the edge. "You up for it?"

She agreed almost too quickly. "Yup. Let's go." The wolf was anxious to get outside.

"Thanks for a great meal," I told Brooke. I nodded at Nick, and he returned the gesture while holding Azura.

"Stay close," he instructed. "Just in case."

"In case what?" Ellie questioned as I closed the patio door behind us.

I laughed. "He's paranoid about wild animals."

Ellie smiled, looping her arm through mine. I'd grown used to the closeness between us, embraced it, even. "Well I'm sure you'll protect me," she said, resting her head against my arm.

We walked through the backyard and toward the trees for privacy. Ellie noticed the charred remains of the gazebo and inquired about it. I struggled with the memory of almost losing Roxy that night.

"Vandals," I explained, leaving out the fact that it was vampires who were trying to send us a message. I'd introduce her to one supernatural creature at a time. "They trespassed and set it on fire."

"Was anyone hurt?"

"Thankfully, no."

Ellie's hand tightened at my elbow, her nails digging in through the sweater I wore. She groaned, stopping dead in her tracks as she bent over a little.

"Ellie? Are you okay?"

The smile she wore when she looked up at me was forced. "Yeah. Cramps. I must have eaten too much."

That wasn't it. I could smell the wolf, could feel the waves of heat starting to roll off her body. She was going to shift any minute.

I needed to bite the bullet and tell her before it happened. Hopefully she'd remain lucid long enough to understand. "Ellie..." She looked up at me, waiting to hear what I had to say. "It isn't cramps."

She laughed. "Yes it is."

I took her hand and pulled her toward the trees. "It is and it isn't. It's so much more than that."

Her dark eyes widened as she looked around. I was pulling her into the cover of trees to offer her privacy to change, but I soon realized it probably looked bad to her.

"Jax, where are we going?"

"I've tried to find a way to tell you this since we met, but I didn't realize just how difficult it was going to be. Or just how much I was going to care about you."

"Tell me what? Jax, you're scaring me." I could hear the tremble in her voice, but I could see in her eyes that the wolf was prancing at the surface of her consciousness, just waiting for her to let go a little.

"The night you were attacked..." She nodded once. "I was there."

"Wh-what?"

"I showed up after. I'd been investigating the strange attacks that have been going on for months. That was the first night we'd had any sort of breakthrough in the case," I explained, embracing the honesty in order to maintain her trust.

"We?"

"My Pack."

Her mouth opened as though she was going to say something, but no sound came out.

"The dreams you've been having, all the cravings? Your increase in strength and the heightened senses? There's a reason for it all, and you've suspected it on some level—you told me as much." I paused, holding both of her hands in mine. "You were just in denial that something like that could ever exist."

Realization sparked in her eyes, and just as she was about to say something, she doubled over in pain. I held her hands through it all, falling to my knees with her as she squeezed.

"Listen to me," I told her as she screamed. "I know it hurts, but you have to go with it. Ride it out and let it take you to your final destination." All I heard was Marcus, and the nostalgia of my first transformation, as well as the grief over my fallen Alpha, threatened to swallow me.

"You're not going to remember this soon, but don't fight it. Open yourself up to it. Accept it. Let the pain take you where you need to go."

Ellie released my hands, dropping them to the

grass. Her fingers curled into the soil, and her back arched toward the sky. The sound of her bones snapping and realigning was almost drowned out by her cries, and I was so thankful that Brooke had suggested we come out here for this. We were sure to draw attention in the city.

"Jax!" Ellie cried, looking up at me. Her eyes were solid amber, the deep chocolate color I'd often lost myself in completely overtaken, and her canines had begun to descend.

I reached out and held her face. My own wolf paced anxiously, wanting to join the shift, but I knew I had to talk Ellie through this, so I suppressed it. "You can do this."

Sweat poured down Ellie's face as the change continued. Her body grew and changed shape, her clothes tearing and falling off her body. Wiry blonde fur sprouted all over her skin, and soon Ellie's cries turned to a howl.

I stared at her for a moment as she took in her surroundings. Her tail was tucked beneath her, head low to the ground and eyes flitting nervously from left to right. When her gaze finally settled on me, she jumped back, pinning her ears down, and the flaxen hair around her neck and shoulders stood on end. A warning growl rumbled in her chest as I sank to her level and dropped my eyes, holding a hand out toward her. I wasn't submissive by nature, but I needed to gain her trust before she took off.

Her cold nose touched the tips of my fingers, and her warm breath trailed across the skin of my hand. I glanced up to find her ears were perked forward and her head was dipped to the right with curiosity. Just as I was about to say something to her, a noise in the distance spooked her, and she took off through the trees.

"Shit," I muttered, standing up and taking off my shirt. I had just reached for the button on my pants when something hit me from behind, throwing me to the ground.

Rocks and twigs scraped my chest. I groaned, pressing my hands into the ground and pushing myself back up, prepared to knock out whoever hit me. I was almost to my feet when whoever it was kicked me square in the stomach, knocking the air from my lungs.

Even though my chest burned, I hopped to my feet, adrenaline pumping through my veins and setting them on fire. I felt the wolf lunging at the perimeter of my self-control. To shift now would put me at a disadvantage. I would be vulnerable and weak. Instead, I harnessed its power, intending to use it against the lowlife piece of shit that was attacking me.

I whipped around, ready for the next assault, but there was nobody there. I could sense I wasn't alone, though. My eyes scanned the area while I inhaled deeply, trying to pick up the scent of my assailant. The scent of tuberose and jasmine hit me hard, surprising me, because I had been expecting stray wolves.

This was the scent of the hunter that Ellie and Nate had encountered last month.

I could smell her—the perfume, her sweat. Once again something in my memory tried to spark to life, but couldn't. It pissed me off.

Her scent hung around me, but I couldn't see her anywhere. Couldn't sense her presence. Had she gone after Ellie? Or would she see me as the bigger threat? I waited a minute, knowing I should shift because I'd be faster on four legs versus two, but could I risk it?

The hairs on the back of my neck stood on end as awareness zipped up my spine. She was close. I clenched my hands at my sides and stood still, pretending I couldn't sense her nearby. I closed my eyes and sniffed the air while I listened for movement.

There was the softest sound of her feet moving through the soft grass, and then something cutting through the air. Opening my eyes, I whipped around, my dark blond hair whipping across my forehead as I blocked her attack. Her forearm hit mine. There was a slight sting, but not enough to throw me off. She moved fast, throwing several punches before trying a kick. She was well trained in combat, but so was I. Marcus made sure of it.

I tried to get a read on her face, hoping I might be able to identify her if she so happened to take off again, but her long blonde hair was loose, falling across her face as she moved swiftly. There was something deeply familiar about her as her eyes burned with fury, though. It was unsettling. She had so much hatred and anger in her, and it showed in the way she fought.

She threw another punch with her left hand, almost getting me right in the throat. Somehow, I managed to block her, grabbing her wrist and turning her so her arm crossed over her chest. I wrapped my left arm around her, holding her shoulders and effectively pinning her back against my chest. We were both breathing heavily, and she struggled against my hold on her.

"Let me go, mutt," she snarled, looking back up at me through a curtain of wind-blown blonde hair.

"What is your fucking problem, little girl?" I demanded with a threatening growl, tightening my grip on her wrist and holding her still.

With a fierce scream, she threw her head back. She was too short to get me in the nose, but she made contact with the lower half of my jaw, forcing my bottom lip into my teeth. I tasted blood immediately.

She probably expected me to relinquish my hold on her arm, but I held firm. She did, however, manage to twist away. Her hair flipped across her face before falling around her shoulders, but before I could get a good look at her, my eyes fell to her left wrist.

I froze, unable to move. My chest tightened for an entirely different reason now. I couldn't breathe, and my vision darkened. That two-inch black spiral against ivory skin had been burned into my memory ever since the first night I saw it. There was no way I would ever forget it.

Another angry cry filled the night sky, and a foot landed square in my sternum with a sickening crack, knocking me back a few steps and forcing me to let go of her.

Disoriented, I shook my head, hoping to clear it enough to process what I was seeing. Then I heard the sound of a blade being unsheathed, and when I looked up, I was looking into a very familiar pair of big blue eyes.

But it was impossible... Wasn't it?

"Ash?"

CHAPTER 11 | FERAL

"Ashley?" I asked again, hoping to get a response. "Sweetheart, is that you?" The rational side of my brain told me this wasn't Ashley—that it was just someone who held a remarkable resemblance to her—but the other part of my brain told me it was absolutely her. Same eyes, same hair, same tattoo.

Sure, she wasn't exactly as I'd remembered her. Fifteen years had passed. While she still looked younger than the forty years she would be today, she'd aged. Add to that, her normally bright blue eyes held a certain hardness brought on by whatever she'd been through all this time.

A spark of recognition flashed in her eyes, but it was gone just as quickly as she raised the sword. "How do you know my name?"

I inhaled a shaky breath upon her confirmation. I wanted to rush to her, pull her into my arms and never let her go, but the moonlight gleaming off the broadsword she held aloft deterred me. Instead, I held my hands up as a sign of surrender and took a step forward.

In response, Ashley took a wary step back.

She was as unsure of what was going on as I was.

"It's me, Ashley. It's Jackson."

"Stop that," she ground out through clenched teeth, her body language threatening again.

"Stop what?"

"Stop talking to me as though you know me."

I continued to search for even a flicker of the woman I married all those years ago. While it seemed she was a little thrown by my appearance, I came up empty. "You're my wife," I finally said, a big part of me hoping that would be all it took.

She only laughed, but never dropped her guard. "Your *wife*?" she inquired, her expression hardening once more as she steeled her stance. "Newsflash, *dog*, I would never marry your kind."

"I wasn't always this."

"Honestly? I don't care!" Her battle cry filled the space between us as she lunged. I deflected every strike, carefully avoiding the sword she expertly wielded. She caught onto my every move quickly, changing up her line of attack and adapting at the last minute. The tip of her sword came down, and I moved just a fraction of a second too late. It cut through the skin of my chest, burning as it sliced deep. Very little blood seeped from the wound before the silver from the blade cauterized the wound.

"Shit," I hissed, looking down at the gaping wound for a split second. When I looked back up, I saw Ashley staring at what she'd done, a horrified look on her face. Then her eyes locked with mine, and I saw the spark of recognition I'd been hoping for.

But it faded in an instant when two vicious snarls ripped through the night. One glance over

Ashley's shoulder, and I recognized the two wolves running toward us: Nick and Brooke.

Nick had about two feet on Brooke, but she was gaining on him, their eyes locked on Ashley and not me. Even though my chest was still burning from her blade, my only thought was to keep her safe.

Ashley noticed the wolves, and looked panicked. I had no doubts that she could take on all three of us at once; she was skilled, highly trained, and unbelievably strong. But she was rattled. Something about hurting me had shaken her.

"Ashley, run," I ordered. She looked at me with confusion, breathing hard. Then her expression steeled once more. I could see the conflict all over her face. Should she stay and fight all three of us? Should she heed my advice and flee?

It didn't take her long to decide. She narrowed her eyes at me once more, her eyes completely void of any and all recognition from before, and she took off through the trees.

Probably because they were confident they'd be able to catch up with her, Brooke and Nick stopped, ears forward and expressions worried as they looked me over. The pain in my chest finally registered fully, and I pressed my hand to the wound. The silver stung, and I knew the wound wouldn't heal properly unless I had it debrided soon. But I didn't have time for that now. "I'm fine. Ellie took off, though. We should focus our attention on her." They both regarded me curiously, heads tilted to the side. "We can find the hunter later. Ellie is our main priority. Before the strays find her."

I stood up and started to remove my pants so

I could finally shift. Because of the silver from the blade, it only took a while before I was on all fours, sniffing the ground and air for Ellie's scent. I also noted Ashley's. As soon as we'd secured Ellie's location, I had every intention of finding my estranged wife and figuring out what the hell was going on.

Nick and Brooke went one direction, following the path Ellie originally took toward the lake. I wasn't sure she'd have continued that way, though. She might be a little disoriented, but she'll crave familiarity. Canines had a keen sense of direction, and my instincts told me she'd head back toward the city.

So that's where I went. Once Brooke and Nick were out of sight, I shifted back and got dressed before grabbing my keys from the manor. I heard Colby and Zach somewhere in the house, and then Azura's soft baby sounds. They all seemed fine, so I slipped out unnoticed.

Not only was my bike the faster option of getting me back to the city, but a human roaming the city was less suspicious than an oversized wolf. I raced back to the apartment, thinking that, even though it would be incredibly risky, the suppressed human side of her might crave home. I was just pulling the bike to a stop when I heard a shrill scream. I inhaled deeply and immediately smelled the blood. The metallic scent was so heavy it stung my nostrils, but beneath it, I smelled Ellie. My bike fell to the ground as I raced toward the alley between our building and the neighboring one.

Before I even hit the mouth of the alley, I saw the blood. It wasn't much at first, just some spatter — probably from a bite if my assumptions were correct. Then blood pooled, and soon it looked as though something had been dragged through it...

Or some*one.*

The last fifteen years as a wolf had been full of unimaginable horror, but at some point, you find yourself a little desensitized to all the gore. What I found in that alley, though, froze the blood in my veins for the first time in over a decade.

The woman who came across the scene bumped into me, calling for help. The streets were pretty empty, but it wouldn't be long before she found someone. I had to act fast.

Her bright amber eyes found me, and the sound of Ellie's teeth sinking into her victim's shoulder, her powerful jaws audibly crushing the bones, made my skin crawl. Arterial spray drenched the flaxen fur of her face when she bit down a second time, this time defensively as she pulled the body further into the alley until her ass hit the wall behind her. She was acting every bit as territorial as any wolf with their prey.

I held a hand out and crouched down again, calling her name softly. Her lips curled back, white fangs deep in the bloody flesh, and a warning growl filled the alley. She was lost to the wolf. I would have to take her down somehow. I couldn't shift, so I'd have to do it as a human, but I wasn't sure how exactly.

Turned out, I wouldn't be given enough time to formulate a plan, anyway. Ellie dropped her dinner and lunged for me. Apparently one kill wasn't enough. I braced myself for the impact, grabbing the fur around her neck and holding her head back away from my face as she snapped wildly. Her slight human frame carried over to her wolf body, thankfully. While she still weighed more than she did as a human, she was no match for me.

Careful not to hurt or kill her, I twisted her body until her back was to me. Her legs flailed wildly, seeking purchase to claw her way free, but I held her firm around the neck. She yelped and growled, but soon her movements slowed until her body fell slack in my arms. I eased up and found her breathing heavily.

With her passed out, I hoisted her up over one shoulder, and just as I was turning around, I caught a glimpse of the man Ellie had attacked, and my stomach rolled. I wasn't sure how I was going to break the news to her that she'd killed a human.

To avoid the main street, I headed to the side entrance of the building with Ellie's fur-covered body over my shoulder. I didn't have keys to this door since it was a service door, so I wrapped my hand around the iron knob and twisted hard. The mechanics inside the knob snapped before I pulled it open. Panicked voices about a savage attack could be heard from the mouth of the alley as I slipped inside, but soon I was taking the stairwell up to our floor as I reached into my pocket for my keys.

The hall was clear, thankfully, but my apartment was all the way at the other end. I would have to hope that no one came upon us suddenly. After several deep breaths, I walked as quickly as possible and was inside my apartment before anyone could find us.

Ellie twitched in my arms as I locked the door

behind me, so I took her to my room and laid her on the bed before moving to my dresser. I opened the top drawer and grabbed the tiny vile Brooke had given me before leaving the manor a few weeks ago.

I twisted the top off and drew some of the silver nitrate into the dropper, pulling Ellie's lips back and dropping a few drops straight into her mouth. The shit stung like a bitch, and I hated doing this to anyone, but it would sedate her and possibly revert her transformation. The sizzle of the nitrate hitting her tongue made me cringe, but soon, her body stopped twitching.

Relieved for the moment, I grabbed the spare blanket from the end of the bed and covered her up, knowing she'd appreciate it in the morning when she woke up naked. Then I sat with my back against the wall, and I watched her sleep, all the while, thinking about how the hell my wife was still alive and what I was going to do once I found her.

It just didn't make any sense. I'd seen her body...held it in my arms as it bled out. The coroner's had reported her neck had been broken and she'd been almost completely drained of blood. There was no way she could walk away from that. Nobody could. Not even a werewolf.

I contemplated some kind of doppelganger situation — maybe shapeshifters who took on the appearance of someone else? — but none of it sat right with me. It was Ashley. I could feel it. *Smell* it. It was most definitely her.

As soon as Ellie was awake and she understood what happened, I would take her back to the manor and head out in search of Ashley. I needed answers, and I had a feeling she was the only one who could provide them for me.

I sat in the dark room, listening to Ellie breathe deeply. Slowly, her body reverted to its human form while I watched over her. By dawn, she was human again, and I was still obsessing over Ashley as she continued to sleep.

My phone vibrated in my pocket for the millionth time since I got back here, so I pulled it out. Brooke.

"Hey," I said quietly.

"Oh, thank God!" she exclaimed. "He answered. He's fine."

"Until I see his sorry ass," Nick threatened in the background. "Bastard could've gotten a hold of someone to let us know where he was."

He wasn't wrong. It was a common courtesy within the Pack—within any family—to check in. I fucked up. I'd been too lost in my thoughts to think of the rest of the Pack.

"Tell him I'm sorry. I meant to check in, but…"

"You found her," Brooke deduced. "Alive?"

I nodded before responding. "Yeah. She's alive, but she won't want to be when she wakes up."

Brooke picked up on my somber tone immediately. "What happened?"

"She killed someone," I explained. "I got to her too late."

"You're sure he's dead? He won't turn next month?" she demanded.

"He won't. She went straight for the jugular, like any hungry animal would. It's in our nature."

"Shit," Brooke muttered.

I sighed, running my hand through my hair. "I had to give her nitrate to sedate the wolf. I hate doing that."

"Oh, Jax. I know you do." She was probably remembering the last time I had to dose someone—her, while we were on a plane headed to Scottsdale to look for her missing parents. It wasn't a pleasant experience for either one of us.

Finally, Brooke exhaled heavily. "Okay. You'll bring her back to the manor after she wakes up?"

"Yeah. I'll let her know what happened, convince her the way Nick convinced you if she has trouble accepting it, and then I'll bring her by. I figure she'll be better off with all of us than with me alone."

"Right." Brooke paused. "I'll have the guys head to your apartment to pack up sometime this week."

Ellie stirred on the bed, her breathing pattern shifting, and soon her eyes fluttered open. She looked around the room, recognizing that it wasn't hers. She was confused, and then the panic set in.

"She's up," I told Brooke. "I have to go." I hung up before Brooke could respond, and I pushed myself to my feet, getting Ellie's attention. "Hey."

Ellie sat up, clutching the blanket to her bloodied chest. Seeing me offered her slight relief, but she still looked really worried. "H-hi." Her voice was low and scratchy, and she licked her lips, cringing when she tasted the dried blood on them. "Wh-what happened? Where are we?"

"My apartment," I explained carefully.

Her forehead furrowed as she likely tried to work out how and when we got here. It wasn't going to be easy to explain. "H-how? The last thing I remember was being at the manor and having dinner."

I nodded along, coming to sit at the foot of the bed next to her. She shifted away, being sure to wrap the blanket around her.

"Did we have sex?" she whispered, a pink blush filling her cheeks. "I can't remember."

With a reassuring smile, I shook my head and held up a hand. "I was a complete gentleman, I assure you."

She seemed unsure, and I couldn't blame her. Nothing would make sense to her until I came clean. About everything.

"Do you remember going for a walk with me after dinner?"

She nodded once. "Yeah. Yeah, I do. And I had some pretty awful stomach pains." Her eyes widened, and I thought maybe she remembered shifting—it wouldn't be the first time someone remembered their first time, but it was extremely rare. "I got sick, didn't I?" She sounded embarrassed, so I reached out and rested a hand on her knee and shook my head.

"No. You didn't get sick, sweetheart." I took a deep breath, and she waited. I could tell she was trying to be patient, but it wouldn't be long until she got upset. I had to bite the bullet. "You changed."

"What?"

"You remember how you told me you thought your dreams after the attack meant more to you than just a dream? How they felt...real?"

"Yes?" she replied warily.

"Ellie, the night you were attacked, it wasn't

just a wolf that bit you."

"Yes, it was," she argued. "I saw it. Clearly."

"You were bitten by a werewolf."

Slowly, Ellie's lips spread into a wide smile, and her crazy laughter echoed off the walls. "You're joking."

I held her gaze, my grim expression never faltering. "I wish that I was."

Her laughter stopped immediately. "I know it's hard to believe, but think about everything you've been through this month—the heightened senses, your increased appetite and food preferences. Your body was preparing itself for your first full moon."

"So, you're telling me that werewolves are real?"

"I am."

"No fucking way," she contested again, though she didn't really sound like she doubted me. It felt like she was fishing for some kind of confirmation. "Where's the proof?"

I reached out and grabbed her wrist, but she yanked it away, still looking me in the eye. "I'm not going to hurt you, I swear."

Slowly, she reached out, and I turned her arm over. Her eyes fell to her arm, noticing the blood for the first time. She moved the other hand out and saw it was covered in dried blood, also.

"Oh, God," she whispered. "What happened?"

"You went hunting."

"Hunting?"

"I was with you when you changed," I started to explain. "You were afraid, but I had you almost trusting me when I was hit from behind."

"By what?" she asked, almost like she was already accepting the news.

"Something that wants to hurt our kind. We'll worry about that later."

"Wait," Ellie interjected. "Our kind?"

I nodded. "I was turned about fifteen years ago. By our old Alpha." I paused, waiting for any other questions she might have, but when she didn't, I carried on. "You took off while I fought our attacker." I tried really hard to not get caught up in thoughts of Ashley again. Right now, I needed to focus on Ellie.

"Brooke and Nick showed up, and she took off. We all went off to search for you, but I figured you'd crave familiarity and try to come home."

Realization started to form in her eyes, and she brought her bloodied hands to her lips. "Did I hurt someone?"

She didn't ask if she hurt some*thing*, and it tore me up inside to have to break this news to her. We may have only known each other a few weeks, but I'd grown to care for her deeply in that time, and I hated to see the pain in her eyes.

"Ellie, honey, Nate's dead."

CHAPTER 12 | DISCLOSED

Ellie stared at me, brown eyes blank with disbelief. "Wh-what?"

I struggled with an explanation. How could I tell her what I saw?

Denial set in before I could begin to explain. Ellie clenched her eyes shut and shook her head. Wrapping the blanket around her, she got off the bed and headed for the door. "No I didn't. You're insane."

I stood, but didn't try to block her way. Doing so would only scare the shit out of her. "Ellie, please. Deep down, you know I'm telling the truth. Like I have been about everything else."

She froze, her hand on the knob. Then, with a heavy sigh, she opened the door and fled my room. I called after her as I followed, but she continued to ignore me, opening the main door to my apartment and turning for hers. She gasped, and once I stepped out into the hall, I saw why: Detective Matthews was standing at her door with a uniformed officer.

The detective looked at her, eyes wandering down to the blanket then back up until they landed on me. "Mr. Devereux?" He sighed, asking the officer to meet him downstairs. Once the officer was done, he took a step toward us, addressing Ellie. "Miss King, I need to have a word with you."

She looked down at what she was wearing—or *wasn't* wearing, more accurately—before heading to her door. That was when she realized she didn't have her keys. They were back in the woods at the manor with the scraps of her clothing.

"Shit," she muttered, pressing her forehead to the door. Then she turned to me, and I nodded back to my place.

"I've got something you can throw on. We can head back to the manor this afternoon to grab your keys," I offered. "If that's what you want."

"Sure. Whatever," she muttered, pushing past me and heading back to my apartment. Her clipped tone stung, but I tried not to take it personally. She was dealing with something pretty unbelievable.

After Ellie went inside, I held my hand out, silently inviting Detective Matthews in as well. This entire situation was growing into something I wasn't sure I could contain on my own.

He walked by me, his hard eyes locking with mine as he stopped right in the threshold and assessed me. "You know, Mr. Devereux, I seem to be running into you a lot when it comes to fatal animal attacks." I swallowed thickly, but maintained a static expression. "I'm starting to think there's more to all of this…and I will figure it out."

My body went numb, but I tried to keep my expression neutral. "I'm not sure what you want me to say, Detective."

"No need to say anything. It's my job to figure out the truth."

I closed the door behind us before showing him to the kitchen. "I'll just go assist Ellie, then I'll come put a pot of coffee on." I realized that kissing his ass was probably only making him more suspicious, but what else could I do? I was going to have to tell Brooke about this. She wasn't going to be happy.

Ellie was waiting in my room, still wrapped in the thin throw blanket. She cast her eyes to the floor when I walked in, and her nervousness and distrust thickened the air in the room. There was still so much we had to discuss, so much she had to accept, but now wasn't the time.

I grabbed a T-shirt and a pair of sweats from my dresser. They'd be too big on her, but it was her only option if she didn't want to talk to the cops in a blanket. Our fingers touched during the exchange, forcing her dark eyes to mine. The amber ring was heavier now, following her first transformation.

"Thank you," she said, her voice barely above a whisper. If not for my heightened senses, I might not have heard her.

I leaned in and pressed a kiss to her forehead. She sighed, resting a hand on my chest. It wasn't long before guilt wormed it's way under my skin, burrowing deep inside me, and Ashley's face popped into my head. It seemed ridiculous to feel guilty over an innocent touch, but with Ashley back, my heart was being pulled in two completely different directions.

My time with Ellie had opened my heart to the possibility of finally letting another woman into my life. I was starting to accept that maybe it was more than just me passing the time like I had in the past, and I sensed that maybe it was more for Ellie, too. There was a deep bond between us that I couldn't ignore…

But…Ashley was my wife, and she was *alive*.

Clearing my throat nervously, I took a step away from Ellie. "I'll, uh, be in the kitchen with the detective," I told her.

I was just about to leave her when she called my name. "You're not lying, are you?"

Releasing a heavy sigh, I glanced back over my shoulder. "I wish I was, Ellie." And I pulled the door closed behind me.

Detective Matthews was looking around my living room at my lack of belongings when I went to put the coffee on. His suspicions were probably only growing, because he knew I lived at the manor. Why would someone leave a place like that?

"Just moved in, huh?" he asked from the living room. "Seems…small compared to the last place."

"It is. Is that a bad thing? I'm only one man."

The detective chuckles. "Not at all, I just can't figure out why you'd want to leave. The house…all that land you're free to roam. It's got to be a difficult adjustment."

I poured two cups of coffee and took them to the living room. Ellie had just appeared, swimming in my clothes and tucking her blonde hair behind her ears nervously. I noticed Detective Matthews look between us, and then he smirked knowingly.

"Coffee?" I offered Ellie, and she nodded.

"Just a little cream…if you've got it."

"I remember," I replied with a smile as I took her hand and squeezed it.

I headed back to the kitchen to grab a third cup, and when I returned, Ellie was standing by the patio window, bathed in the early morning sunlight. Her arms were wrapped around her torso protectively until I handed her the coffee.

From his place in front of the mantle, Matthews cleared his throat. "Miss King, can I ask your whereabouts last night between ten and eleven?"

"I, uh… I was…"

"She was with me." I set my coffee down on the nearest table and wrapped an arm around her shoulder like we were together. Which we were— *are?* "I took her to the manor for dinner, to introduce her to Brooke and Nick. We got back to the city around…" I thought back to see if I could recall a time. "It had to be around eleven-thirty."

Detective Matthews hummed contemplatively.

"Why?" I asked. "What's going on?"

His eyes drifted from me to Ellie. "The last time we spoke, you were with Nate Baxter."

Ellie trembled next to me, so I ran my hand over her arm supportively until she relaxed. "I was. We broke up a couple weeks ago."

"I'm sorry to hear that," Matthews said before releasing a sigh. "Look, there's no easy way to say this, Miss King, but Mr. Baxter's body was found in the alley outside your building last night."

Ellie's expression fell, finally accepting the truth. Her hands shook, so I took the coffee mug from her and eased her to the floor as her knees gave out. Tears fell from her eyes as she looked up at the detective. "How?"

"From what the coroner's report could confirm, it looks like another animal attack." He paused. "And the witness who called the authorities confirmed that it was a large white wolf."

"This far into the city?" I questioned, feigning innocence.

"It's not unheard of for some of the local wildlife to wander into the city." Another pause as he looked at Ellie with sympathy while she sobbed into her hands. "Animal control will be on the lookout for the wolf."

I believed him, so it was a good thing I planned to convince Ellie to move to the manor until she could control the wolf. This would also mean she would have to take some time off work. I wasn't sure how she would feel about that, but thankfully she could site bereavement as a reason.

When he realized that Ellie was unable to form a coherent sentence, Detective Matthews suggested he leave. "I'll be in contact," he said, handing me the half-full coffee mug. He stopped in the hall, turning as I started to close the door. "You know, Mr. Devereux, you always seem to be around when these animal attacks occur."

"Oh?" My heart pounded, and my palms began to sweat. I wasn't usually nervous around authoritative types, unless it involved being exposed for what I really was.

Matthews nodded and lowered his voice. "I've heard from several witnesses, and even saw with my own eyes last month, that these aren't normal wolves. They're bigger, more aggressive, and they seem to act on very specific nights of the lunar cycle."

I forced a laugh, hoping he'd think his unspoken insinuation ridiculous. "Detective Matthews, are you implying what I think you're implying?"

Color filled his cheeks, and he shook his head. "I know how it sounds, but I know there's something else going on here, Devereux." He leaned in close. I could taste his determination just as potently as I could smell it. "And I will figure out exactly what's going on."

His promise hung between us as he walked away down the hall. When he reached the elevator, I closed the door and went back to Ellie. She hadn't moved. In fact, she was staring blankly at a spot on the carpet, breathing slowly. It was almost as though she was in some kind of catatonic state.

I knelt next to her and placed a hand on her back. She jumped, startled out of her trance, and when her eyes met mine, fresh tears flowed over her cheeks.

"Oh, Jax," she said, throwing her arms around my neck and hugging me. "What did I do?"

I ran a hand over her hair and made soothing sounds, trying to calm her sobs. "Ellie, what happened wasn't your fault."

"What was he doing here?"

"We shouldn't worry about that right now," I told her. "You need to focus on controlling your emotions. Any extreme shift in them can trigger your change, and we can't have that here." She lifted her face from my shoulder, and I wiped at her tears with my thumbs. "What we are, Ellie? Humans can never know."

I spent the next hour explaining about the Pack and how we all lived at the manor in an effort to stay united. Obviously she clued in to the fact that this wasn't really my home, which only brought up more questions revolving around why I chose to live here.

"I was there the night you were attacked," I explained. Even though I told her this last night, she still looked shocked. "I was only there to track the strays that have been rallying against our pack."

"What do you mean?"

"A few months ago, there was a surge in bizarre animal attacks. The Pack was investigating them, and we realized that it was probably a bunch of non-pack wolves who were moving in on our territory without permission from our new Alpha. Brooke."

"*Brooke* is your alpha? But, she's so…small."

I laughed. "She is, but she's good at what she does," I assured Ellie.

"So these strays, they're just attacking random people, to what? Turn them?"

"We've been led to believe this is their intention, yes. When I heard you'd been bitten, I followed you back here and figured out who you were so we could keep an eye on you." I realized just how creepy it sounded, and the look on her face confirmed it. "We've been watching the survivors we've been able to track down in hopes of getting to them before the strays can. That many new wolves under the wrong guidance could be bad for us."

"You're trying to turn the tables on them by snatching up their new recruits."

"Exactly. You're the first we've been able to make contact with. I have a feeling that's because the wolf that made you was snuffed out that night."

Ellie gasped. "By that blonde woman. Is she one of you...us?"

My stomach rolled, remembering my encounter with Ashley again. The need to flee the apartment so I could try to track her down grew quickly. But I shook it off, knowing I needed to get Ellie to the manor first. I could head out tonight. After last night, I had a feeling she wouldn't be far from me. I could draw her out.

"She's human," I finally replied. "We think she might be a part of something called The Order. From what our source tells us, they're an elite group of demon assassins."

"Demons?"

I nodded. "Ellie, there are things in this world that are kept hidden from humans. Occasionally, bits of information get leaked or someone sees something they shouldn't, and that's how the rumors get started. Everything you know about the monsters in horror movies is true—to a degree."

Ellie stood suddenly, pacing in front of me and wringing her hands while she looked around the room, her eyes never settling on any one thing for long. Her anxiety affected me, too, but I stayed in place so as not to spook her.

Finally, she stopped and looked down at me. "So what now?"

I cleared my throat. "Well, that depends."

"On what?"

"On whether or not you trust me."

"I-I think so," she replied.

I hopped to my feet and took her hands in mine. "The next few months are going to be hard for you. Your emotions will be out of control. The wolf will want out, and if you don't learn to accept and control it, you could hurt someone."

"You mean someone *else*," she said, her voice a strained whisper.

"That wasn't *you*. It was just a part of you. The sooner you accept the wolf as your equal, the sooner you'll be in control. If you deny her access, you'll black out, and her baser instincts will take over." I paused, placing a finger beneath her chin and coaxing her eyes to mine. "The Pack will help with this."

"How?"

"They'll walk you through it. You'll learn more about our kind, maybe understand what it is you've become."

Ellie bit the inside of her cheek hard as she contemplated what I was telling her. "So, you want me to live there?"

"It would be easier, yes," I told her. "You'd be far enough from the city that an accidental shift wouldn't hurt anyone. The house is big enough that you'd still have space if you needed to be alone. And, more importantly, you'll be safe from those who targeted you last month."

"And…you'll be there?"

I inhaled sharply. Yes, at some point, I planned to return, but first, I had to search for my wife and figure out how she was still alive.

Ellie was still waiting for an answer, so I just nodded. "I still live there, yes, and I'll be moving back as soon as I get things sorted out here. But you should go as soon as possible."

She shook her head, her eyebrows pulling together. "What about my job?"

"You'll want to take time off. It won't be forever — some of us still hold day jobs — but until you can control the wolf, being in close quarters with humans is dangerous."

I gave Ellie time to think about it. I couldn't force her to move to the manor, but I could make it the more appealing option by reminding her that staying in the city right now was too dangerous.

After a few minutes, Ellie nodded her head. "Okay. When do we leave?"

We pulled up to the manor on my bike a few hours later. Brooke and Nick came out to greet us, Azura nestled in her mother's arms while she slept.

"Nice to see you again, Ellie," Brooke greeted with a careful smile. "How are you feeling today?"

"Exhausted and confused," Ellie replied honestly, and Brooke nodded with understanding. "Guilty."

"Oh, I remember that feeling all too well." Ellie eyed her curiously, so Brooke elaborated. "I was changed last year. Attacked in a park, actually."

"Did they...kill the one who bit you, too?"

Brooke bit her lip and scrunched her nose while Nick dropped his eyes to the ground. Biting Brooke wasn't his proudest moment, and it was no secret that the truth behind the attack had caused some strain between them. The night she found out was the night she took off and got herself abducted. The entire Pack was franticly searching for her, but we failed for weeks.

"No," Brooke said. "My attack was accidental. There was a vampire nearby, and he was trying to protect me from it."

Ellie shook her head before staring at Brooke with wide eyes. "I'm sorry, did you say *vampire*?"

Nodding, Brooke wrapped a free arm around Ellie and led her inside. "I did. There's so much for you to learn. I look forward to helping you through this the way this pack and our old Alpha helped me."

I stayed by my bike while the girls went inside. Part of me wanted to go with them, but there was a much stronger desire to head back to the city and search for Ashley. The sun would be setting soon, I could smell it, feel it in the way my skin burned and my muscles tightened.

Nick had taken a few steps to follow them when he realized I wasn't behind him. He turned around and nodded once toward the house. "You coming?"

I smiled. "Actually, I'm going to head back to the city. Keep an eye out for strays."

The look he gave me told me he knew I was up to something, but instead of calling me out on my bullshit, he grinned. "That's cool. But you get to tell Brooke. She was looking forward to a big pack meal to welcome Ellie tonight. She's been cooking all day."

I sighed, defeated. He might not have called me out, but he definitely guilted me into staying a little longer before I went out tracking. "You're right. I'll head out after dinner."

"That's probably for the best," Nick agreed.

I followed Nick, stopping just inside the foyer and turning around to stare into the distance. I wasn't looking for anything in particular, but my thoughts were definitely on what I might find out there later.

"I'll find you, Ash," I whispered, gripping the edge of the door tightly. "I'll find out what happened to you."

"Jax?" Brooke called from the dining room. I turned to find her setting the table with Colby, Roxy, and Corbin. The rest of the Pack was in the dining room already, too, talking and laughing, welcoming our newest member. "Dinner's almost ready. Are you coming?"

I caught a glimpse of Ellie, who smiled and waved. I waved back and closed the door. "Yeah I'll be right in."

CHAPTER 13 | SEARCH

After dinner was over, Brooke suggested I show Ellie to her new room. Colby had moved out of her old room and into Vince and Layla's old one back in March. She claimed she was unable to sleep, knowing her little sister shared that room with her while plotting their parents' deaths with the vampire coven. I couldn't blame her. It would be hard to sleep peacefully with that lingering in there.

Ellie wouldn't have any of that plaguing her. To her, that room was a fresh start.

"It's not much," I said, leading her into the room. "But you're free to do whatever you like to it."

Ellie walked around the room, looking at the bare white walls, the solid oak furniture, and the simple blue bedspread. She ran her fingertips along the smooth fabric before sitting down. "It's nice."

With a nervous laugh. I scratched the back of my neck. "We'll head back into the city in a few days and pack up some of your things to bring back. I want you to feel at home here."

Ellie glanced down at her fidgeting hands.

They were shaking, and soon the tremors moved through her body. She was anxious, and soon her scent changed.

"Hey," I said, moving to her side and taking her hands in mine. "You're going to be fine here. Trust me — trust the Pack."

Ellie's dark eyes found mine, and before I knew it, her lips were on mine. There was desperation behind the kiss, a desire to forget about what had happened in the last twenty-four hours, and I let her have it. Focusing on this feeling would suppress her anxiety long enough for the wolf to go dormant.

Caught up in the blanket of her lust and the recent familiarity of her touch, I surrendered completely, bringing a hand up to cup her jaw and wrapping my fingers around the back of her neck. I curled my fingers, twisting them into her hair, and she sighed against my lips as the intoxicating scent of our growing arousal wrapped itself around us.

Slowly, her hands moved to my thighs, pressing firmly and sliding up. My ability to form a coherent thought was lost as my groin swelled in response to her thumbs grazing the zipper of my jeans. I tipped her head back, dragging my teeth, then tongue along the column of her throat. Her skin was hot, burning as the wolf treaded the surface of her consciousness with my own. They were in control now. Their desires trumped any rationality either of us might have.

I fell deeper and deeper into the chasm of lust, spiraling way past the point of no return, when she gasped. "I want you, Jax."

And that was all it took to force the wolf back

into the darkness. All I could hear was the way Ashley said those same words as her hands tugged at my clothes, her sweet scent wrapped around me the way Ellie's was.

Eyes clenched, I wrapped my hands around Ellie's and pulled my face back. I took a deep breath before meeting her confused expression. "I'm sorry," I managed to say, my voice gravelly with lust.

"No," Ellie said, her cheeks darkening with her embarrassment. "I'm sorry. I don't know what came over me."

"Part of it's the wolf," I explained.

She stared at me, the tip of her tongue slipping out and licking her bottom lip. "And the other part?"

"It's you. Your human desires."

Ellie nodded along. "And you? Is it all wolf, or is there…a part of you that wants me as much as I want you?"

Sighing, I pushed myself to my feet and paced in front of her. "Both," I told her honestly, watching her confidence rise. "But…"

And just like that, her expression fell. "Is it because of what I did last night?"

"What?" I demanded, baffled she could even think that. "Of course not, Ellie."

"Then why does it feel like you're pulling away? I thought everything was going really well between us?"

"It was… It *is*," I amended. "I just think we need to be careful until we teach you how to control your emotions and urges. We don't want to trigger a change until we're ready to tackle that."

Ellie stayed silent for a bit before nodding and

changing the subject. "So, which one is your room?"

I was grateful for a slight change in topic. Sure, it was only a small detour, but it was enough. "I'm just next door. End of the hall."

"So, close if I need you?"

"Ellie…"

"No," she quickly interjected. "Not like that. But I still don't know the others. I'd be more comfortable knowing you're nearby."

I smiled, but it was forced, and Ellie knew it.

"What?"

"I hate to do this, but you should know I need to head back into the city tonight. There's some unfinished business I need to look into before I can come back."

Ellie's eyebrows pulled together. "The hunter?"

Her intuition was impressive. "That's a large part of it. She was here last night and attacked me after you shifted. I need to draw her away from here. Try to…stop her before she has the chance to hurt any of us."

"You're going to kill her?"

I swallowed the lump that formed in my throat. Kill Ashley? I couldn't. I *wouldn't*. "I'd like to try and reason with her."

"And if you can't?" It wasn't Ellie who asked.

I turned around to find Brooke and Nick in the doorway, and I inhaled deeply. "Then I'll do what I have to do."

Brooke's gaze drifted past me to Ellie, and she smiled brightly, despite the annoyance I picked up. "Do you mind if we steal him for a moment?"

Ellie shook her head. "Not at all."

I ran my hand up and down her arm, hoping to soothe her nerves. "I'll come see you before I leave."

Brooke and Nick followed me into my room, closing the door behind them. "Are you seriously going after her?" Brooke demanded, crossing her arms and looking up at me fiercely.

"I have to, Brooke," I replied.

"Why?"

I wanted to tell her the truth, but until I knew more about how Ashley survived, I couldn't bring myself to do it. "It's dangerous to have her here. Alistair's barrier spells aren't going to keep her out. She's human."

"You don't know that," Nick interjected. "He could tweak the cast."

Frustrated, I turned away from them, running a hand through my hair. "You have a baby. I won't put her life at risk. Or yours. This pack has been through enough. We won't lose another member. I'm certain she can be reasoned with."

"And what makes you think that? The five-inch slash across your chest?" Brooke hissed, stalking toward me.

"You're being dramatic."

"I saw the wound last night before you shifted, Jax. I'm not being dramatic. This chick has the strength and knowledge to destroy us, and you want to run after her?" Brooke's rage was quickly rising, the green of her eyes erased by the bright amber color.

My chest tingled at the memory of the blade burning me as it sliced through my skin like a hot blade through butter. It still hadn't closed properly, and I wasn't sure if it was fixable now. I cringed, and Brooke took notice immediately.

"We can't risk losing you either." She took a deep breath, unfolding her arms and placing them on my upper arms. "I'm asking you to wait until someone can go with you. Please."

The obedient wolf in me wanted to submit to her request, but the husband in me was stronger. But I wouldn't worry her unnecessarily. "Fine. I'll leave her alone." Brooke released a heavy breath of relief, her lips curling up into a small smile. "I am heading into the city for a bit, though."

She took a step back, shaking her head. "Jackson—"

"I should do a little more digging. See if I can find anything else out about the strays. Any information I can dig up only helps us."

Her hesitation was obvious as she looked back at Nick. He only nodded. I couldn't tell if it was in my favor or not until Brooke looked at me, defeated. "Fine. But for the love of God, be careful. And call us if you run into trouble."

"You know I will," I promised, pulling her into a hug.

She groaned, folding her arms around my waist. "You're such a pain in the ass. Isn't disobeying an Alpha's direct order a crime?"

Nick and I both laughed, and I let her go. "It's not, but I can tell you it is difficult, if that helps?"

She rolls her eyes. "It only helps if you're being honest."

"It is a little. You get stronger and more confident in your new role every day. I'm sure before any of us know it, we'll be doing exactly what you tell us to."

She slapped my arm and shook her head.

"Shut up and get gone. And don't forget to check in this time."

After agreeing once more, I went to see Ellie and let her know I'd be back soon. She seemed worried, but was appeased when Brooke assured her I wasn't going after Ashley. I kissed her good-bye, and tried to ignore the ache in my chest as I put more distance between us. It wasn't easy, and Ellie was never far from my thoughts. With every day that passed, I was starting to believe this was what a mated pair experienced.

When I arrived back in the city, I went straight to Glenmore and walked around. I tried to look like I was just wandering, but I was always on alert. The park was quiet. Even the few homeless people who camped out here were nowhere to be found. I would bet my life that it had everything to do with the animal attacks as of late. Seemed the city was finally taking the threat seriously.

I stayed in the open, hoping to draw Ashley out. What did I plan to do if I was successful? I had no idea. I needed to talk to her, but would she stop trying to kill me long enough to listen?

"Well, look what we have here," a rough, un-familiar voice said from behind me. The hairs on the back of my neck prickled, and my body tensed. It was the equivalent of my hackles raising when threatened while human. Slowly, I turned to face the man, inhaling deeply and not recognizing the scent beyond that it was wolf.

He stood about fifteen feet away, but I could tell he was larger than me. Same height, but he was thicker across the shoulders and was packing a few extra pounds. His dark hair was almost black and cut short, and his face sported a full beard.

"It would seem you've strayed from home," he fired at me, crossing his arms. His leather jacket groaned in protest as it was too small for a man his size.

Containing the warning growl that was building in my chest, I smirked, taking a few steps forward. "In case you haven't heard," I said, spreading my arms wide, "this here is our territory. I believe you and your pathetic band of merry bitches are the ones trespassing on Pack territory."

"Newsflash, asshole," the stray said, tilting his head to the side and cracking his neck. "We're here to claim it. Way we heard it, your alphas are dead — killed by vamps. Looks like new leadership is in order. Listen like the good little bitch you are, and maybe we'll let you stay in the area."

I laughed dryly. "You must not have heard. We have a new alpha."

"The bitch? Yeah, she looks like she'd be fun when she's in heat... Or whenever the mood strikes, really."

Anger flared inside me, emanating outward until the fever set in. My natural instinct to defend and protect my Alpha was taking over, and all I could do was fantasize about ripping his fucking head off and shoving it up his ass.

My body prepared itself for a fight, the wolf laying just below the surface of my awareness so I could utilize its strength. Always aware of him, I gauged my surroundings as best I could. I didn't sense any others nearby, so I could only assume we were alone. The asshole didn't stand a chance.

"Speaking of bitches, Boss says you have something that belongs to him. Pretty little blonde thing with an ass that just won't quit. My words, not his." He flashed a slimy grin after alluding to Ellie in such a crass way, and it only made me want to kill him, then bring him back and kill him again.

My lips pulled back into a snarl, and I glared at him. "You'll stay away from her," I warned. "You'll stay away from the entire pack if you want to live. Leave. Leave Canada and don't come back. Once word travels through the other packs, they'll be hunting you, too."

"So you all just expect us to continue living like this? Moving from place to place, never settling down?"

"No one said you couldn't put down roots somewhere, but you can't really think any pack would welcome you into their ranks after a stunt like this," I pointed out. "They'll force you to shift and skin you alive as a message to all the other greedy shits just like you."

It sounded barbaric, but it was a popular way to get the point across that treason amongst our kind wouldn't be tolerated.

The stranger stepped forward. We were only a few feet apart now, and we started walking in a wide circle, never taking our eyes off one another. I didn't really expect him to just walk away from this fight; it would make him weak to those he was plotting with. They'd kill him if I didn't, and my killing him might rattle his cohorts enough to make them rethink their plan.

"We've been watching you for months," he announced, his dark eyes glowing amber in the dark.

I looked at him like he was an idiot. Because

he was. "We know. You shitstains aren't exactly discreet. You've left a trail of corpses behind you in your mission to build the world's weakest werewolf army. A shower once in a while wouldn't hurt either." I laughed dryly. "Did you really think an army of feral wolves stood a chance? They aren't even aware. Whoever your ring leader is must be a special kind of fucking stupid."

My statements got under his skin like a bad case of jock itch, just as I'd hoped they would. He closed the distance between us with a feral scream, reaching for me. His claws had engaged, tearing through my shirt and skin. He was strong, but he didn't have proper training. He fought like he was in a bar fight, and not like his life was on the line. My instincts told me he was new; maybe a few months since he'd been turned.

I got in several solid hits to his temple that sent him stumbling back a few steps, shaking his head like he was trying to clear it. His nose was bleeding and likely broken, and he glared at me menacingly once he regained his balance.

"You're going to pay for that."

I cracked my neck and sneered. "If you ask me, it's actually an improvement."

"You sure like to wag that tongue of yours, don't you?" I smiled in response. "I'm going to enjoy ripping it out and feeding it to y—"

Before he could even finish his sentence, blood sprayed from his mouth, some of it splattering onto my face and neck. It all happened so quickly that I had trouble registering exactly what happened until I heard the sound of metal scraping against his teeth. That was when I saw the blade between his lips slowly being extracted from the back of the stray's head.

He remained upright for a few seconds, gurgling and choking on his own blood, before his eyes rolled back in his head and he fell into a heap at the feet of the very woman I came here to find.

CHAPTER 14 | CONFRONTATION

Ashley's blue eyes gleamed with the thrill of the hunt. While I didn't exactly relish the fact that she seemed to get off killing my kind, I understood the high she was experiencing as the adrenaline coursed through her veins. Because I felt it each and every time I ran with my Pack.

Even with a couple feet between us, I could hear her heart pounding heavily. Her scent changed slightly, a hint of worry haloing the heady scent of her excitement. It wrapped itself around me, momentarily making me forget that she was still gripping the hilt of her bloody sword.

Ashley stared me down. The smell of the stray's blood hung in the dry, late-summer air. I could hear each drop as it hit the grass after dripping off the pointed edge of her blade.

She twisted her wrist, catching the moonlight on what little silver wasn't covered in thick, red blood. "You don't seem too surprised to see me, mutt," Ashley said, her voice so familiar, yet foreign in how hard it sounded. The smile that crossed her face was both confident and deadly. "You had to know I'd find you."

"I was counting on it, sweetheart," I informed her, relaxing my rigid posture just enough that I came across as non-threatening.

"Is that so?" Her confidence wavered for just a second before it slid back into place. "And why is that?"

"I want to talk."

Her laugh carried through the park. "Talk?" Her expression turned serious just as quickly. "And why would I talk with a worthless *thing*?"

My jaw clenched in frustration. "Because I'm your husband, and you owe me that much after disappearing fifteen years ago without so much as a damn word."

I thought I saw another flicker of recognition, but she shook it off. "Married? I would never stoop so low."

"Ash…" I took a step forward.

Her eyes went wide, and her breathing picked up. Part of her was scared. Instead of trying to hurt me, though, Ashley held up her free hand and gripped the sword tighter in preparation of defending herself should I become a threat. Blood trailed down the blade and dripped onto the ground. "Don't come any closer."

"What happened to you? This isn't you." I raised both hands in front of me, hopefully convincing her that I wasn't a threat to her. Her expression softened, and hope flooded my chest. "I was hoping you'd show," I replied gently, taking small steps toward her. "I have…so many questions."

Her big blue eyes flitted from mine to my hands nervously. I could see the conflict in her expression. She wasn't sure if she could trust me. I took another step, and she lifted the sword between us. "I said stop!" she shouted.

The point of the sword was directed at my jugular, mere inches away from piercing my skin. I stopped, determined to get through to her somehow. "Sweetheart," I said, lowering my voice. "It's just me."

Ashley's eyes hardened, her eyebrows pulling together. "Who *are* you?" She paused, shaking her head slightly. Her hand began to tremble until the tremor reached the tip of the blade. "Why...why can't I stop thinking about you?"

Even though she seem shaken, she didn't back down with the sword, and if it was going to give her some semblance of peace, I wasn't going to try to disarm her.

I said try, because I had a feeling I might not succeed.

I knew I had to choose my next words carefully if I didn't want to spook her or worse: make her angry. One flick of her wrist, and she'd slice my carotid.

In less than a second, my hope turned to ash like curtains engulfed in flames, and I was only given a split second to react, stepping back, before Ashley lunged for me. She released a feral scream, leaping over the body between us and pointing the blade at my chest.

My reaction speed impressed even me as the blade sliced my shirt, singeing the skin of my left pectoral. Ashley didn't relent, moving gracefully as though this was nothing more than a well-choreographed dance for her. Something she practiced daily to perfect. The sword was an extension of her arm, whistling through the air with every swing. If I wasn't busy trying to survive, I might have found it beautiful.

When she didn't relent or seem to tire, I realized I might have to actually fight back. Hitting a woman wasn't exactly something I relished having to do—especially when that woman was my wife—but I had a feeling I would have to defend myself. I let my instincts take over, raising my arms and blocking her attack by grabbing her wrist, the edge of the sword stopping just inches from my neck.

She raised her blue eyes to mine and smirked, trying to pull free. "So, you don't just roll over, do ya, Spot?"

I snarled out of instinct. "I'm not really into tricks, sweetheart."

Ashley shrugged her left shoulder and smirked arrogantly. "Something tells me you'll be playing dead soon enough."

"Don't count on it." I lifted my right leg, pressing my foot into the middle of her torso, and pushed hard.

Ashley gasped for breath, the fire in her eyes flaring. I'd made her angry. Her bantering came to an abrupt halt, and she resumed her attack. I blocked her again, this time dislocating her shoulder and sending the sword flying. The tip of the blade speared the earth several feet away. She looked at her fallen weapon, then at me as she grabbed her right arm and snapped it back into place.

Before she could get to the sword, I ran toward her. She responded by showing off the extensive training she'd obviously gone through over the last fifteen years. Her fists collided with my face, much harder than I'd expected. She wasn't the same woman I'd fallen in love with. Whatever had happened—whatever brought her back from death—had changed her.

You wouldn't have known it to look at her, but she was pretty evenly matched to my strength. Possibly stronger, which was a major shot to my ego. I didn't have to hold back, and for every kick and punch she landed, Ashley took as well as she gave.

I could tell she was running out of steam, her eyes darting around with desperation as she looked for an escape route. I couldn't let that happen. I drew on the wolf, accepting a fresh surge of adrenaline and blocking an incoming right hook. Grabbing her forearm, I turned her body until her back was against me and her arm was across her chest. She struggled; I didn't expect anything less.

"If you think killing me will stop the mission, you're seriously deluded."

I inhaled deeply, bringing my free arm up and wrapping it around her neck. My eyes burned with tears as I tightened my hold on her, feeling her pulse speed up against the crook of my elbow. Her fear flowed off her in waves, and panic caused her to thrash her legs as I lifted her off the ground. I released her left arm so I could use my other hand to hold the back of her head. Her breathing slowed, and her body stilled in my arms.

A tear slipped from my eye, rolling down my cheek and onto her shoulder as her head fell forward and she fell slack in my arms. "I'm sorry," mumbled as I slung her over my shoulder and grabbed the hilt of her sword, accepting the burn of the silver etching on my palm as punishment.

CHAPTER 15 | CONFLICTED

My apartment wasn't equipped to hold prisoners—not that I wanted to view Ashley as such. I should have taken her to the manor. There we had restraints and a cage in the pit that would hold her. The thought of caging my wife made me nauseous. Of course, binding her arms and legs with the cords I ripped out of perfectly good lamps didn't exactly nominate me for world's best husband either. Another reason I didn't take her to the manor was because bringing her there would put our entire pack at risk. We had children—babies—there. They were the future of our pack.

My phone blew up with missed calls and texts all night. Mostly from Brooke, wondering where I was, and eventually starting to express how worried they all were that I hadn't replied. It wasn't my intention to worry them, but I didn't know what to say. So, instead of manning up, I sat in my room, watching Ashley sleep...like I'd done with Ellie only twenty-four hours ago.

Ellie...

Thinking about her amplified the twist in my gut, and I realized the longer I was away from her, the more uncomfortable I became. Since bringing Ashley back to my apartment, Ellie hadn't been far from my thoughts. I worried about her first night in the manor after everything she'd learned, and I wondered if she felt the ache of being apart as intensely.

Ashley stirred, drawing my focus from Ellie again. How and when had my life gotten so damn complicated? In just one short month, I'd gone from single and resolved in my decision to be the male equivalent of a spinster to considering the possibility of Ellie being my mate. And then my dead wife showed up...*alive.*

The sun had barely broken through the curtains when Ashley groaned. Bruises had formed on her face and arms where I'd hit her. Guilt weighed me down like cinder blocks chained to my ankles. I struggled against the pressure around my heart, and it made me sick to think I'd laid a hand on her that way.

I watched as her eyes fluttered open, taking in her surroundings. She looked confused as she took in the bare walls, the basic black headboard and the window above it. Then her eyes grew wide with panic when she went to move her arms and legs and realized they were bound together. She pulled against the restraints until they cut into her skin.

"I'm not going to hurt you," I assured her as I stood from the still-dark corner of the room.

Her heart beat frantically, the air turning sweeter with her fear. I didn't mean to find it appealing; it was purely instinctual.

"Where am I?"

"My apartment in the city," I told her honestly. She seemed shocked.

"Why?"

"Why, what?"

"Why didn't you kill me?"

I sighed. "Because I can't, Ash."

She stopped struggling, her eyebrows pulling together. I could smell the blood on her ankles and wrists, and a part of me wanted to release her. But I knew that would be suicide.

"Why do you talk to me like you know me?"

"Because I do. We go back twenty-two years." I watched her expression change as she searched her memory, trying to figure out if I was lying. "We met when you were seventeen. You'd run away from your family, and I gave you a place to stay. We became...close.

She picked up on my allusion immediately, her nose wrinkling with disgust. "I would *never* get involved with a werewolf," she spat with seething hatred I knew went beyond knowing me; it had been programmed into her.

"I wasn't always this." I walked toward the bed. Nervous by my proximity, Ashley scooted back, her ass hitting the edge of the mattress. "I was turned the night you died."

Ashley scoffed. "I didn't *die*."

I reached out, using a finger to tug at her restraints to assess her wounds. Naturally, Ashley flinched, but she eventually complied with my silent request. They'd need to be cleaned, so I went to the washroom and wet a cloth with warm water.

I returned, sitting next to her and reaching for her wrists. She yanked them toward her chest, but I eased them away and dabbed at the lacerations with the cloth. Ashley winced, but allowed me to continue.

"I don't know who you are, but I'm not who you think I am."

While I'd been caught up in the smell of her fear before, this was the first time I'd seen it in her eyes at the same time. Trying to remain sympathetic to her fears, I ran the cloth over the tattoo on her inner wrist, remembering how secretive she'd been over it all those years ago.

"You're exactly who I think you are. I just don't understand *how*. I buried you."

"Look," Ashley said, propping herself up on one of her arms. "If you let me go, I'll tell The Order you've been dealt with. They won't come after you again."

I laughed dryly. "You work for a secret organization that hunts down all otherworld beings. Somehow I doubt it'll be that easy."

A knock at the door pulled my attention from Ashley. I chose to ignore it in hopes that whoever it was would go away. The knocking only grew more persistent.

"You should get that."

"They'll give up and leave," I told her. "We need to get this figured out."

"What's to figure out?" she demanded, thrashing back on the bed again and aggravating her wounds all over. "You've kidnapped the wrong girl!"

Her shirt rode up, showing off the tiniest bit of her stomach, and I caught a glimpse of the thin silver scar from her C-section.

Tired of not being heard, I reached for the hem of her shirt. "This here," I began, pulling the fabric out of the way.

"Get your damn hands off me, mutt!"

"This is from the day you gave birth to Tyson."

She froze, her eyes widening, but it wasn't with panic or fear. It was the fierce desire to protect something.

"H-how do you know about him?" Her voice shook, and I wanted to hold her. I wanted to tell her that I grieved his death, too.

Instead, I looked at her bound wrists, ignoring her question for a second. "If I untie you, do you promise to hear me out?"

After a moment of contemplation, she nodded once, so I removed the cords from her arms and legs and stayed sitting while she stood. She rubbed her wrists, turning to me and asking again, eyes narrowed. "How do you know about my son?"

"I've told you, Ash." I stood and placed my hands on the side of her face. She didn't even try to pull away this time. "We were together." Her eyes moved between mine, searching for answers she for some reason didn't have. "You're my wife."

CHAPTER 16 | HOSTILE

Another knock forced Ashley a few steps away from me. Her posture stiffened as her guard went back up, and I sensed her tension. Smelled the physical change in her. She was ready to hunt. Ready to kill.

Her eyes flew to mine when the knocking grew more impatient again, pupils dilated. I was afraid of two outcomes: she'd either run or try to kill me.

"I'm sure it's nothing," I told her calmly. "Can you just...wait?" Truthfully, her only way was out the window, and we were six floors up. Something told me that wouldn't stop her, though.

She gave no indication one way or the other what she would do, but the next knock was far less patient and a lot more forceful. I opened my bedroom door and knew why as soon as the scent hit me.

Mixed emotions passed through me—annoyance, anger, and pants-pissing fear—but I didn't have time to properly process each one.

"Open the damn door, Jax. I know you're in there. I can hear you moving around."

My hand froze on the knob, not afraid of who was on the other side, but what she might do once she realized why I was actually here. I didn't want to appear weak or ashamed—because I wasn't—so I took a deep breath and opened the door.

Angry green eyes stared up at me, and Brooke pushed past me without an invitation. Not that she needed one. "What the hell are you doing here? You were supposed to come back to the manor," Brooke scolded. She seemed more agitated than usual, and I felt like it had to do with more than just me being here.

Because it's what I always did, I deflected her interrogation. "Where's Azura?"

"With her father. At the manor…where she's *safe* with her pack."

"Brooke…"

"Don't you *Brooke* me, Jackson." It wasn't often she used my given name, so I knew I was in deeper shit than I thought. I felt like I was a child. "We've been calling, texting. You didn't reply. Do you have any idea how worried we've been?" I was instantly fifteen again and getting my ass chewed out for staying out past curfew.

Closing her eyes, Brooke took a deep breath. When she opened them, she was a little more calm. "Where have you been?"

Before I could reply, something registered in her eyes. Her nostrils flared, and her eyes snapped toward my closed bedroom door. She knew what I was hiding. What she didn't know was *who* it was. She recognized the scent as the hunter she and Nick had helped me with the other night.

"Jackson…" There was a rumble in her throat as a defensive growl slowly gained momentum.

"Tell me that isn't—"

"It isn't what you think," I interjected, stepping in her path.

"Really?" she fired back. "Because I think you're harboring the very thing that tried to kill you... That killed another wolf a month ago."

"A stray," I corrected.

"Still one of our kind." Brooke pinched the bridge of her nose, frustrated. "Tell me she's bound."

"She was."

"Was? *Was*? So you have a known killer of our kind loose in this apartment?"

Brooke's anger continued to escalate. I could tell she was about to lay into me again when the door to my room opened and Ashley stepped out.

Her blue eyes found me before they drifted to Brooke, assessing her. Brooke's anger dissolved, instantly replaced by confusion.

"Jax," Brooke whispered. "I don't know if I'm just sleep-deprived, but isn't that...?"

"Ashley," I concluded. "It's Ashley."

"How?"

Ashley continued to look between us, never moving, never talking. I could tell she was trying to get a read on the situation.

"I don't know," I replied, watching my wife carefully.

"So this is why you didn't come home?"

I only nodded, noticing Brooke move forward through my periphery. It took less than a second for everything to go sideways.

Clearly feeling threatened, Ashley sprang forward, reaching for the hilt of her sword that I'd left in the hall the night before, and Brooke reacted on her survival instincts. With a growl, she ran toward Ashley, aware of the sword as she blocked the downward slash, gripping Ashley's wrist with one hand and her neck with the other. Brooke slammed Ashley up against the wall, cracking the plaster and securing the reality that we'd never see our damage deposit again.

Ashley might have towered over Brooke by a few inches, but Brooke was strong. A force to be reckoned with. She was everything an Alpha should be — in a tiny little package. With every day that passed, she became stronger and more skilled in hand-to-hand combat.

"Relax," Brooke told Ashley. "I'm not going to hurt you."

Ashley scoffed. "You couldn't, even if you tried. One flick of my wrist, and you'd be at my mercy."

Brooke's confidence was her undoing. Ashley flipped the tables and had Brooke against the wall, the edge of the blade resting at her throat. I could smell Brooke's skin singeing as Ashley pressed the blade harder.

"Ashley, stop," I commanded firmly.

"I don't take orders from animals," she spat. "I put them down."

"Don't," I warned, a growl building in my chest, the wolf not about to let her hurt my Alpha. It's loyalty to Brooke seemed to be stronger than my promise on our wedding day to take care of her.

Ashley turned to look at me, her smile sinister. "What's wrong? Can't stand to see your bitch be put down?"

Brooke struggled, careful to not force the

blade deeper. A lone drop of blood trickled down her neck before the wound cauterized.

"We aren't the enemy."

"You're all the enemy!" Ashley shouted. She was beyond reason. Whatever drove her to be the hunter had taken over, and all traces of the woman I'd reached moments ago was gone. While I still felt obligated to her as my wife, I had a stronger obligation to my Alpha.

In two giant strides, I had Ashley's sword arm in my grasp. I pulled it back, accidentally nicking Brooke. I wrapped my other arm around Ashley's neck, constricting her airway until her body fell slack against me, and I let her fall gently to the floor.

Brooke touched her neck, wincing. "What the hell, Jax? What took you so long?"

"I had the situation under control before you showed up. You spooked her."

"So this is my fault?" She gestured to Ashley's unconscious body, and I only looked at her, pissing her off. "Since when do we go off and take care of shit on our own without checking in with the pack?"

Glaring down at Brooke, defiance burned through my veins. I crossed my arms. "So, are you the pot or the kettle today? Need I remind you of when you took off after Gianna against Nick's orders? Or the time you got yourself abducted and held captive for weeks?"

Brooke's eyes blazed yellow, and her hands shook. "Don't push me, Jackson. You fucked up. You've been hiding out with the thing that's been picking us off one by one…"

"Strays!" I barked. "She's killed strays!"

"But she's gone after members of this very pack! She tried to kill *you* just the other night."

"She's my wife, Brooke."

"And Bobby was my brother. Cordelia? Colby and Corbin's sister," she shot back firmly, "and when push came to shove, they were taken out—for the safety of this pack. Jesus, Jax." Brooke turned away from me and pinched the bridge of her nose. "Another body was found last night. In the same park Ellie was attacked in," she said, changing the subject.

"It was a stray," I told her. "He and I exchanged words before Ashley ran him through."

"Detective Matthews called the manor." I froze. "Said he wanted to talk to you about it." Brooke paused, eyebrows furrowed with worry. "Tell me he's not involved on the wrong side of this whole thing, Jackson. That he only called you because he thinks this is related to Ellie's attack somehow."

She was my alpha; I couldn't lie to her. But I wanted to. "He hasn't said anything one way or the other, but I think he suspects something."

"Oh, Jax…"

"Not because I said anything. He came to his own conclusions. I know the rules and the consequences. I wouldn't risk the safety of this pack." Brooke's eyes fell to Ashley's still form before rising to meet mine again. "More than I already have," I amended.

A small breath from Ashley spooked Brooke. When she didn't wake, Brooke looked at me. "Bind her. We need to get her to the manor and put her in the cage."

"I'm not putting my wife in the pit," I argued

defiantly.

"If you want to figure out how she's back, you'll do as you're damn-well told."

I cast my eyes to the floor, submitting to my alpha out of instinct versus free will.

"I'm not saying you have to torture her for information, but we stand a better chance at finding out more about her—and maybe The Order—if she's not trying to decapitate us all."

"Fine." I went to the bedroom to grab the cords I'd used earlier and tied her arms and feet again.

Brooke looked at the sword, and I shook my head. "Leave it. We can't bring it to the manor."

Transporting Ashley to the manor in broad daylight meant we couldn't use my bike. It was too risky. Instead, I carried Ashley like she'd simply fallen asleep, a blanket draped over her unnecessarily to hide her restraints and we slipped out the back entrance where Brooke had moved Nick's truck. Brooke opened the back door, and I slid Ashley in.

"We can come back for the bike later," Brooke offered.

Worried Ashley might wake up while we were driving, I sat in the back seat with her. It would be easier for me to keep her subdued in a worst case scenario.

Brooke focused on the road, and I wasn't sure what to talk about. I knew she was still upset, and I was worried that anything I might say would only make her mood worse. After a few more minutes of awkward silence, I couldn't take the silence anymore, and I needed to pacify my earlier pangs of worry.

"How's Ellie?"

Brooke sighed, her eyes catching mine in the reflection of the rear-view mirror. "That's actually why we've been calling you." She paused, biting her lower lip. "Ellie took off last night."

CHAPTER 17 | MISSING

"What the fuck do you mean, she took off?" I demanded, the discomfort in my chest returning. While the events of the past fourteen hours offered me brief moments of reprieve, now that I knew she was missing, the pain of our separation had magnified until I felt physically ill. "Why didn't you say something sooner?"

Brooke's eyes met mine in the mirror again, clearly not impressed. "Oh, I'm sorry. I must have forgotten, what with a sword pressed up against my throat." Another pause as she rolled her eyes. "Zach and Colby are tracking her. I doubt she's gone far."

"Unless she's shifted."

"You know her best. Once we get Ashley settled, you can head back out. If you want."

We arrived at the manor a short while later. Ashley was still unconscious, so I hoisted her over my shoulder and followed Brooke inside. Nick was on us as soon as we walked in, handing a fussy baby to her mother.

"Any word" Brooke asked, likely referring to Ellie.

"Nothing yet," he supplied, his eyes drifting to Brooke's neck. He reached out, his thumb barely grazing the cauterized wound. "What the hell happened?"

Brooke winced and grabbed his hand to keep him from touching it again. "It's fine. I'm fine. I'll get Layla to clean it so it heals properly."

That was when he noticed Ashley over my shoulder, and his eyes narrowed angrily. "Is that the hunter?"

I made my way for the stairs, but Brooke stopped me. "Jax. The pit. She can't be loose."

"She's tied up."

"I don't care. She nearly took my head off," Brooke argued, and Nick's nostrils flared, his eyes glowing a bright yellow and his hands clenching into fists at his sides.

Brooke was right, of course, but I hated the idea of caging my wife. With a childlike grumble, I headed for the basement instead.

The last time we'd used the pit was when we had Corbin and Colby's little sister caged following the attack on Marcus and Miranda. The original wooden door had been broken when the vampires showed up to save her—their ultimate hybrid weapon—so after a bit of discussion and planning, we replaced the door with an inset bookcase that locked in place.

Brooke was the one with the new idea to extend the shelving unit along the length of the basement so it would blend, building it right into the wall. We'd never needed something so *007*, but after Marcus and Miranda's death, humans had been in sniffing around our home, and it had come too close to being discovered. This was definitely the best way to keep our secret torture chamber and prison hidden. We wouldn't want anyone thinking we were distant relatives to Leatherface or anything.

I placed my hand around the red vase, listening for the electronic click as it registered my finger prints. The bookcase unlatched, popping out a couple inches until I could grab the inlaid handle along the edge and pulled it open the rest of the way. I flipped the light switch before descending the stairs into the cool cellar.

My stomach twisted with every step I took. Everything human in me screamed that this was wrong, but the wolf rationalized with its Alpha. We were all safer with Ashley locked up. At least until I knew what the hell was going on and why she was back.

I used my foot to swing the cage door open, knowing the silver-infused bars would burn my still-healing hands if I touched them. Ashley groaned as I eased her down onto the small bed, but she didn't wake. Knowing how sturdy the cage was, I made the decision to unbind her arms and legs. Once the cords were removed, I brushed the blonde hair from her face, tucking it behind her ear before letting my fingers trail down her neck and over the faded scar from the night the vamps fed off her. She sighed, her weight shifting until the tattoo on her left wrist was exposed. I traced the black lines, remembering she said it was a family crest of sorts, and then it hit me. like a train emerging from a thick blanket of fog.

"The Order," I mumbled, Ashley's pulse strong against my fingertips. "This was what you were running from."

I backed out of the cage and carefully pulled the door shut, the lock clicking into place as soon as it was closed. I watched Ashley for a few more seconds before the front door slammed upstairs and Colby and Corbin called for Brooke.

"Ellie," I said, heart pounding with hope that they'd found her.

Knowing Ashley was locked safely away, I left the pit, securing the door before racing upstairs to check in with Colby and Corbin. When I reached the main floor, I followed their voices to the dining room where everyone was seated around the table.

"We lost her somewhere in the city," Colby announced.

"What do you mean you lost her?" I demanded, insides twisting with anxiety. "Her scent couldn't have just vanished."

Colby turned to look at me, her eyes narrowed. "Coming from the only one she knew here. Where the hell were you, Jax? Because it sure as shit wasn't here."

"Colby, enough," Brooke warned.

"No!" Colby fired back angrily. She wasn't always this confrontational; ever since her parents and sister were killed, she'd been different. Angrier. "She needed someone she could trust, and he just fucking left."

"Colby!"

"Let her speak," Nick cut in, earning him a shocked look from Brooke. "She wants to know where he was. Make him tell her." His eyes shifted to me from his spot at the end of the table. "Tell the entire pack where you were. What you brought into our home."

This time, everyone's eyes were on me. "I was looking for the hunter," I replied. She knew where we lived. I left to stop her from coming back."

Nick released a dark laugh, and I glared. "I'm sorry, but tell me you see the irony of bringing a killer into our home when you claim to have left to prevent that from happening."

My hackles went up, and I took a threatening step toward him from the doorway. "This coming from the guy who released a fucking vampire in our home when we were interrogating him," I challenged. "Tell me, Nick where did that get our pack?"

Nick stood up quickly, sending his chair clattering to the floor. I could sense his wolf was close to the surface, and so was mine. While I knew I should back down, I couldn't help myself. "Let me refresh your memory: a six-year-old member of our pack was taken and used as their little lab rat."

"Enough!" Brooke shouted. The energy in the room changed. Anger still thickened the air between Nick and me, but the tone Brooke used forced us to back down. Even if we didn't want to.

A sniffle pulled my attention, and I turned just in time to see Colby brush a tear from her cheek. Bringing up her sister had upset her, and why shouldn't it? She was the one who'd been forced to put her down to save our new Alpha.

"Colby, you're free to leave if you'd like," Brooke told her gently. She'd definitely taken on a more maternal role with the girl since Miranda died. "The rest of you, too. We'll check in later."

Nick and I moved to leave. I planned to go look for Ellie, and I didn't give a shit where Nick was going.

"Not you two," Brooke ordered. "Sit." Nick and I did as we were told, glaring at one another the whole time. "What the hell has gotten into you two? Do you really think *now* is the time for us to be divided?"

"He brought a killer into our home, Brooke," Nick argued.

"She's my wife!" I shouted, though something about the proclamation felt weak.

"Your wife is dead!"

I stood up, my chair violently scraping the tile floor. Nick met the movement, leaning forward on the table, eyes wide and flaring yellow.

With a groan, Brooke pressed her face in her hand before moving them up and through her hair. "I am aware of who—and *what*—she is." She took a deep breath. "She's locked up until we can figure out what the hell is going on. We'll try to find out more about The Order, but first, we have to find Ellie and get her back here before the strays get to her. Arguing like this will get us all killed. Our enemies will see it as the chink in our armor, and they'll use it to their advantage. Pull your shit together."

She was right. She usually was. "I'll go back into the city. Check her usual spots."

I didn't wait for either one of them to say anything else, but as I grabbed the keys to Brooke's white mustang off the key rack, I heard her scolding Nick further, and I smirked. I knew I would have my ass chewed out later upon my return, but for now, I took sadistic pleasure in Nick's discipline.

I was back in the city by one. I checked Glenmore park first where I picked up traces of her scent. They were faint, and I was going to head to the apartment next when I picked up the scent of blood. At first, I passed it off as the stray's blood from the night before when Ashley ran him through, but I recognized it as Ellie after a moment.

Panic wound its long gnarled fingers around me, tightening until I struggled to breath, and my vision blurred. Just as quickly as it had started to darken, my eyesight sharpened, zoning in on several large drops of blood pooled around one another. Soon they spread out, lessening in number, and the way the drops had landed told me that Ellie had been running when struck.

I followed the trail into the thick brush, but all I found was a much larger pool of blood that had mostly soaked into the dirt. Gut twisting, I knelt at the site, gently running my fingers over the spot. Bone dry. It wasn't wet or tacky, which meant this probably happened last night. Likely after I'd taken Ashley back to my apartment.

Had Ellie tracked me here? Was that why she was in the park instead of back at the manor with the pack? What had found her? Stray? Another member of The Order? Whatever it was, did it have her, or had she managed to get away?

My panic only grew with every unanswered question. In a city as large as Calgary, it would prove difficult to track her... Difficult, but not impossible. I pulled my cell phone from my back pocket and dialed Brooke.

"Hello?"

"Brooke, I need you to call around to the hospitals, see if Ellie's been brought in."

"Jax, what's going on? Is everything okay?"

I stood from my spot and looked around, trying to focus beyond the trees. "She was attacked at Glenmore." I felt sick as the words left my mouth.

"By what?"

I ran my hand through my hair, pulling tightly enough to make me wince in pain. If I hadn't been distracted, this never would have happened. How had I been so negligent? "I don't know." I grew more and more frustrated and angry with myself for taking off when I did. "I'm going to look around some more, maybe head back to the apartment to see if she went there to recover."

"Okay," Brooke agreed. "I'll call you if I find anything out."

"Thanks." I hung up the phone and slipped it back in my pocket. I took another detailed look around the small clearing, noticing the wolf tracks at first. It looked like she was in wolf form when she sought cover, and when I went back to the dried up pool of blood, I noticed small *human* foot and hand prints.

"She managed to shift back," I deduced aloud to myself, trying to get a deeper understanding of what happened here. I looked for another set of wolf tracks, but found none. I did, however, come across a set of shoe prints. They were large, likely male. The tread was fine, leading me to believe they weren't a sneaker or a boot. They looked like they might belong to a dress shoe, and they seemed almost perfect, like whoever they belonged to came in here after Ellie cautiously.

"You looking for Miss King?" The voice startled me, and I mentally kicked myself for not picking up his scent before he managed to sneak up on me.

I slowly turned around, forcing a friendly smile. "Detective Matthews. This is an unexpected surprise."

His expression read skeptical as he stepped closer. "Is it? Didn't Miss Leighton tell you I've been looking for you?"

"Oh, right." Having actually forgotten made my reply believable. "Something about a body?"

The way he smiled told me it wasn't the body found in the park he wanted to talk to me about— or not *just* the body. I cast my eyes down, my keen eyesight taking in the style of his dress shoes, and the tracks behind him...

They were a perfect match.

"Why don't you follow me down to the station, Mr. Devereux?" A smile slowly spread across his face, unnerving me slightly. "I think we have a lot to discuss."

CHAPTER 18 | EXPOSED

I followed Detective Matthews down the long halls of the police precinct. He didn't say much after I climbed out of Brooke's car about why we were here, and he continued to remain tight-lipped as he led me through the building. Finally, he opened a door, holding it open and allowing me to go first, looking down the hall in both directions. It was almost like he wanted to make sure we were alone, and my guard was instantly up.

I stepped inside carefully. It was dark in the room, save for the light shining from the other side of a window. I looked through it, and inhaled sharply to find Ellie sitting at a table on the other side. Her blonde hair was a mess, grass and leaves scattered in it. Her hands and face were smeared with dirt, save for the streaks on her cheeks from where her tears had wiped it away, and there was a blood stain on the left shoulder of the over-sized gray sweatshirt she wore. She looked terrified and exhausted, like she hadn't slept since the night before. My guilt returned with a vengeance, tearing at my insides, and I just wanted to collect her and take her back to the manor.

"What is she doing here?" I demanded.

Detective Matthews sighed. "I found her at Glenmore," he replied.

"Yeah, and?"

The door closed, and I heard the lock engage. I turned to him, eyebrows raised. The way he looked at me wasn't angry, it wasn't intimidating. He wanted answers.

But answers about what?

"I arrived at the park around midnight, after receiving a call about another dead body," he began. "I was driving by on my way home when the call came through on the scanner, so I figured I'd get there first and wait until the crime scene unit and more officers could arrive.

"Everything was fine at first. I inspected around the body without disturbing it, and as I was checking out an unusual pattern between two different sets of footprints, I heard a deep growl." His eyes drifted to Ellie. "When I first saw the white wolf, I panicked. I drew my gun, because the way it's yellow eyes were trained on me didn't feel overly friendly. When it lunged, I fired. Got it right in the shoulder. It was enough to scare it off." Detective Matthews walked over to the window and continued to watch Ellie. I looked at her, too, and noticed she'd placed her forehead on the backs of her hands as they rested on the table.

"Then what happened?" I urged, already sure I knew the answer.

"I followed it to the brush where it'd taken cover."

"You planned to kill it?"

Looking more tense than before, he shook his head. "No. I actually don't know why I followed it—keep tabs on it, maybe? Make sure it stayed away from the body? Make sure it didn't suffer should it be bleeding out?" His heart rate picked up a little, and I could smell his anxiety.

"But you didn't find a wolf," I finished for him. "You found her. You found Ellie."

"Naked. And...and bleeding," he whispered hoarsely, glancing my way. "In the exact same damn spot I'd shot the wolf." He turned to me fully this time, his gaze burning into mine and seeking confirmation. "Tell me I'm going crazy, Mr. Devereux. That what I think happened is nothing more than my imagination getting the better of me after almost forty-eight hours with little to no sleep."

I went back and forth on what to tell him. Humans weren't supposed to know about our kind, because it was a secret we didn't want getting out there. Unnecessary fear that we might go on a hunting spree could cause chaos amongst the humans. We'd been living peacefully among them, hidden beneath their world. Some of our kind had been exposed, but lack of proof has made our existence nothing more than an urban myth or material for a B-list horror movie. The vamps got the A-list movies. For whatever reason, humans found them mysterious and sexy. I would never understand it. They were nothing more than a parasite.

There were a few humans that our kind could trust with our secret, but they were guarded by those they knew about, and they knew the fatal consequences that awaited them should they ever slip up and tell anyone else. We had to do whatever we could to protect our world from the pitch-fork-toting humans of the world who were too narrow-minded to accept our kind.

"In January," Detective Matthews continued, "when I came to the house on the double homicide?"

"Yeah. I remember."

"The blood from the scene had traces of canine DNA in it. We figured it had been contaminated at first..."

I clenched my jaw, nervous about just how far his theory stretched throughout the precinct. "Uh huh..."

"The body of that wolf in the woods on the night of Miss King's attack had traces of *human* DNA, and the body in the park last night has shown traces of canine..." He turned to me fully, eyebrows pulled together and arms crossed. "If I take a sample of Miss King's blood to the lab, what do you suppose I'll find?"

"Is that a threat?" I demanded, the wolf suddenly feeling defensive and leaping forward to assert dominance.

Matthews recognized his mistake and backed down immediately. "Not at all. I just want answers. I want to know if we're up against something we have no fucking right to be."

I knew I should talk to Brooke about Detective Matthew's suspicions, but I was backed into a corner—almost literally—and Ellie was alone in that stark white room, probably confused and scared.

I took a deep breath. "Ellie's blood would show traces of canine DNA if you were to take it to the lab."

"How?" he asked. "I don't understand."

"I think you understand perfectly, Detective. You just don't want to admit it to yourself."

He stared at me for a moment, taking it all in and probably working toward acceptance, but then he laughed and shook his head. "It isn't possible."

"It is," I assured him, keeping my tone even and serious.

His laughter died suddenly, and his eyes drifted back to Ellie. She was staring at the window now, almost like she knew we were behind it. There was a good chance she could hear and smell us; I could smell her.

"So Miss King…?"

"Is a werewolf. Bitten by another werewolf the night of her attack four weeks ago."

"The wolf we found was a…"

I nodded. "Werewolf, Detective. It's easier to accept if you can bring yourself to say it."

Ellie stood up and moved around the table and toward the window. Her nostrils flared as she raised her hands to the glass. Her lips moved, and my name reached me softly, muffled by the soundproofing between the rooms.

"I'm here," I said in a low voice, placing my hand against hers.

Relief filled her eyes in the form of tears, and she nodded. She was falling apart, and I was desperate to get in there and comfort her.

"She can hear you?"

Ellie's head shifted toward Detective Matthew's voice.

"She can. Enhanced hearing comes with the gig." I turned to him and nodded toward the window. "Can we get in there? Or are you holding her for something?"

Matthews shook his head. "Just…for her own

protection and because I figured you'd be looking for her."

Before Matthews could open the door, I placed my hand on the door, holding it closed to stop him. "Who else knows?"

"I'm sorry?"

"Don't play stupid."

The detective's eyes widened, and his fear thickened the room. "I assure you, Mr. Devereux, I'm not."

"You didn't tell anyone else what you saw?"

"No. I wasn't even sure what I saw myself. I didn't want people to think I'd gone insane."

He really had no reason to lie at this point, so I released the door and we headed to the interrogation room where Ellie was being held. The instant I was through the door, Ellie's arms were around my neck, and the ache I'd felt when I left the manor last night finally eased. I felt whole again.

"Oh, Jax. Thank God," she mumbled into my shoulder. "You won't believe what happened last night...who I saw."

"It's okay, Ellie," I whispered, wrapping one arm around her trembling body and running my other hand over her disheveled blonde hair. I inhaled deeply, letting her scent calm me further, and while it did, I picked up on something else. I couldn't quite place it before the copper smell of her blood singed my nostrils, reminding me that she'd been shot. I released her, hooking a finger into the neck of the oversized sweater. She seemed reluctant, but eventually conceded to my silent request.

The wound had already closed, but an angry welt remained. There was a possibility of infection, but her immune system would fight it off quickly. She'd be fine. Physically, anyway. She'd probably be a little skittish for a while.

"You left," she said, hurt and anger lacing her tone. Accusation stared back at me, and I grew confused.

"I told you I had to," I reminded her gently. "There's something out there that's after us."

"What?"

I'd almost forgotten about Detective Matthews. I opened my mouth to explain when a couple uniformed officers walked by. "This isn't the best place for this. I should get Ellie back to the manor. Detective, you're welcome to meet us there. I'm sure Brooke would like the chance to talk to you about all of this."

Detective Matthews had some work to do, but he said he'd be by in a few hours. This worked out perfectly, because it would give me time to talk to Brooke and hopefully she'd be able to keep Nick from losing his fucking mind, as he so often did. He thought he was so damn perfect. It was exhausting.

I respected him as my alpha's mate, and I would follow his orders if Brooke wasn't there to give them, but the two of us just didn't get along. I doubted we ever would.

Ellie and I arrived back at the manor a little while later and sat in the car for a few minutes before going inside and facing the inquisition. She'd had a rough enough night—we both had; this was the least I could do for her. When we did finally walk through the door, Brooke was on us immediately. Ellie, clearly embarrassed, mumbled something about needing a shower and ascended the stairs to her room.

"Is she okay?" Brooke asked, worried.

I nodded. "Some shit went down last night," I started to tell Brooke when Nick entered the foyer. "The three of us should talk."

I led them straight ahead between the two curved staircases and into the sitting room where I told them about Detective Matthews. Brooke was concerned, and as I suspected, Nick was pissed off.

"I had no choice," I told them both. "He'd already come to the conclusion based on having shot a wolf and then coming across Ellie. What else was I supposed to do?"

"Nothing," Brooke said, placing a hand on Nick's forearm and turning to him. "He did the right thing. He did what I would have done." She looked back to me and smiled. "How did he take the news?"

"I'm sure he still has questions. I invited him over to talk to you tonight."

"Good," Brooke said. "You should go check on Ellie. I'm sure she needs a little comforting after her night."

"Right." I turned to leave the room, but then remembered something else. "How's Ash?"

"Contained," Nick said, sounding less angry than he had earlier. "She's been restless and tried to bust out, but the cage held up."

"Good," I said, but I wasn't sure if I believed it. There was nothing "good" about having to cage my wife. "Well, I'll go see how Ellie's doing."

As I left the room and turned to ascend the stairs, I briefly contemplated heading down to the pit instead to see Ashley. Ultimately, I decided to focus on Ellie for right now, and I would go down to see my wife in a little bit. I owed Ellie that much after all she'd been through, and I found I needed to be with her for my own peace of mind, as well.

I knocked on the door before pushing it open. Ellie was wrapped in a big white robe, her blonde hair hanging down her back in wet waves. She looked up from whatever she was holding in her hand and smiled.

"Hey," she greeted.

"Hi," I replied. "How was your shower?"

"Good."

"And your shoulder?"

Ellie shrugged. "Better. Burns a little, I guess."

"I'll have Layla come up to take a look at it in a bit," I told her.

"Layla?"

I smiled at her and sat next to her. "She helped Miranda with a lot of the medical stuff, and has taken it over since…"

"Since what?" Ellie asked innocently.

"Since Miranda died earlier this year."

Ellie's expression fell. "I'm sorry. That must have been awful."

"It was hard, but we're doing all right." I paused, leaning over and bumping my shoulder against hers. "I'm more concerned about how you're doing, though, Ellie. You had a pretty rough night."

Ellie dropped her eyes again, and when I let my gaze follow, I saw that she was holding a photo.

"What's this?" I asked carefully, not knowing if she was as protective of her past as I was.

She offered it to me. "That's my friend Sarah

and me at Spruce Meadows a couple years ago." She pointed at the brunette in the photo and then her, bypassing the blonde woman in the middle completely. "Did you know I used to ride?"

I nodded. "Kind of. We looked into you a little before I moved into the building," I confessed, hoping Ellie wouldn't be too upset. She wasn't.

"I was pretty good, too. I had dreams of one day competing at a professional level."

"That's kind of cool," I told her. "Who's the other woman in the photo with you?"

"Only my idol," she replied as though I should know this. "Madison Landry. Meeting her and getting to talk to her was incredible."

"Did you ride often?"

Ellie nodded once. "A few times a week. Up until the attack. After that night, I went out to the barn, but the horses…they freaked out whenever I was around, so I stopped going. My friend has been riding my horse since I couldn't even get near him. I didn't understand it at first, but I do now."

I could tell that this really upset her, and I wasn't sure how to help ease that. "Animals react better to us over time. In those first weeks, the wolf is volatile and unpredictable. Once you harness it and accept that you're one and the same, everything gets a little easier."

Ellie nodded along, but her mood didn't seem to lift at all. Something else was weighing on her.

"I'm sorry I disappeared last night. I should have waited until you were more comfortable with everyone here — comfortable in your own skin."

"No, Jax. It's okay. I know you were doing something important. I can't hold that against you." She looked up at me through her thick eye-lashes, her big brown eyes soft and the thin amber ring around the pupil flaring slightly. "You were just trying to keep us safe. I didn't mean to go back to the city. I was only going for a walk when…"

Resting a hand on her lower back, I shook my head. "Ellie, you don't have to explain yourself. I don't blame you for feeling like you needed a little space. This place is huge, but at times it can feel claustrophobic."

Ellie placed a delicate hand over mine, the look in her eyes telling me she had more to say but wasn't sure how to. A jolt of electricity shot through me, awakening the wolf and my desire for her. I tried to tell myself it was wrong to be having these thoughts and feelings — especially knowing that Ashley was alive and in the manor — but Ellie's lips were on mine before I could say anything.

With a low moan, she was in my lap, discarding the photo to the mattress next to us. The bottom of her robe was open, partially exposing her to me. Her temperature rose in time with mine, and soon, I wasn't thinking about how wrong this was. I was letting my urges drive my actions after years of forcing them into submission.

My hands ensnared Ellie's hips, guiding her against me and enjoying the friction between our bodies, and she curled her fingers into my hair. My right hand moved up her body, feeling her heartbeat through her ribcage as it found its way around and slipped beneath her loose robe. My thumb grazed the underside of her breast, and Ellie responded enthusiastically.

"Yes," she murmured into my mouth, arching

her back into my touch.

Every time the two of us were together like this, the rest of the world slipped away into oblivion. There was no one left but us, and everything was perfect. Normally, I was a take-charge kind of man, but Ellie's determination turned me on until I was no longer in control of my own body and was willing to let her lead. Until there was a knock at the door.

"Oh!" Brooke exclaimed, caught off guard as she pushed the door open a little further.

Ellie looked embarrassed as she climbed off my lap and adjusted her robe, avoiding Brooke's gaze entirely. I wasn't sure what to say to help ease her humiliation, or if anything even would, so I just sat there like a clueless lunkhead — mostly because my brain had yet to receive blood flow from my lower half.

"I didn't mean to interrupt," Brooke continued, casting her eyes between Ellie and me. I could see the questions burning in her eyes. "You're needed downstairs." She was only looking at me now.

"Downstairs?" I questioned, not certain why I would be nee —

"The pit, Jax," she clarified. "You're needed in the pit."

I paused, unsure how to explain the importance of my having to deal with Ashley to Ellie. I hated feeling so torn. I much preferred when my life was simpler…but at the same time, I didn't.

"It's fine," Ellie told me. "Go. I'm kind of tired anyway. I think I'll just crash."

I stood up, but before I left the room, I leaned over and kissed the top of Ellie's head, inhaling the scent of her freshly washed hair. "I'm just down the hall if you need me tonight," I assured her. "Sleep well."

I stepped out of the room, feeling Brooke's eyes on me the whole time. She was only a step behind me, her growing curiosity prompting me to stop at the top of the stairs. "It's confusing, okay?"

I turned just in time to see Brooke holding her hands up in surrender. "Hey, you don't have to explain yourself to me," she declared. "You forget, I was in a similar position not too long ago."

I collapsed on the top stair and buried my face in my hands. It didn't take long for Brooke to join me, placing her hand on my back supportively.

"She's been dead for fifteen years," I said, un-prompted. "It took a while, but I'd accepted that. I chose to be alone—to not seek out a mate, out of respect for her."

"And then you met Ellie," Brooke tacked on.

"And then I met Ellie." I sighed. "These last weeks with her have been incredible, Brooke. Un-like anything I've experienced in a long time."

"You bonded, Jax, and that's okay."

I turned to look at her. "But now Ash is back."

Brooke eyed me skeptically. "Is she, though? Jax, I might not have known the two of you back then, but I have a feeling she's not exactly the same girl you fell in love with when you were kids." She wasn't wrong, but I found I was still grasping onto that small bit of hope that she wasn't completely lost to me.

Feeling my chest tighten with the onset of anxiety, I stood up. "I should head down and check on her. You'll let me know if Ellie needs anything while I'm down there?"

Brooke nodded once. "I will."

I left Brooke at the top of the stairs, not looking back, and I made my way to the basement where I opened the secret hatch and descended into the pit. I didn't know what to expect once I got down there, but it sure as hell wasn't what I found.

Ashley was sitting on the edge of the cot, blonde hair hanging around her face like a curtain as she looked at something in her hands. When I was a little closer, I noticed it looked like a photo. Was it something she kept on her?

She looked up at me, and for a brief second, she looked like the woman I remembered. The hate and disgust she harbored for my kind earlier seemed to have vanished as her eyebrows pulled together. I glanced down at the photo in her hand and recognized it as the one from the frame in my room back at the apartment. The one of our family.

"Jackson, right?" I nodded once, swallowing the lump that formed in my throat. "I've...been dreaming of you. For a long time."

CHAPTER 19 | IMPRISONED

I looked at Ashley, letting what she'd just said sink in. But I still didn't understand.

"How is that even possible?" she asked in response to her own confession. "I don't know you. We've never met, but I've been dreaming of you for weeks. When I wake up, there's this annoying itching sensation in my brain as more information from the dreams comes back." Ashley pointed at her head, her eyes glazing over as she relived the moments she was talking about. "The more I try to push them away, the more incessant the sensation becomes until it burns. That's...not normal." She looked down at the photo, running her index finger over the image of our son. It seemed she wasn't really looking for answers, or maybe I was just too shocked to formulate any right now. "And yet there's this." Her eyes found mine again. "Where did you get this?"

I sighed sadly. "It was taken shortly before the accident."

"Accident?"

I nodded, but didn't say anything else. She'd been resistant to hearing me before. It was possible

I'd have to let her lead this conversation if she was going to accept the truth for what it was.

"I still don't understand." She lifted her face, her blue eyes filled with questions. "I don't know you, but this photo says otherwise. How is that even possible?"

Even though I was sure to regret what I was about to do, I grabbed the key off the table, unlocked the cage, and stepped inside. Ashley watched as I avoided touching the bars, the look in her eyes curious and calculating. I closed the door and tossed the key back toward the table. I overestimated the distance, and it hit the far end of the table before sliding off and onto the floor with a *clang*. I shrugged it off, deeming it low on my list of priorities.

Ashley stood up, and my posture stiffened, waiting for her attack. She only looked at me, but I kept my guard up, because I was afraid the second I didn't, she might strike.

It was what I would do if the roles were reversed.

"It's all so confusing," she said, her forehead creasing. "All I've ever known was that your kind is evil. That they should be eradicated…"

"That's not all you've ever known," I offered, staying in place as she walked toward me.

She stopped six inches from me, looking up and meeting my gaze. Her blue eyes danced back and forth between mine, and she swallowed thickly. "It's not?"

Without really thinking it through, I reached out and took her hand. She flinched at first, but allowed it. My entire body relaxed as the familiar hum that accompanied Ashley's touch thrummed through me. It was as though the last fifteen years never happened. Like we'd never been apart. I was captivated by her intense blue eyes, and nothing else seemed to register.

"I know everything is a little hazy, Ash"—she inhaled a shaky breath, and I saw a glimmer of recognition in her eyes at hearing her nickname—"but those dreams you're having? I think they might be memories." Slowly, my hand released hers, my fingers softly stroking her skin as it ascended her arm. I stopped at her neck, cradling it, and moving my thumb over her jaw like I used to before I would kiss her.

Ashley exhaled softly, her eyelids dropping slightly, and then her hand covered mine as she leaned into the touch. "Jax…"

Being this close to her after all these years sparked something I thought had been lost forever, and I let myself forget everything that had happened since. All I could see was her. All I wanted to see was her …

My lips were on hers before she finished speaking, and I swallowed her soft moan as I wrapped my other arm around her waist and pulled her close. Her body molded into mine, her arms winding up around my neck and shoulders, and her fingers twisted into my hair. Relief and happiness consumed me as I got lost in the familiarity of her embrace, and I basked in the moment for a split second before Ellie's face appeared in my head. Unbearable guilt weighed down on me, forcing the air from my lungs until my chest burned, and I was about to pull away from Ashley when shit went sideways.

In a fraction of a second, Ashley's body went

rigid. I opened my eyes to find hers were wide, her pupils dilated. The recognition I'd seen in them before was nowhere to be seen, and she pressed her hands against my chest and shoved me back.

"What the hell are you doing?" She wiped her mouth with the back of her hand, the disgust on her face obvious. Her posture had changed, too, reminding me of our first couple encounters.

Just like me, there were two parts at war within her, both fighting hard for control. Ashley was gone. I was with the hunter now...in a cage with silver-laced bars, and the key somewhere on the floor outside. Solid plan, Jackson.

"Ash—" Her fist connected with the side of my face before her name even reached her, the pressure in my eye socket almost explosive as my body followed the momentum. Before I fell, I caught myself on the cage, burning my hands and swearing loudly. I had just found my footing when Ashley launched her second attack, kicking the backs of my knees and forcing me down.

"How dare you violate me like that," she snarled, her voice unrecognizable.

"Ashley," I tried again, choking on her name when she wrapped her right arm around my neck and squeezed.

Her warm cheek was pressed against mine, and I felt her smile. "I noticed the way you handled the door when you came in here..." She paused. "Saw how you reacted just now when you touched the bars..." Ashley's knee pressed into my spine, her left hand reaching out and wrapping around one of the bars as she forced me closer.

I could already feel the heat from the silver, but as Ashley forced me closer, I heard the sizzle and smelled my skin beginning to singe. "Ashley, please."

Her laugh was dark, haunting. "Begging? I thought you didn't do tricks?"

Out of instinct, my hand shot up to keep my face from connecting with the bars, but I recoiled in an instant when my palms burned and blistered. The distraction as I focused on my hands was all Ashley needed as she pushed harder, pressing my face to the bars. I howled in pain, reaching behind me and grabbing a fistful of her blonde hair. I pulled her forward, smacking her head into the bars as hard as I could. My strength waned as the silver in the bars weakened me a little, but I fought as best I could. Ashley remained unfazed, demanding to be set free.

Soon, footsteps thundered down the stairs above, sounding like a herd of elephants as they raced across the basement. The hidden doorway clicked and shifted out of the way before several pack members came to my rescue.

"Where's the key?" Nick demanded, looking on the table, then at me. He looked worried. If it wasn't for the flames of hell lapping at my face, I'd bug the shit out of him for it.

"Fl-" I started to say, before Ashley constricted my airway further.

"Alistair!" Brooke screamed, and when the dark edges of my vision cleared, I saw him next to her. Had he been there the whole time, or had he teleported?

"*Recedite.*"

I didn't understand what he'd said, but soon

Ashley's arm fell slack around my neck, and I heard a loud crash behind me as I fell to the floor, gasping between coughing fits. All I could smell was my burned flesh, but I could feel it slowly starting to knit itself together. Very slowly. The Silver would keep it from closing entirely unless I got it looked at immediately.

Ashley cried out, and I turned just in time to see her lunge toward me.

Alistair's voice was clear, echoing off the walls of our hidden dungeon. "*Ligabis.*"

Not yet at full strength, I braced myself for impact, but was stunned when she seemed to hit an invisible barrier. The way she struggled made it look like she was stuck in tar up to her shoulders. I felt safe when I realized she couldn't get free, and I pushed myself to my feet.

While Brooke and Nick searched for the key, I walked toward Ashley, staying a little further back this time and never dropping my guard. She stopped struggling as she looked up at me, her eyes widening with concern and remorse.

"Oh, God," she breathed. "What did I do? Jax…"

"*Somnus.*" That word I knew. Alistair often used it to sedate Colby since he came to live here after his circle of shamans shunned him. Her nightmares were becoming too frequent, and she'd stopped sleeping. This cast forced her into a dreamless sleep.

Ashley's body went limp in a second, her head falling forward while her invisible restraints held her upright. I backed away from her slowly, hearing the key in the lock before the metal groaned as someone opened the cage door. I stepped through it backwards before turning to my Alpha and Nick. Alistair closed and locked the door again.

"Thanks," I said, my voice strained.

Brooke stepped forward, reaching for my face. "You're a fucking idiot." It wasn't often she swore—usually just when she was angry. "What the hell were you thinking?"

I recoiled when she grazed one of the blistered marks on my cheek with her fingertips. "I was trying to get her to remember…and she did."

"So, she's always wanted to kill you?" Nick asked smugly. "Why am I not surprised?"

I ignored his attitude. "No. Something in her snapped."

"What triggered it?" Brooke asked, sounding legitimately concerned.

"I kissed her."

Brooke shook her head, clearly disapproving, but before she could tear into me, I jumped to justify my actions. "She remembered me. It might have only been brief, Brooke, but she remembered. I only kissed her because I was hoping to help jog the rest of her memory about our past."

Brooke looked over at Ashley, shaking her head. "How do you think any of this is even possible?"

I didn't have an answer, because I was still trying to figure that out myself. I opened my mouth to tell her as much when Alistair spoke up.

"Magic."

I turned to look at him. He stood at the foot of the stairs now, his arms at his sides, his dark hair pushed back, and his glasses resting high on his nose. He looked like someone who might have been made fun of a lot in high school back in my day, but would now pass as trendy or some shit. Regardless, he was a pretty cool guy, and he'd proven himself a useful member of this pack — even if he wasn't a werewolf. Especially tonight.

"Magic?" I inquired.

He nodded. "I've been doing some reading on The Order, and I had some questions. I'm hoping we can get her to open up."

"By the looks of Jackson's face, I don't think she's in the mood to cooperate," Nick said with a laugh. Brooke slapped his arm in my defense. Not that I cared what he thought.

"I don't know how you hope to accomplish that," I told Alistair. "She's not exactly volunteering information."

Alistair opened the cage and stepped in. I was worried for him until I remembered how effective his casts were. He circled Ashley's unconscious body, stopping behind her and holding his hands on either side of her head. His eyes closed as he focused, eyebrows pulling together.

"What is it?" Brooke asked.

"I don't know," he replied. "It looks like a block of some kind." He opened his eyes. "Whoever put it in place wasn't messing around. Their magic is stronger than mine...but it's not permanent. Like any cast of this magnitude, it needs to be regularly maintained. It's already starting to fade, which is probably why bits of her past with Jax has been slipping through. Without someone to recast, it's possible all the memories could flood back at once, which could be extremely painful."

I stepped toward the cage. "Can you reverse it? Without hurting her, I mean?"

Alistair looked at me, and I could see the concern in his eyes. "I don't know. Maybe? But Jackson, they probably put it there for a reason."

"Yeah, because they're controlling bastards," I argued. "She ran away from them before. I know if she could just remember what her life was before they brought her back, things would be better. She'd have a choice."

Alistair didn't seem so sure as he exited the cage and walked toward me. "Look, I'll do what I can, but you should ask yourself if it's worth it."

"Worth it?" Angry, my head snapped in his direction. "Of course it's worth it. She's my wife."

"Right, but I wouldn't just be uncovering her life with you." He let his sentence hang for a moment, waiting for me to piece whatever his thoughts were together.

Just as I was about to ask him what the hell he was talking about, Brooke placed a hand on my arm. "Her death, Jax. Removing this barrier would force the memory of her death, too. And everything she's done since then would still be there."

The revelation sucked all the air from the room. My stomach rolled, and my heart hurt to even think she might remember the night she died. How our happy laughter soon turned to screams of terror as we fought for our lives against Gianna's coven of hungry vampires.

"You said it was fading, anyway," I pointed out. "She'll remember either way, right? Unless we let her go so they can repair it?"

Alistair only nodded.

"Jax, we can't let her go," Brooke reminded me. "She's picking us off one at a time."

There were too many variables and, it seemed,

not enough time to weigh them all. If we let her go, she'd go back to The Order, forget about me, and start hunting us again. If I asked Alistair to find a way through the barrier around her memory, I'd be forcing her to remember the worst night of our lives.

"I'll help her through it," I spoke up without thinking.

"What?" Brooke looked up with me, equal parts worried and confused. "Jackson, I think you have enough on your plate without adding this."

Ignoring her concerns, I looked past Brooke at Alistair. "Break through whatever mystical wall they put inside her head. I'll help her cope with the unpleasant memories."

"Jackson..." I looked down to find Brooke's eyes wide with concern. "Are you sure about this?"

A groan from the cage drew my attention, and I turned to find Ashley coming to. Alistair waited until she was lucid before releasing her from the binding cast he'd used. Once she was steady on her feet, she ignored everyone else in the room, staring only at me. I saw the same spark of recognition, but it was buried deep, and it only stoked the fires of determination to get her back.

"Do it."

CHAPTER 20 | RETRIEVAL

"You're sure about this?" Alistair seemed nervous about what he was preparing to do. Not that I could blame him; I was feeling pretty rattled, too.

We left Ashley in the cage while the four of us congregated in the library. The others had gone for a run, wanting to secure the perimeter in case anyone came looking for Ashley. They still didn't agree with her being here, but none of them were about to argue with Brooke. While I knew she was concerned about our safety with our new houseguest here, she had my back. I appreciated it, but I couldn't help but wonder why.

"How's everything going in here?" Roxy asked, entering the room.

"I thought you went out with the others?" Nick inquired.

Roxy shrugged. "I'm about to. I just wanted to check in." She acknowledges me. "Ellie is fast asleep. Poor thing must have been exhausted."

"Thanks for checking in on her," I said, relieved to hear it. While I felt this deep desire to find out what happened to Ashley, my need for Ellie to be safe under the same roof as me was just as strong. Maybe even stronger.

With a sigh, Alistair crossed the room and pulled Roxy into his arms. With their foreheads pressed together, she ran her fingers through his short hair and quietly assured him that everything was going to be fine. His tension seemed to lift, the air in the room clearing slightly, before she kissed him and left us alone again. Before he came into the picture, Roxy was angry—and who could blame her, really? She thought she and Nick had something between them before he bit Brooke.

Despite her past, though, it was nice to see she'd found someone. He might have been her polar opposite in every way, but they complimented each other perfectly.

"Okay," Alistair said, turning to face the three of us. "Let's do this before I lose my nerve."

The four of us left the library together, Alistair carrying an old, thick book beneath his arm. It was all written in Latin, so I had no clue what any of it said, but Alistair claimed it contained the spell he would need to help him retrieve Ashley's memories.

We had just hit the stairs to the basement when there was a knock at the door. We froze, wondering who it could be, when I suddenly remembered...

"Detective Matthews."

Brooke looked at me, "You and Alistair head down. Nick and I should talk to him."

"You sure?"

She nodded. "Yup. Go."

Alistair and I retreated for the pit, securing the door before making our way to the cage. Ashley was still asleep again, but she didn't exactly look peaceful. Her forehead was glistening with a thin layer of sweat, and she was mumbling in her sleep. She must have been having a nightmare…or another lump of memories were resurfacing.

We entered the cage together, Alistair securing it behind us so she couldn't escape if something went wrong; she was still a huge risk to the pack, after all. I sat on the cot next to her and held her hand. It was clammy against mine.

Alistair kneeled at the head of the bed, placed his hands on either side of her head, and closed his eyes. We sat in silence for a minute before he opened his eyes and looked at me. "The wall is deteriorating on its own."

"That's good…" I paused, gauging his worried expression. "Isn't it?"

Alistair released a heavy sigh and shook his head as he reached for the ancient tome at his side. "Nothing about this is good, and it most certainly won't be easy. She's in a lot of pain." He flipped through the pages as Ashley's head moved from side to side, her discomfort growing by the minute.

I gave her hand a squeeze, but it only calmed her for a fraction of a second. I felt useless.

"I'm going to have to wake her up for this, and if she's already uncomfortable with the barriers coming down on their own, there's a really good chance my tearing them down altogether could be worse." He held my gaze. "I'll try my best to minimize it, but are you ready for that?"

The thought of Ashley being in pain didn't sit well with me, but I didn't think we had much choice. "Rip it off like a Band-Aid, right?"

Alistair nodded. "*Exitare*."

Ashley's eyes fluttered open and she took in her surroundings calmly...until she realized she couldn't move. Panic and fear soon took over as she struggled against Alistair's cast. "What the hell is going on? Why can't I move? What have you done to me?" She fired off question after question, never leaving an opportunity for us to answer.

When her eyes found mine, I saw the panic lessen slightly, so I offered her a soothing smile as I squeezed her hand gently. I didn't know if she could feel it, but I hoped she could. "Ashley, Alistair wants to try to help you remember everything you were struggling with before." She swallowed thickly, her nerves setting in again. "I'm here to help you through it," I assured her, my voice smooth and controlled.

"And if I say no?"

"The memories will come back either way, but this will be faster and, I hope, far less disorienting," Alistair interjected, drawing her focus above her. He held her gaze. "I can't promise it won't hurt, but I can hopefully tweak the incantation to make the discomfort less."

"What if you're both wrong and these are just the remnants of old dreams?"

"Ash," I said softly. She looked at me, her eyes hard all of a sudden. "I think you know they're more than that."

"Some of your memories have been blocked and replaced with fabricated ones. It's very convincing, but it needs to be maintained regularly or everything starts to deteriorate, and the old memories start to slip through." Alistair smiled at her. "Think of it like a car needing scheduled maintenance."

"And I'm just supposed to believe you? How do I know you're not just feeding me whatever bullshit the wolf told you to?"

Alistair looked at me, then back at Ashley. "You don't, but can you really tell me with absolute certainty that you don't believe what he's told you? With all the proof before you, you still deny it?"

"I don't...I don't know what to believe anymore."

"All the more reason to let him try, Ash," I said without thinking. I expected her to lose her mind, but all she did was nod her head, her expression softening once more.

"Okay," she replied. "Let's do it."

Glancing down at the worn pages, Alistair took a deep breath, rubbed his hands together, and then held them at her temples again. Ashley took a deep breath and closed her eyes in preparation as Alistair's lips started moving, the words so soft they barely reached me.

"*Levate velum.*" He repeated himself over and over again, closing his own eyes as the words came faster, soon blending together until I couldn't tell where they began and ended.

With a gasp, Ashley's grip on my hand tightened, and her eyes snapped open. Her jaw was clenched shut, and beads of sweat had begun to form on her forehead. I could see the pain in her eyes and her fear tainted the air. Feeling otherwise useless, I spoke soothingly to her, but I wasn't sure she could hear me through her discomfort.

"*Receptui!*" Alistair said firmly, ending his cast.

Less than a second later, Ashley's body stiffened, her spine arching away from the cot, and she finally released a cry of agony so sharp it sliced through me.

I looked up at Alistair, angry and ready to pummel him. "I thought you said you'd be able to lessen the pain."

His eyebrows rose with remorse, and he spoke simply. "I did."

Ashley's cries tapered off to moans and groans as Alistair and I watched her start to settle. Her eyes closed slowly and her breathing eventually evened out. Alistair stood and collected his book, but I remained next to Ashley, monitoring the pulse on her inner wrist. Its quickened pace soon regulated.

"That's it? Why isn't she awake?"

"I imagine the stress of bringing the wall in her mind down sent her into shock. She'll be fine after some rest." He opened the cage door and turned his head to me. "You coming?"

I considered leaving her, remembering that Detective Matthews was here speaking to Brooke and Nick, but didn't think I could bring myself to until I knew she was okay.

"I imagine she'll sleep for a couple hours. You should come upstairs and recharge. Eat, go for a run. Do whatever you have to do to release your energy before she wakes. The last thing you want is to let your own stress trigger a volatile reaction while you're in here with her."

He'd been with us long enough to understand our physiology, and what sorts of things triggered the wolf. I nodded, placing Ashley's hand at her side, and followed Alistair out of the cage. He pushed it closed, turning the key, and I was about to protest when he said, "She's still a risk to the Pack. Brooke wants her locked up until we're certain she's been neutralized."

The way he spoke made her sound like some sort of weapon. I looked at my wife, basked in the serenity on a face I hadn't seen in fifteen years, and remembered my most recent encounters with her. Alistair was right. Everyone, including Ashley, was safer with her locked up.

Alistair and I parted ways when we reached the main level. He went off to the library to return the book, and I went to the kitchen to find food in hopes it might help the unsettled feeling in my gut; I couldn't recall the last time I'd eaten. As I neared the kitchen, I heard Brooke talking, followed by the voice of Detective Matthews.

"I still can't believe all this."

I cleared my throat as I entered the room so as not to startle the human. Brooke nodded in my direction. "How'd it go?"

"Alistair assures me it all went fine. She's resting now."

"Miss King?" Detective Matthews inquired.

I opened the fridge and grabbed a bottle of water. "No. She's fine. This is…someone else." I took a drink before changing the subject. "How's everything here?"

Detective Matthews looked into his mug. "Enlightening."

I shrugged. "Well, you're not running scared, so that's a good sign."

He laughed. "I've seen some pretty hairy shit in my years — more so in the last couple. What happened with Miss King was…unexpected, but not the worst thing I've seen."

"He's handling this better than you did, Brooke," I teased.

Brooke glared my way, opening her mouth to fire off some witty retort, I was sure, but Azura's cry filled the kitchen from the monitor on the table. Nick reached for it and shut it off. "I'll go get her."

Brooke stepped around the island. "No, I'll go. She's probably hungry." She excused herself, telling the detective to call or stop by any time.

He remained quiet for a few minutes before Brooke called down for Nick. When it was just the two of us, Detective Matthews looked at me. "How does that work? With babies?"

I raised an eyebrow and smirked. "Pretty much the same way it does with humans...or is that a talk we need to have?" I joked.

Embarrassed, he shook his head. "No, I meant, is the baby...?"

"Because both parents are wolves, she's considered a full-blood, meaning she'll gain the ability to transition once she reaches puberty."

"And if both of her parents weren't?"

I shrugged. "There'd be a fifty-fifty shot she'd be one of us if that were to happen. Can I get you another cup of coffee?"

He looked down at his cup again and shook his head. "No, thank you. I should be heading out. You'll give my best to Miss King?"

"I will," I assured him as I walked him to the front door. "Please call us if there are any more attacks."

Detective Matthews turned to me. "I will. And thank you for being so honest about all of this."

I paused for a moment, not wanting to scare

him, but also wanting him to know how important it was to keep this information to himself. "I assume Brooke told you about the rules? How only a select few humans are aware of our existence and what could happen if word were to spread?"

He nodded once. "She did."

"So you know the consequences if you were to slip up?"

"Trust me, no one would believe a word of it anyway. Your secret is safe with me."

After watching Detective Matthew's car pull out of the driveway, I went back through the house and headed for the patio where I started to strip down. My tension from earlier had returned, and I needed to release it before I went down to see Ashley again. My transformation didn't take long, and soon I was running through the countryside as fast as I could. The warm summer air whipped through my coat, and soon I picked up the scent of a hare. Salivating, I followed it, chasing the surprised animal through the forest until I finally caught it.

Belly full and energy spent, I jogged leisurely to the manor where I changed back and got dressed. Brooke and Nick were in the small sitting room off the kitchen, laughing and admiring their daughter.

"Hey," Nick greeted with a smile. Fatherhood changed him. It was unsettling most days.

"How was your run?" Brooke asked. "Feel better?"

"I do, actually. Have you checked on Ellie?"

"Still asleep," Brooke assured me.

I nodded. "That's good. She's had a rough few days." Standing in the area between the two rooms, I stared out the window awkwardly. It was no secret just how socially inept I could be at times. After losing my family, I'd withdrawn from the world as a way of protecting myself. I figured if I didn't allow myself to care about someone else, I wouldn't be putting myself in a position to be hurt. It made sense at the time. Even if it was a lonely way to live.

"I haven't heard anything from downstairs," Brooke said softly, intuitively knowing what I was thinking about. "You should take the opportunity to go catch some sleep. You look exhausted. We'll wake you if there's any change."

It was then I realized I hadn't gotten more than a few minutes of sleep at a time the past couple nights. First, because I'd been watching over Ellie, and then Ashley the next night. Exhaustion fell down around my shoulders like a weighted blanket, so I excused myself and headed upstairs.

On my way to my room, I glanced into Ellie's room and found her fast asleep. I paused in her doorway for a moment to admire her as she slept. She looked so peaceful. It was hard to believe she was still within the first forty-eight hours of her transition. Most of us continued to have the dreams that woke us up feeling anxious.

Pleased by this, I went to my room and laid down on my bed, fully clothed. I was too exhausted to change, and I wanted to be ready to go in case something happened. It didn't take long after my head hit the cool pillow for me to fall asleep, all of my concerns melting away for the moment as I slipped into a dreamless sleep.

Warmth shrouded me as I slowly breeched the surface of consciousness. I was so comfortable,

I momentarily considered letting myself fall back asleep, enjoying the feeling of the woman beside me…

Confused, I opened my eyes to find blonde hair splayed across the other pillow and Ellie smiling at me. "Good morning," she greeted softly.

"Hey." My voice was still hoarse with sleep, so I cleared my throat. "How'd you sleep?"

"Good. I woke up a few hours ago and saw you'd come to bed." Reaching out, she laid a hand on my chest and started moving it. When she reached the hem of my shirt, she slipped her fingers underneath and started teasing the waist of my jeans. "I've missed you." Her breath was warm on the shell of my ear as she whispered. Then her lips pressed against my jaw and she started a slow trail toward my mouth.

Remembering Ashley in the basement, I sat up abruptly, and I felt every last bit of Ellie's disappointment. "Sorry," I apologized quickly, looking at her as she sat up, looking crestfallen.

"Jax?" She looked up at me with furrowed brows. "What's going on?"

I paused, feeling like a total asshole.

"Ever since…that night, it feels like there's this wedge between us, and I don't know how to fix it."

I turned to her, taking her hands in mine. "Sweetheart, I'm sorry. There's so much going on right now, and I'm just trying to figure it all out."

There was a knock at the door, and I was happy for the interruption. Brooke popped her head in, smiling. "Breakfast is ready."

After changing our clothes, Ellie and I joined the rest of the Pack in the dining room, and I smiled happily as I watched her get caught up in a conversation with Layla. She seemed to be fitting in quickly, and that made me hopeful for her overall integration into the Pack.

"I like her," Brooke said, sidling up next to me. "She seems eager to learn about how this all works. She might get the hang of all this quicker than I did."

"You were kind of stubborn," I teased, watching Ellie ask question after question.

"Damn skippy." Brooke looked up at me. "You should slip out while she's occupied. We haven't heard anything, but that doesn't mean she isn't awake. You should go check on her."

I excused myself, leaving them to do the bonding thing while I went to see if my wife was...well, my wife, or if she was still the hunter that was trying to kill us all. I made my way down into the pit slowly, the knot in my stomach returning, feeling tighter than before. She was still on the cot, but she had rolled onto her side, her back facing the stairs. I resisted the urge to say her name, not wanting to wake her before her body and mind were ready for consciousness.

"Do you remember the first time you kissed me?" her soft voice called out, followed by a sniffle. I could smell the salt in her tears.

"Do you?" I replied, picking the key up off the table as I approached. I fisted it in my hand, letting the teeth dig into my palm to keep me rooted in reality instead of swept up in the past.

Ashley turned her head, her blue eyes brighter against the redness from her crying. "We were in your apartment, and we'd had too much to drink. I confessed to having never been kissed before." She stood, keeping her eyes locked on mine as she walked toward the cage door and wrapped her fingers around the bars. "Your fingers brushed my cheek, pushing my hair back over my shoulder, and you licked your lips before leaning in."

I was just over a foot away from the cage, still far enough back in case this was a trick; the wolf remembered what happened last time and refused to be fooled again because my human emotions put us in danger. "You tasted like tequila and lime," I said with a breathy laugh.

Ashley's head tilted to the right, resting against her hand as she smiled fondly. It was a smile I recognized, but the wolf remained cautious. Ash recognized this and frowned. "I'm sorry I was so awful." She sounded sincere, and I couldn't pick up any traces of deceit in her expression or her body language. There was still a hardness in her eyes, but if I was being entirely honest with myself, it had always been there. I just didn't recognize it for what it was.

"Jax," she whispered, a tear falling from each eye.

That was all it took for me to unlock the door and yank it open, ignoring the brief sizzle of my skin as I grabbed the silver bars. I'd barely stepped into the cage before her arms were wrapped around my shoulders and my fingers were twisted in her hair, our lips mashed together. Even though I felt guilty, I pushed it down to embrace the joy I felt in having my wife back.

Her soft whimpers shot through me like little jolts of electricity, igniting the kindling of my broken past and bathing me in the warmth of a life I thought I'd lost. I could feel the heat between us beginning to escalate, and while every part of me always ached to be reunited with my wife in every way, there were just too many complications.

With one last kiss, I pulled back, smiling down at her as I moved my thumbs over her cheeks. "I thought I'd lost you."

She moved her hands over my shoulders and up my arms until she was gripping my wrists gently. "I'm right here," she whispered.

I nodded, standing upright, but not letting go of her; I didn't want to break our connection. "How are you feeling?"

Ashley groaned, dropping her hands and taking a step back, forcing my hands to fall to my sides. She sat on the cot and looked up at me. "Hungover. My head is...clouded."

"But you remember everything? What Alistair did...?"

"It's slowly coming back to me," she replied. "I mean, it's all there and a little more clear now. Less dream-like. It doesn't hurt anymore, either. It's kind of like...an irritating buzzing."

Relief washed over me in waves, and I dropped next to her on the rickety bed. I picked her hand up and turned it over, tracing the lines of the tattoo. This time, she didn't pull away; she watched my finger move.

"Now you know why I was so reluctant to talk about my past."

I chuckled lightly. "Ash, you made it sound like you had been raised in some kind of cult."

She turned to face me, bringing her leg up onto the bed between us, and she looked into my eyes. "It wasn't too far from the truth, Jax. The things they do... It wasn't a life I wanted."

"Ashley, you could have told me."

"And you'd have believed me? Jackson, you were a nineteen-year-old boy who'd taken in a minor runaway. There's no way you'd have believed me if I told you I was one of many being trained to become hunters of the supernatural world."

I kissed her forehead and pulled her close, allowing her to rest her head on my chest. "I loved you, Ash. I would have believed you."

She laughed, then sniffled. "No, you wouldn't have," she fired back lightly, pressing a hand to my chest and pushing back a few inches. Her big blue eyes searched mine, her eyebrows pulling together with fear and concern. "But you're one of them now. How? When?"

"The night you died," I responded simply. "I'd been bitten by a wolf that had come to stop the vampires that killed you and would have killed me."

Her lips curled with disgust as she muttered, "Vampires. I still can't believe that's how I went out. They were one of the first things The Order taught us to fight. I was thirteen when I bagged my first vamp, for crying out loud. Talk about irony."

There was no easy way to ease into the next question I had, and I probably should have waited until she brought it up, but I was never really known for my patience. "How much of that night do you remember, Ash?"

"I can still hear the glass break, feel their cold hands on my skin, the pull in my neck before it broke." She shuddered in my arms. "I tried fighting them off, but it had been years since I'd trained properly, and there were so many of them. They were strong, and I was out of shape. Then I heard Tyson scream for me, but it was too late... Everything went black."

I swallowed thickly, preparing myself to tell her that Tyson hadn't survived that night when she gasped sharply. "Oh, my God. Tyson."

Eyes burning, I gripped her shoulders in hopes of supporting her before I delivered the devastating news of our son's death. "Ashley, there's something I have to tell you."

Ashley just shook her head. "We have to go get him."

I offered her a sad smile. "Ash, we can't."

Her eyes widened with shock and anger. "Excuse me? What do you mean we can't?" She didn't give me a chance to expand on that before her next words stunned me even more than her initial arrival. "I won't leave him behind to be further brainwashed by The Order."

Chapter 21 | Reclaim

I stared at Ashley, dumbfounded, as I tried to process what she'd just told me. "What are you saying?" I asked, my voice strained. "Are you saying Tyson's alive?"

Ashley's eyes narrowed as though she didn't understand. Her mouth opened, then closed before her eyes widened, likely remembering what else happened that night. A tear slipped down her cheek as she brought her hand up to cover her mouth. "Oh, God. All this time…you thought—"

"I was alone," I interjected, dropping my eyes from hers. "I'd lost you both."

Ashley's hand slipped into my view, resting over mine. Her fingers wrapped around mine and she squeezed. "I can't begin to imagine how awful that must have been. To think…"

My head snapped up. "Think? Ashley, I *watched* them kill you. Both of you. I held your bodies until I couldn't anymore. Your necks were broken, blood flowed from your veins until the snow turned red…" Everything about that night came flooding back in an instant. I could feel the weight of their bodies in my arms again as anxiety constricted within my chest, and I stood up. "I didn't *think* I lost you, Ashley. I *did*." I turned to her then, the one question I'd been dying to ask for days. "How are you both alive?"

The cot creaked as Ashley stood. She walked toward me slowly, her posture relaxed and non-threatening. "A resurrection spell." Something seemed to be plaguing her as she took my hand in hers. Her skin was soft compared to mine, rough and calloused not only from hard work throughout my life but also from running as a wolf. "The Order is able to sense the death of one of their own. It's like a ripple effect throughout the hunters when one of us has been killed. Normally, when a hunter dies, The Order accepts it as the way of life. They're celebrated as a loyal soldier who fought valiantly."

"And you?"

Ashley inhaled deeply. "My parents are the leaders of The Order. I was next in line to inherit their responsibilities, to carry on the mission to kill demons. But I was seventeen, and it wasn't the life I wanted, so I left. Because I had run away in the middle of the night almost a decade before, my parents demanded a locating spell was done to retrieve my body when they sensed my death."

I worked to process what Ashley was telling me. It wasn't easy to hear that she had been living this whole other life for the last fifteen years, but I imagined she might have felt the same way as she remembered who she was and what we once had. "And now? What do you want now?" I slowly raised a hand, carefully brushing her cheek with the backs of my fingers until her blue eyes locked with mine.

"If you'd have asked me yesterday, I would have told you I planned to rule over The Order even more fiercely than my parents and theirs before them… But that was before I remembered why I left and what you and I had before it had all been taken away so violently." She brought her hand up to my face, her eyes dancing back and forth between mine. "There's still something here, isn't there?"

Focusing only on her words, and not on anything else in my life, I slipped my arms around her waist and pulled her to me. Our lips collided passionately, her fingers threading through the strands of my hair so she could hold me close. Arching her back, she forced her chest against mine until I could feel her heartbeat. I smelled the spike in her pheromones, tasted it on her tongue as desperation wound itself around us, driving us deeper into desire. Before we could get too lost to our urges, the door to the pit opened. Breathing heavily, Ashley and I took a step back from one another, and I smiled when I noticed the pink hue in her pale complexion before she turned away, licking her lips.

I glanced toward the stairs just in time to see Brooke and Nick come into view. The looks on their faces told me they knew what they'd just walked in on, and Brooke looked both apologetic and concerned. Their eyes flashed amber as the heady scent of lust hit them hard and awakened their own desire.

"Sorry to interrupt," Brooke said, shaking off the feeling. "We just wanted to check in." Her eyes flitted to Ashley. "See how everything is going?"

"I'd like to apologize for how we first met,"

Ashley spoke up.

I glanced toward Brooke, who regarded Ashley carefully. It was probable she was trying to gauge whether or not Ashley was being sincere. After the way she was attacked back at the apartment, I couldn't blame her.

"You seem to be doing better than you were earlier," Nick spoke up next to Brooke. "Less psychotic."

My lips curled back out of instinct, and I felt the growl starting to build in my chest. Before I could let it out, Brooke reached out and put a flat hand on Nick's chest.

"Stop it," she scolded gently. "Now isn't the time."

"No, it's fine," Ashley interjected. "I deserved that."

I shook my head, eyebrows pulled together angrily. "No," I stated firmly, glancing down at her. "You really didn't."

"Jax, it's fine. Really. I know what I am — what I tried to do." Ashley returned her gaze to Brooke and Nick. "And I am sorry. Had I known…"

"You'd have refrained from killing our kind? We know what you are, what it is you do." Nick was relentless. I knew he was angry — I could feel the heat of his rage thicken the air — but I didn't like the way he was attacking her.

"Yes," Ashley said, seeming unfazed by Nick's seething hatred for all that The Order stood for. "I hunted and killed your kind as well as other creatures and supernatural beings who deserved it. But believe me, this isn't what I wanted my life to be like. I tried to leave it all behind. I *did* leave it all behind. Until they found me again. If they hadn't altered my memories of my years with Jackson, I assure you I wouldn't be a threat."

Ashley's confession caught my attention, and I turned toward her, desperate for answers. "So, you never questioned where the father of your child was?"

Nervous, Ashley bit her bottom lip, struggling with her reply. "I didn't have a reason to question it," she finally confessed, her voice so quiet I might have struggled to hear her had I been human.

"What do you mean?"

"I didn't have to question it, because I thought I was living with the father this entire time."

The room fell silent, Ashley's more recent confession stunning us all. Finally, after I let what she said sink in, I asked, "What?" It wasn't the most thought-out intro to my next line of questioning, but I was still a little floored.

Ashley turned away, unable to look me in the eye as she confessed to having been with another man all this time. I had to try and remind myself that she didn't remember me, that if she had, she wouldn't have been with someone else, raising our child. It helped. My anger toward her instantly shifted to The Order. Those sons of bitches kept my wife and child from me and let her believe their fucked up story about her life. I wanted to burn their entire organization to the ground.

"His name is Carson. He's a hunter, like me, and he's a good man, Jackson." The cot creaked beneath her weight.

"We're going to give you guys some time to talk through this," Brooke interrupted, turning and pushing Nick toward the stairs. He seemed reluctant to leave, but Brooke forced him to with an aggravated look.

When we were alone again, I focused on Ashley, and she looked up at me with sadness and regret. "I had been promised to him upon birth. Our marriage and subsequent rise to lead The Order was to happen as soon as I turned eighteen. Just a few short weeks after we met."

"You never said anything," I replied softly.

She laughed, but it was a dry, humorless sound. "How could I? You wouldn't have believed me back then. It was easier to let you think they were…whatever you thought they were."

"I had several theories ranging from abusive to polygamist cult," I told her with a cheeky smirk.

Ashley stroked my cheek and smiled. "If it makes you feel better, both aren't too far off. Several of the elders have more than one wife, and their training practices are barbaric, to say the least. No twelve year old should be locked in a dark room for days at a time without food and water. It's enough to drive a person insane."

I couldn't help but gawk at her. I didn't want to imagine her at such a young age, sitting in a windowless pit, hungry and crying out for her parents…

"Tyson… Did he…?"

Tears slipped down Ashley's cheeks before she pressed her face into her hands. "You have to believe me when I say that, had I been in my right mind, I never would have let that happen." She looked at me. "But it's their way. While I rebelled at a teen, I see the value in their methods now — the good they do in the world. It's true, I hated everything they stood for, but I finally get it." She broke down again, and I pulled her into my arms to try and soothe her suffering.

"Is he...okay?"

Ashley sniffled against my shoulder, her head moving up and down. "He's fine. One of the best hunters The Order has ever seen."

"And you think he'll want to leave the life he's known for the last fifteen years? What about you?"

Ashley lifted her head and met my stare. There was a brief pause between us, and I could see her uncertainty as much as I could feel it. "He might if we can make him remember the way you helped me."

"And you? What do you want?"

"It doesn't matter what I want." Her voice wavered as I stared at her, eyes narrowing with inquiry. "We're married. The three of us should be together."

A flood of disappointment swept over me. I had doubts that Tyson would want to leave a life he'd known for so long. He was only seven when he died. The Order wouldn't have had to work very hard to wipe those memories from his mind. He probably didn't require the same level of maintenance as Ashley, given how young he was when it all happened. I stood up quickly and turned from Ashley, not wanting her to see my hesitation.

"It'll work," she argued, coming after me and placing her hands on my back. Then I felt her rest her forehead between my shoulder blades. "I'll go in and entice him under the guise of a hunt."

My entire body tensed. "You'll do no such thing," I commanded, not exactly relishing the idea of sending my wife back into the belly of the beast. "I'm not going to allow you to go back in there, Ash. What if I never see you again? They have to know something is wrong. What if they wipe your memory again?"

Still resting against me, I felt Ashley shake her head before she used her strength to turn me around. "I remember the last fifteen years well enough to fake it, Jax." She lifted her hands and cradled my jaw, eyes securely locked on mine. "I'll come back. I'll bring our son to you."

Hope filled my chest, swelling until it felt like I couldn't breathe through it, and I nodded. "Fine," I agreed. "But I'm going with you."

Ashley's head moved from side to side, and she took a step back. "No, you can't. There are mystical barriers in place. They'd be warned of your presence as soon as you stepped over them."

I imagined the barriers were similar to the ones Alistair kept in place around the manor to safeguard us against intruders. The high frequency sirens were deafening and never failed.

"There has to be a way," I argued. "I can't let you go in alone."

"I promise, Jackson, I'll come back to you...no matter what."

"And if they don't let you?"

"I got away from them once. I can do it again."

Frustrated at the thought of losing her again after having just gotten her back, I started pacing in the small cage — regardless of the fact that it was open. "No. Absolutely not. We'll find another way."

"There's no other way, Jax!" Ashley shouted. "If I don't go back now, they'll do the locator spell and find me with your pack. They'll send in Carson and Tyson's teams, and they'll obliterate you all without a second thought. It's what they were trained for. Let me go." Ashley grabbed my arm and stopped me in my tracks. I still couldn't get over how strong she was. "Let me bring our boy back to you."

I placed my hands on her cheeks and leaned forward, pressing my forehead to hers. "I don't feel right letting you go in alone," I confessed, my anxiety returning.

"I know." Her hands gripped my wrists. "But I'll be fine."

"And if you're not? If I lose you again?"

Her eyes burned into mine. "I have no doubts you'll find me."

"I will capture and kill any hunter I come into contact with."

Ashley smiled. "You've gone kind of dark, haven't you?"

"Comes with the new fur coat."

Ashley pulled back, shaking her head in disbelief. "It's still so strange that, even though I tried to run from it, our paths still eventually crossed. It wasn't how I pictured our lives together, but I guess fate had other things in store for us."

That twinge of guilt returned as the word "fate" registered, the pressure building until it filled my chest painfully. Yes, Ashley was my wife, and I still loved her, but then there was Ellie. My feelings for her—feelings that had started before I found out my dead wife was very much alive—were real. The bond we shared was deeper than anything I'd ever felt. It felt old…primal.

After a beat of silence, Ashley sighed, knocking me free of my turbulent thoughts, and I took a couple steps to put some space between us. It was possible she took offence to this given the sullen expression on her face. "I should go."

More conflicted than I was before, I watched as she made a move for the cage door. The realization that this might not go the way we planned hit me hard, so I grabbed her hand and pulled her back toward me. Her body slammed into mine, my fingers weaving tightly into her hair as I kissed her firmly for a few seconds. I loosened my hold on her, and we exited the cage together and went upstairs. When we arrived at the door, I opened it for her, but couldn't find it in myself to let her leave.

"Let me drive you to the city," I offered.

Ashley sighed heavily. "Jackson... It isn't safe. I'll be fine."

"I really hate this."

"Me, too."

"Then let's find another way..."

"Jax..."

Ashley and I were so focused on one another that we didn't realize we'd acquired an audience until Alistair spoke.

"I might have a way that you can go with her without being detected."

CHAPTER 22 | CONVERGENCE

I was still a little dizzy from the teleportation cast that Alistair had done to get us here quickly. Ashley figured The Order would probably do a locator spell since she'd been gone for so long without checking in. We let her lead the way, stopping only once she did.

"This is as far as you can go. The barrier isn't far from here."

Alistair nodded. "I can sense it," he confirmed.

Ashley stepped toward me and took my hand. "I'll get Tyson out, and we'll find a way back to you. You should get back to the manor before another hunter shows up. We patrol the woods often to keep the compound safe."

Reaching up, I caressed Ashley's cheek. "I'll be with you the entire time."

Ashley nodded, then looked at Alistair. "And no one will know?"

"As long as you don't speak aloud, no one will be the wiser."

Ashley took my hand in hers and gave it a tight squeeze. "Go. Now. I'll wait right here until the cast is done."

Within minutes, Alistair and I were back in the manor. My knees buckled beneath me, but instead of fighting it, I gave in, sinking to the marble floor of the foyer.

"Jax?" Brooke's panicked voice drew my focus, and I looked up at her as she barreled down the stairs. "What happened? Are you okay?"

I pushed myself to my feet, still a little wobbly. "Just dizzy." I glanced to Alistair. "That ever get easier?"

With a smirk, he just shrugged. "I feel fine," he teased. "Okay, where do you want to do this? You'll want minimal distraction, because too much interference could cause you to lose the connection."

"My room," I decided.

Alistair followed me up the stairs, and as we turned the corner to my room, I saw Ellie stepping out of hers, looking refreshed. I froze, not knowing what to do or say. I instantly felt my guilt return, knotting tighter and tighter in my gut. There was a good chance all this secrecy was giving me an ulcer. Could werewolves get ulcers? Would our bodies heal them like they did everything else? Why the hell was I thinking about this right now?

I swallowed the lump in my throat and met Ellie's eyes. She looked excited to see me, and I'd be lying if I said I wasn't just as happy to see her, but I had to help Ashley right now, and I didn't think Ellie would understand that.

"Jax." She beamed, her smile stretching across her face. She noticed Alistair and nodded. "What are you up to?" Her elated expression quickly shifted to concern as she reached up and touched my face. "You look exhausted. Is everything okay?"

"Not really," I replied, leaning into her touch, before Alistair nudged me.

"We need to do this now, Jax."

I nodded. "Sorry, Ellie. I promise I'll explain everything as soon as it's all figured out." She nodded as I leaned in and kissed her softly; until I could sit down and talk to her properly, it was best I didn't upset her. I couldn't risk her shifting in the manor. Sure, I felt like a total asshole, given all we'd been through and that we had feelings for one another, but I was low on options at this point. Besides, I didn't even know what I was going to say. My feelings for Ellie hadn't changed even though Ashley was alive, but I couldn't deny the obligation I felt to my past life.

"I've got some stuff to take care of, Ellie. I think Brooke's downstairs with the others, getting a head start on lunch already. I'm sure she wouldn't mind if you went and hung out."

With a smile that wavered slightly, Ellie excused herself and turned away. I could tell she sensed something was off, but she was giving me the space I needed to deal with it. Even if I could practically taste her upset.

"She'll understand," Alistair said in an effort to comfort me.

I sighed, pushing open my bedroom door. "Will she? I thought maybe she was my mate."

"Perhaps she is," he suggested, holding a hand out, signaling for me to sit on one of the chairs by the window.

"My wife is alive."

"And you weren't a wolf when you met her.

227

Now you are. That changes everything."

I thought about this for a second before brushing it off. "I love her, I know that."

"Your human side does, but what about the wolf? What does he want? His needs run far deeper than your human ones now."

Honestly, I was trying to ignore the wolf's desires, because I'd known the answer since the first time Ellie kissed me. "We should do this. Ashley's waiting."

Alistair stepped forward. "Close your eyes and breathe deeply. Keep it steady. Calm your heart. Now shift that focus to Ashley." Heat pulsed around my temples; I imagined Alistair's hand hovering inches from them. He began chanting words I didn't understand as my thoughts returned to my wife. Her smile, her touch, her voice...

"Jax? I'm freaking out here..."

"I'm in," I said aloud.

"Oh, thank God," she said. I could feel her relief almost as though it were my own, and I was sure some of it was, but as my eyes took in my surroundings, I realized I was back on the outskirts of the city where we'd left Ashley.

Alistair's cast to psychically link my consciousness to hers had worked. We were both skeptical when he'd first suggested it, but it was the only way for me to go in with her — to keep her grounded and focused on the mission to gather information on The Order — without being detected.

"There are several of them out here patrolling," Ashley reported quietly. *"I can't see them, but I can tell they're here. It's only a matter of time before we*

cross paths."

"I'm here now, just let them find you. The sooner you get in, the sooner you can come back to me."

There was a brief pause where I sensed Ashley's hesitation and fear, but she was quick to shake it off. I scanned Ashley's surroundings with her, momentarily startled when a tall figure stepped out in front of her. She had to look up at him, which put him somewhere around my height, and he had dark, almost-black hair, cut short, and piercing green eyes.

"Carson," she said, his name coming out a little strained.

Relief washed over his face, erasing the hardened look of a killer, and he sheathed his sword into the scabbard that was secured to his back. He pulled Ashley into his arms, and my jealousy flared. My shared view with Ashley flickered slightly until more heat pulsed at my temples.

"Focus, Jax," Alistair said calmly.

"Ashley, thank the gods you're all right," he said. When you didn't come back or check in, we all became very worried. We tried a locator spell, but all we got was static." He sounded genuinely concerned for her, and the vibes I was getting off Ashley's subconscious were unexpectedly warm and…loving.

Then I picked up on her guilt as she pushed away from him. She was wrestling with her past with me and her present with this guy. I was afraid it might happen, but I found myself surprisingly understanding, given my own similar predicament.

"I'm okay," she assured him. I could feel her

heavy pulse in her ears; hell, I could practically feel it in my own veins.

"Where have you been?"

"I ran into a local pack, so I kept a low profile while I hunted the wolves new to the area that are behind the attacks."

Carson's eyes narrowed, almost like he didn't believe her.

"Easy, Ash. He looks uncertain." Ashley cleared her throat, possibly responding to me without a word.

"You...*hid* from a pack of wolves?" He regarded her, eye dancing between hers. "Why didn't you just take them out?"

Ashley tried laughing him off as she walked past him. "Why instigate a war with creatures that aren't responsible?"

"Because it's the mission." He sounded suspicious and annoyed.

"The mission is to kill the animals behind the attacks. Not to wage war on a pack we aren't equipped to handle." It was Ashley's turn to sound irritated.

Carson grabbed her upper arm and whipped her around to face him, her blonde hair getting in her eyes before she brushed it away. "The *mission*, sweetheart, is to take them all out. They're dangerous."

"Ashley, careful," I repeat. "Don't let him suspect anything..."

Ashley took a deep breath, and I think she smiled up at him, because he seemed to relax minutely. "Carson, my love," she cooed, placing a hand on his chest. "I am simply prioritizing based on the threat level. The local pack isn't as big a threat as the ones that are rising up against them and their new alpha."

"What the fuck, Ashley?" I demanded. "You can't just feed him Pack information like it's candy."

"I'm sorry..." The words were barely a whisper, in fact, I thought maybe I imagined them because I wanted an apology.

"She's communicating telepathically," Alistair assured me quietly, clearly inside my head. It was feeling a little crowded.

Ashley stepped up onto her toes and kissed Carson's cheek. The desire to rip him limb from limb and burn his flesh was all I could focus on, and I felt my connection with Ashley waver.

"Jax..." Alistair warned.

I pushed my jealousy aside again and focused on my wife. I focused on our final embrace, her warmth, the sound of her laugh, the spark of hope in her blue eyes. Our connection grew stronger, and I paid attention as she looked around while Carson led her toward a large Land Rover.

"Somebody's overcompensating," I quipped, and Ashley fought to suppress a laugh, sloughing it off as nothing more than her clearing her throat. Carson didn't suspect it was anything more.

They drove through the countryside for a while until they arrived at a huge fortress-like structure built into the mountainside. Ashley blinked, and there was a shimmer across her vision, making the fortress disappear.

"Interesting..." Alistair said. "That's an impressive glamour."

Ashley looked around the building as they crossed the threshold. "Where's Ty?"

"He and his team are on their way back from searching for you. The entire Order has been out of their minds with worry — your parents, Ashley."

I could taste Ashley's guilt and shame as she swallowed hard. Now that she remembered her past, she remembered how desperate she was to escape them, but that didn't erase all the good she felt she'd done since then. "I didn't mean to worry you all," she assured him.

Carson stopped dead in his tracks, sighing heavily before turning to her. His hands moved over her body until he was cupping her jaw, and he leaned down to kiss her. "I felt your fear, waited until the moment I would feel your death — again — and then..."

"Nothing," she finished, wrapping a hand around one of his wrists and leaning into his touch. It felt like I was intruding on a private moment, and I could still feel her internal struggle with this whole thing.

For the first time since he'd happened across Ashley, Carson smiled — but I didn't like the look of it. "You know," he said, his voice low as he looked around. "Almost everyone is out hunting...we're practically alone, and I've missed you terribly."

I could feel Ashley's protest swelling in her chest as Carson's lips connected with hers, but soon her body melted into his embrace. Her conflict flared, but she couldn't seem to pull herself away. Carson pulled Ashley closer, his hands gliding down over her body, stopping when they reached her breasts. A whisper of an apology reached me, Ashley's inner voice cracking with her deep remorse. I hated being mentally present for this, but I knew I couldn't break our connection.

Thankfully I didn't have to…

The sound of a door opening behind Ashley broke her away from Carson, and when she turned around, I was face-to-face with a slimmer, much blonder version of myself. It was a little jarring.

"Mom," Tyson said, removing his scabbard and dropping it to the floor as he rushed toward her and pulled her into his arms. She held him tightly. "We were so damn worried."

Ashley pulled away and looked up at him. "Language," she chastised softly, and Tyson rolled his eyes. I found myself smiling.

"Where have you been? We lost track of you—even the shamans couldn't locate you," Tyson demanded.

Ashley tucked her hair behind her ears. "I was staying low so as not to engage in a battle I wasn't ready for. I was being a smart hunter."

"Grandma and Grandpa will be so happy you're all right," he said, kissing his mother on the cheek.

"I'm sure they will be," she replied, but I could feel her uncertainty prickle beneath every inch of her skin.

"I'll go get them," Carson offered, clapping a hand down on *my* son's shoulder.

"Thanks for finding her, Dad."

"I told you we would, Son."

I wanted to scream, I wanted to throw things, but I didn't. Instead, I took several deep breaths and focused on Ashley and our son, knowing she'd get him out of there soon enough.

Ashley looked around, almost frantically, and Tyson watched on, seeming confused. "Mom?"

Ashley laughed it off. "Sorry. I guess I'm a little on edge. I think I need to shower and grab a bite to eat before I head back out."

"Head back out?" he asked. "Mom, Dad and I don't think that's such a good idea."

There was a brief second where Ashley panicked, but she pushed it aside to maintain her composure. "Ty, honey, I'm sure you know by now that no one tells me what to do. There's still a job to be done."

"Yeah, and you disappeared for two days," he argued boldly. While I was worried she would be kept from finding her way back to me, I admired our son's protective nature over his mother.

"Then come with me," she suggested. "It's been a while since the two of us went on a hunt together. It'll be fun."

Tyson's eyebrows pulled together. "What about Dad?"

"He'll want our teams in different areas of the city. I'm sure he'll be fine with it."

"Fine with what?" asked a woman's voice.

When Ashley turned around, I saw a woman over twice her age, silver hair pulled back in a tight bun. She looked like Ashley, only older. "Mother," Ashley said, dropping her head and bowing before she kissed her mother on both cheeks. It was odd for me to witness a mother and daughter reunited this way. It was so cold.

"Fine with Tyson accompanying me on the hunt tonight, Ma'am," she replied firmly, finally meeting her mother's penetrating stare.

Ashley's mother looked straight into her

daughter's eyes, reading her. She stared so intently, I was sure she'd pick up on the changes in Ashley's demeanor. There was a split second where I thought she'd figured it out when she looked toward Tyson and Carson, and they cleared the room in an instant. "Ashley, your father and I don't think it's a good idea for you to leave the safety of the compound."

Ashley looked beyond her mother. "Where is Daddy?"

"Your father is strategizing before sending the teams out to find the animals who had you."

There was a moment where Ashley froze, but she shook it off and told her mom the same story she'd told Tyson. Her mother regarded her skeptically, and I figured we'd been found out. "Head on up to your room to rest, honey. I'll have Roberta bring you up something to eat and a cup of tea."

Probably not wanting to tip her mother off, Ashley listened, climbing the never-ending flight of stairs until she entered a room. I gasped when I took in the color and décor — it looked almost identical to our old room; clearly The Order hadn't been able to wipe everything from her memory. Some things were just too deeply ingrained.

She closed the door behind her and moved to the mirror above her dresser. For the first time, I could see how panicked she was just as well as I could feel it. *They won't let me out tonight.*

"They will. Just keep acting like everything is fine."

"And if they don't?"

"Then I'll come for you both." I did my best to keep Ashley calm, but I'd be lying if I said I wasn't freaking the fuck out myself. If I could feel her panic, I had a pretty good feeling she could feel mine.

About fifteen minutes later, there was a knock on her door, and a portly little woman with dark hair walked in. "Here's the tea your mother wanted sent up, Miss Ashley."

"Thank you, Roberta."

Roberta didn't stick around long, leaving quickly when Carson came into the room.

"How are you feeling, darling?" he asked caressing the length of her hair as they sat side-by-side on the edge of the bed.

"I feel great. Ready to get back out there."

Carson sighed. "Ashley…"

With an aggravated groan, Ashley stood up. "Carson, I'm stronger than the rest of you." I took pleasure in the shocked look on his face. "I can handle myself. You know I can."

"We could have lost you," Carson said, raising his voice out of fear—a fear I understood, having lived through losing Ashley before, and Ellie very recently when she took off.

"But you didn't. I'm fine."

Carson frowned, looking Ashley over for a moment. "Where's your sword?"

Without missing a beat, Ashley replied, "I stashed it somewhere safe so I wouldn't be caught with a weapon and arrested. I'll go back for it tonight."

"You're not going."

"The hell I'm not! You can't keep me here. I'm not your prisoner…I'm your commander."

"You tell him, Ash," I interjected.

"My commander? So now you're going to pull

rank on me? I thought this was a partnership?"

"So are you the pot or the kettle today, Carson?" Ashley demanded. "Because you *ordering* me to stay behind while you're all out there hunting sure as shit feels like we're not partners."

"Ashley!" a deep male voice declared.

Ashley slowly turned to find an older man with salt and pepper hair standing just outside her room. "Daddy, hi." She walked over and hugged him, but it felt forced on her end.

"What's going on in here?"

"Ashley thinks she's going hunting — even after you and Corrine forbade it," Carson said. I wanted to punch him for acting like a little snitch.

"I told you, I'm fine. I need to see this mission through. Why are you all acting like I'm some fragile little flower?"

"Because we couldn't locate you," her father interjected harshly. He looked pissed and paranoid. "We knew you weren't dead, but we couldn't get a read on your location. That's some pretty powerful magic at play."

There it was: his suspicion had reared its ugly head.

"You're acting insane," she said, shaking her head. When he didn't back down, she rolled her eyes. "Then send Tyson with me."

Her father's eyes narrowed, looking deep into hers. Something sparked in them before he ordered Carson to leave. I didn't like his expression.

Once they were alone, he turned back to her. "Your mother said you were pushing for Tyson to accompany you... Why?"

"What do you mean? He's my son — the future of this entire organization. It would be good for him."

His eyes met hers again, but this time there was something sinister behind them. She didn't have time to react before he grabbed her roughly around the arm and pulled her closer. It was then I realized he was looking through her eyes...

And he was staring right at me.

CHAPTER 23 | FRAGMENTED

"RELINQUO!"

That was all it took. One word from Ashley's father, and a flash of light blinded me, forcing my psychic link with Ashley to snap like an over-stretched elastic and recoil painfully. I felt the sting through every inch of my body, and my vision was compromised. Once the haze cleared, I stood up and turned to Alistair, the word still echoing in my head.

"What the hell just happened?" Rage and confusion coursed through my veins.

Alistair looked just as confused and disoriented as I was, stammering and trying to find an explanation. It was obvious this caught him by surprise.

Not wanting to wait for him to try and explain it, I sat back on my bed. "Take me back, Alistair. Do…whatever it is you did to link us."

I tried calming my mind and body while Alistair chanted behind me, but twenty minutes later, we were unsuccessful.

"Someone put a barrier in place," Alistair said, sounding out of breath as he adjusted his glasses. "I can't seem to get past it."

"How did he even know? You said this would work." Heat flared beneath my skin as I glared at Alistair, the wolf creeping to the surface and wanting retribution. I could smell his fear, and the look on his face instantly sobered me. "Sorry," I mumbled, looking away as I focused on calming down.

"I understand your frustration, Jackson," Alistair said. "Unfortunately, I didn't foresee the possibility that the coupling cast would be detected." He removed his glasses and cleaned them, a nervous habit of his I'd noticed over the months he'd been with us. "The way he was able to disrupt my cast concerns me."

"How so?"

Replacing his glasses, Alistair's eyes rose to mine. "I'm an extremely powerful Shaman," he reminded me. "One of the most powerful in my old circle. It takes great power to disrupt my spells."

"So...?" I had no idea what he was trying to say, and to be honest, I couldn't really force myself to care, because every second we stood around talking about it was another second Ashley was alone with The Order. And who the hell knew what they were doing to her.

"This can only mean The Order has been dealing in magicks. And based on the force with which we were ejected from her mind, I'd hazard a guess that they're leaning a little on the dark side."

I let this information sink in for a moment. "Then what are we waiting for?" I demanded. "We need to get the hell out of here."

Alistair was on my heels as I flew from my room and down the stairs. Having probably sensed my growing anxiety, the Pack filtered into the foyer.

"Jax?" Brooke asked, looking from me to Alistair. "What's going on?"

Ellie came into the room last, and my guilt returned, but not enough to kill the concern I had for Ashley.

I filled everyone in as best I could, watching Ellie carefully. She looked confused, but the flash in her eyes told me the wolf was itching for some action.

"Nick, you should go with him," Brooke said, looking around. "Take some of the others."

I expected Nick to argue with her, tell her that there was no way we were going to risk a majority of our pack rescuing someone from an army of hunters. Especially when the person I wanted to rescue was one of them.

To my surprise, he turned toward the pack. "Roxy, Vince, and Corbin, let's go."

While they made their way for the front door, Ellie approached me. "I want to help."

I appreciated her offer, but there were several reasons she couldn't come.

"Ellie, it isn't safe. You don't have control yet. We'll need to shift at a moment's notice, and you haven't mastered that yet. You're vulnerable right now. It'll come with time," I assured her, cradling her face in my hand and kissing her forehead. "We'll work on it as soon as things settle down."

Ellie's lips curled up into a tiny smirk. "Something tells me this is all pretty normal around here."

"Only on days that end with Y," I joked lightly before catching Nick's impatient gaze. "We should go. I'll be back soon, okay?"

I was just about to turn to leave when Ellie reached up and pulled my face to hers, kissing me. I could smell her fear—could feel it in the way she held onto me like she might never see me again. She was petrified, and I couldn't blame her.

"I'll be back soon," I promised again, looking beyond her at Brooke who nodded once.

"We're good here," Brooke assured me, resting her hands on Ellie's shoulders. "Go."

Within moments of being outside, Alistair was chanting. The wind picked up, swirling around us like a vortex, and soon the ground was dropping out from under us. My stomach flipped as though I was on one of the rides at the Stampede. I had never been a fan; those rides always made me nauseous. This teleportation cast, while damn effective, often left me feeling a little queasy.

When the world finally stopped spinning, and I was able to gain my bearings, I looked around. While most forests looked the same, I could smell faint traces of Ashley lingering in the evening air, so I knew this was where we'd been before parting ways.

I went back to the memory of Ashley walking through the woods and followed her scent. Soon, another scent joined hers that I assumed was Carson's from when he found her. We followed the scent, Alistair keeping up as best he could, and when we finally reached the end of the line, we stood at the perimeter.

"If we cross the barrier, they'll be alerted," Alistair reminded me.

I nodded. "Is there anything you can do?"

Alistair reached out, ripples appearing around

his hand with a low hum. As the waves worked their way outward, the glamour flickered, eliciting shock from the others who hadn't seen it before.

Alistair remained this way for a few seconds, concentrating, before pulling back. "Unfortunately, their spell is beyond my abilities."

"Jax, how fast can you track her once we're inside?" Nick asked.

I closed my eyes and envisioned the inside of the estate, remembering the direction Ashley walked, every turn she took, the door she opened and stepped through. "I can get to her room, but I doubt she's still there."

"Then we rush in and fight our way through," Roxy said confidently. I, however, was less confident.

"Wait, wait, wait," Alistair said. "Let's not be reckless."

"We don't have time to debate this," Roxy said. "Jax?"

Before I could respond by rushing across the barrier, Alistair grabbed my arm, gaining my attention. "We trip the alarm, draw them from the building and see how many we're up against. Then, I'll teleport us inside, and you can track her from there while the others draw The Order away."

I tried to find a flaw in his plan, but couldn't, so I nodded. Until I remembered Tyson was in there and would probably fight any threat to their home. I turned to Nick. "My son will be with them," I told him, watching as his eyes widened. "He's tall, blond...don't hurt him. We can break the spell The Order cast over him."

Nick nodded once. "Consider it done. Let's do

this," he said before stepping over the invisible barrier.

Nothing happened at first, and I wondered if maybe Ashley had been wrong. That was when I heard something. It started off a quiet hum, but quickly grew to an incessant buzz similar to a horde of bees until it took on the distinct sound of orders being given.

Nick ordered the pack to disperse, so we all scattered. Alistair and I stuck together, and he used his own glamour incantation to camouflage us until we knew we were safe. Within minutes, a wave of about twenty hunters flowed from inside and around the building. Among them was Carson, and not too far behind him was Tyson. I wanted to run to my son and take him away from here, but I couldn't risk blowing my cover. I needed to get Ashley out, and then we'd get Tyson together.

Fights broke out all around me. I heard my Pack fighting with the hunters, and I could only hope that none of them were seriously hurt because of me.

As soon as the coast was clear, Alistair nudged me. "We need to move."

Alistair chanted quickly, and before I knew it, we were inside Ashley's room. Her scent was heaviest here, lingering on the drapes and bedding. Intermingled with her scent was another that was just as prominent, only male, and it made me see red, even though I had no right to. I knew these last fifteen years weren't her fault. She hadn't brought herself back from the dead. She hadn't wiped her own memory, and she sure as shit didn't shack up and play house with some other asshat for shits and giggles.

Her family did this in order to keep controlling her so they could get what they wanted.

"She's not here," Alistair said.

My gut reaction was to thank him for stating
the obvious, but I knew it would be an asshole
thing to do. Instead, I inhaled deeply before walking around him and out into the hall. I followed
the scent of Ashley's fear back down the stairs,
taking them two at a time.

My blood boiled in my veins, heat flaring beneath my skin as the wolf sprang to life. I held him
there, just below the surface, so I could utilize it
when the time was right. A few steps behind me, I
heard Alistair chanting. I could feel his power emanating off of him as we came to another set of
stairs that led to a basement, and we took them.

"Stop!" I heard Ashley plead. "Daddy, please.
Don't do this."

"I knew we were pushing it by waiting," I
heard him mumble, ignoring his daughter's frantic
cries.

I smelled blood as I hit the bottom of the stairs
and recognized it as hers. She was tied to a chair in
the middle of the unfinished room. It closely re-
sembled the pit back at the manor, except the
walls were decorated with ritualistic symbols instead of adorned with weapons used for torture.

I was ready to go in there, claws at the ready,
but Alistair grabbed my arm to tell me to wait. I
didn't understand why until I noticed his lips
moving in a silent chant. I couldn't make out what
he was saying, but I hoped to hell whatever it was,
worked.

"Sweetheart, this is for the best. Remember

how happy you've been since coming home. With Tyson and Carson?" her mother said in a soft, soothing voice.

Ashley was anything but soothed, however, fighting back against her restraints. "This isn't right! You know this is wrong!"

That got her father's attention, and he turned to her. "Wrong? Being with your family is... *wrong*?" He approached her, gripping her face between the thumb and forefinger on his right hand. "You have a responsibility to your people...to The Order, Ashley."

"Fuck responsibility," she spat. "I never wanted any of this, it's why I left."

"It's why you wound up dead!" he shouted, pushing her face away from him and standing upright. Had the chair not been bolted to the floor, it probably would have fallen backward. "Had you stayed with your family and continued your training, you'd have been prepared... Instead, you went gallivanting around, got yourself pregnant, and then thrust into the middle of werewolf affairs!"

"At least I was happy. Even death was better than this."

Ashley's mother gasped while her father swung around and slapped her across the face. He seemed just as shocked as she was—maybe even a little remorseful. When she raised her blue eyes to him, they danced with the fires of rage, but before she could say anything else, I flew out of hiding with a growl, and stalked toward the three of them.

"This must be the hitchhiker," her father said, staring me down like he was unafraid. He looked at me carefully as I stood before him, slowly letting disgust settle across his aging face. "A werewolf, Ashley?" She didn't say anything, so he turned his full attention back to me. "No matter. I was wondering just how long it would take you to find us." His lips twisted up into a sadistic smile. "I even waited for you before we started. *Ligabis!*"

I felt the wave of his cast hit me, slowing me for only a second before I was able to move past it. That was when I saw a hint of panic in his eyes. He cast again, and the sensation of moving through a wall of molasses returned, but only for a second. Behind me, I could hear Alistair still chanting something in Latin, and I suddenly realized he was cloaking me with a protection spell to counter any attacks they might try to throw at me.

I smirked. "Nice try."

"Start the incantation," he ordered his wife before trying a different spell on me.

This time, I felt an immense pressure in my body. It didn't take long to realize he was feeding more power to the wolf; he was hoping to force a shift. If he did that, I'd be vulnerable for an unknown amount of time, and he could try to kill me.

My knees buckled as the spell started to take effect. My bones started to shift, muscles tensing, but I managed to fight the feeling and took another shaky step. It took everything in me to keep the wolf at bay.

"Those are some effective counter spells," he said, sounding partially impressed as he drew his sword from the scabbard on his hip.

"Jackson, go," Ashley said.

"Not likely."

Her father pointed the sword at me, and I stopped, gauging my next move carefully. "Do you have any idea how hard it's been to keep you out of her head? Most memories don't need this much upkeep, but you...you just keep popping up every few years. You're really a much bigger hassle than I'd bargained for."

He lunged forward, the heat of the silver blade barely caressing the skin of my neck as I twisted away. For an older man, he was in incredible shape; I could tell he trained regularly. I paid attention to his technique, and waited for the moment he would feign left, so I could go right. When that happened, I reached out, wrapped my hand around his throat, and used my other hand to knock the sword from his grip as I pressed him against the wall. My claws sliced through the skin of his neck, his warm blood trickling down over my fingers.

He struggled to draw in breath while I held him, and I heard Ashley's mother stop chanting immediately. All I would have to do is squeeze a little tighter, and...

"Jackson, stop," Ashley cried out. "He's...he's still my father."

I knew if I let him live, this would never be over, but if I killed him, I risked Ashley never forgiving me—regardless of how evil this bastard was in my eyes. What was I supposed to do?

"Release her," I ordered, staring at Ashley's father while addressing her mother. "Release her, and I'll let him live."

"How do I know I can trust you, you filthy mutt?" Ashley's mother questioned.

"You don't." I squeezed a little harder, making her husband's eyes bulge.

"Okay! Okay!" I watched through my periphery as Ashley's restraints were removed, and she stood up and looked at her mom. I could see the pain in her eyes, and I understood her conflict. They were still her parents, and no matter what they'd done to her, she still held onto some of the good memories. She always would.

"Ashley, don't," her mother pleaded. "You belong with us."

Ashley looked at me and smiled, though I definitely saw discord in her eyes. "I'm sorry, Mom."

I opened my hand, letting Ashley's father slide to the floor, gasping for air. "Pleasure to meet you both after all these years," I told them, piling on extra layers of sarcasm just to piss them off, then I took Ashley's hand in mine. "Let's go."

We followed Alistair back up to the main floor and toward the front door. Ashley grabbed a samurai sword from the rack beside the door, and unsheathed it, prepared to battle for our survival. We could hear the fight still going on, so I tried to figure out where everyone was. I smelled blood, both human and wolf, and I panicked, hoping none of my own had fallen. As we ran toward the fray, I whistled, hoping to get everyone's attention.

It worked. A little too well, actually.

The battle soon shifted, some of the members of The Order coming for us. Ashley stepped up and fought against some of her own people, much to their surprise.

"Stop! Everyone stop fighting!" The voice, though loud, was familiar, and I turned toward it to see Carson. "Ashley, what are you doing?"

I took a quick look around to see every member of my pack that I'd brought with me, a little banged up and bloody, but they were all breathing and had all their limbs attached. That was a relief. I didn't see Tyson, though...

Ashley kept her sword raised in front of her, breathing hard from the fight. "I'm leaving, Carson. You can't stop me."

Carson only smiled. "Leaving?" His eyes moved around the clearing in the forest. "With these savages?"

I stepped up next to Ashley, ready to fight should he make the first move. Wouldn't want him to be right about the "savage" label, after all.

"Jackson is my husband, Carson."

He released a laugh and took another step toward her. I growled in response to his advance. "You're confused, Ashley. *I'm* your husband. We have a son."

Ashley shook her head, her face contorting like she was fighting between the old memories and the fabricated ones. "No. I remember. I remember what my parents did to me — to Tyson. And you allowed it. You let them rip my memories from me. You let them violate the most private parts of my mind."

Carson's expression changed in an instant. Gone was the loving concern he showed for his wife, and in its place was fear and what looked like defeat. "I swear to you, Ashley, I didn't know what was going on. They told me all they were doing was helping you forget the night you died."

To my disappointment, the conviction in his voice indicated he was telling the truth. I wanted him to be a lying sack of shit so I could hold him responsible as an accomplice in forcing Ashley back into a life she tried to escape.

Ignoring me completely, Carson took a step toward her. "If you think they're just going to let you walk out of here…"

"You'll what?" I challenged.

Carson's expression hardened as his eyes drifted up to mine. "I don't believe I was speaking to you, dog."

The air around us shifted suddenly, the tension escalating as the fight threatened to pick up again. Before anyone could raise a sword, however, a loud, dry laugh echoed through the forest, frightening the birds that had chosen to settle in the branches above. They sensed danger—a predator.

Slowly, we all turned to this newcomer, and every member of my pack growled when we realized he was another werewolf. The fact that we'd never seen him before could only mean he was part of the group that was looking to take over our territory.

His dark eyes flashed a dark shade of amber as he grinned sinisterly, flashing his elongated canines. "Well, lookie what we have here," he said, eyeing us each carefully. "I've got about half of Marcus' infamous pack and…" he looked at Ashley and the rest of the hunters, waving his hand up and down dismissively "…whatever the fuck you guys are." Pulling his lips back, he released a shrill whistle, and soon we were surrounded by about fifty feral strays.

CHAPTER 24 | OUTNUMBERED

We were surrounded and severely outnumbered. Even if we presumptuously counted the hunters on our side. The leader of the strays — their Alpha, I guess — was about my height and build with curly dark hair that grazed his shoulders. Not that this didn't make him look intimidating. If I had to guess based on the scars covering his exposed arms and face, he'd been a werewolf a while; he might have even been a pureblood.

"I'm sorry," he said, a sardonic lilt to his tone. "Allow me to introduce myself. I'm Alex, and this here is my pack."

I looked around at each of the werewolves before us and chuckled. Some of them were pretty scrawny still, and they reeked of inexperience. Regardless, based on everything I'd learned over the last fifteen years with my pack was that their size didn't necessarily matter. They were new wolves, and their strength would be what they relied on over skill. They were volatile creatures who weren't in control, and therefore held very little remorse — especially given they were recruited by a total sociopath. I didn't want to let him think we were intimidated by him or how he had us out-numbered, though.

"You call that a pack?"

He stopped and looked me dead in the eyes. He was trying to shake me up, leaning in close as his eyes moved between mine. There was something familiar about them, but I couldn't place it. "In case you haven't learned how to count, I've got ten wolves to every *one* you have here." He paused before clapping his hands together. "Now," Alex continued, his voice steady with confidence as he took a step forward and paced in front of his pack. The way he spoke and moved was almost charismatic, which might explain why so many would follow him so blindly. "This is going to go one of two ways." He held up two fingers as though we were all incompetent. Or maybe he just needed his own reminder. He did look a little slow. "One, my pack kills you all…"

"Or two," I interjected, crossing my arms, "*You* die."

Beside me, Roxy chuckled. I hadn't even realized she was there. "I'm putting my money on option two."

A smile slowly stretched across the wolf's face as he looked at us, his eyes drifting around to the rest of the Pack and the hunters before settling back on me. "Come on, now," he said, holding his hands out to the side as if to gesture our surroundings. "We just came here to talk. Maybe strike a deal…"

"You brought an army to have a conversation?" Nick said, stepping from the shadows to my left. His arms were at his sides, fists clenched. "Seems a little…aggressive." I couldn't help but snicker.

With a loud, obnoxious laugh, our rival raised his eyebrows. His shifty blue eyes glimmered, and he pointed. "You must be Nick, Brooke's mate...your new alpha, if I'm to understand correctly."

The smile fell from my face instantly, and when I looked at Nick, his confident demeanor remained, but blood dripped from between his fingers as he clenched his fists tighter, and the muscles in his jaw feathered with tension. We knew they'd been hanging around for a while, but none of us had realized just how closely.

Neighboring packs, and the strays between territories, all knew about Marcus and Miranda's deaths, but we had yet to announce Marcus' successor. With Brooke being so new to our life, getting pregnant, recovering from her abduction, watching her brother die for a second time, then having her baby...it just hadn't been the right time. And the one stray I did tell wound up dead at the end of Ashley's sword; he didn't get the chance to tell anyone.

But this guy knew. He knew more than the other Packs we trusted. What was worse was we left our Alpha at home with limited defenses and her newborn child.

"Alistair," I said without taking my eyes off the wolf in front of us. "Get back to the manor."

"I'm not leaving you."

"Get back to the manor. Make sure they're safe," Nick commanded. Because Alistair wasn't wolf, he was under no obligation to listen to a direct order from Brooke or Nick, but he did it anyway.

There was a shift in the air as it pulsed around us, and Alistair was gone.

"Well, ho-*ly* shit!" With a stupefied expression, Alex looked back at the two members of his pack that flanked him when they arrived—his betas. "Did you see that? Hot damn, that was incredible. We gotta make sure we keep that guy around when we take over."

"Take over?" Roxy said with a scoff.

Alex eyed her up and down, licking his lips appreciatively. "That's right, sweetheart. I might just keep you, too. How would you feel about being my bitch?"

I glanced over at Roxy as she cocked her head to the right and contemplated his offer. "Mostly…like I want to vomit."

I smirked. Trust Roxy to spit in the face of the man who threatened her packmates. She was never one to just roll over and take it.

Alex shrugged off her defiance. "No matter. I'm not really a stickler for consent these days."

I took an angry step forward at his implication, but Roxy grabbed my wrist and stopped me. "Jax, don't. He's not worth it. I'm not easily rattled." Alex took note of this, and cocked his head to the side.

"Interesting," he said, wagging his finger between Roxy and me. "And here I thought you were into the little blonde." With just my eyes, I glanced over at Ashley, who was still several feet away. Alex laughed again. "No, not her—though, let's come back to that. I meant the other one. The new wolf in your pack…Ellie, I believe her name is."

"Jax, he's baiting you." Nick spoke calmly.

"Don't fall for it."

I wanted to tell him I wasn't stupid—that I recognized Alex's tactics for what they were—but the truth of it was, I wanted to rip his damn throat out and show it to him. I didn't though. I knew that one wrong move could get us all killed, leaving Brooke at their mercy. And we had no way of knowing which side The Order would take. I wanted to believe they would fight against the stray threat, especially since it was the increased attacks that brought them here, but now that we were taking off with Ashley... There was really no way of knowing until a fight broke out.

Alex started walking again, moving past Roxy and me and toward Ashley. My body tensed as I watched him approach her. She didn't move, showing no fear as he stopped inches from her.

"You intrigue me," he whispered, reaching up and pinching a lock of her light hair between his thumb and forefinger.

Ashley's right hand tightened around the hilt of her sword, turning slightly as she prepared to attack. She clenched her jaw, the muscles feathering beneath her pale skin. When Alex raised his hand to touch her face, she brought her free hand up and grabbed his wrist, shoving it away from her as she leaned in.

"You'd be wise to keep your paws to yourself, dog," she told him menacingly, slowly raising the point of her blade to his jugular. I could see the smoke rise from his skin as the silver blade rested against his throat.

He didn't flinch, instead, he leaned into the blade until it pierced his skin. "Go ahead, blondie. Run me through like you did my subordinate the other night in the park. See what happens to your band of merry men and your werewolf pet..." He smirked again when her resolve didn't waver. "Of course, I could just bring out the new chew toy we've stumbled upon."

"Mom!"

Ashley and I both snapped our eyes to the left and found Tyson being shoved by a huge man in a leather jacket. He probably had about fifty pounds on me and his neck was covered in tattoos. One of his huge mitts was wrapped around the back of Tyson's neck, claws sinking into the flesh and blood seeping from the wounds. His face was bloodied and bruised and starting to swell.

"He smells like you, blondie. But also a little like the wolf—not much, but there's something familiar there. Isn't that against your rules?"

Alex's voice drew my eyes back to him, but Ashley's were still on Tyson, and a tear slipped from one of them. Her right hand started to shake until she let up with her sword.

"Run him through, Mom," Tyson said, his voice strong with conviction. "Don't let emotions get in the way. You know this is one of the risks we take."

I couldn't believe what I was hearing. And, yet, I could; the Pack would sacrifice one of our own if it meant saving our alpha. "Ash..."

"Do it," Carson spoke up through gritted teeth. "Cut his fucking head off."

The wolf holding Tyson closed his grip even more. Tyson hissed, clenching his eyes shut. "Listen to Dad..."

Hearing Tyson acknowledge someone else as his father made my anger boil hotter. My skin started to tingle and crawl as tension set into my bones. If I didn't get a hold of this, I would shift, and that was too risky. I took a few deep breaths, clenched my hands until the pain of my nails biting into my palms grounded me. I could still feel the wolf lying in wait, but I managed to stave off the change for now.

"Tyson," I started. His name fell off my tongue, bringing back every feeling of grief I experienced over the last fifteen years.

"Hmmm... Seems to be some conflict in what to do," Alex said with a cocky smirk. He had so many opportunities to get out of this position, to kill Ashley and start ripping us apart, but he didn't. He was toying with us, reveling in the anguish he incited.

"Ashley, we don't negotiate with them," Carson said from somewhere behind me.

"Whatcha gonna to do, blondie? You going to sacrifice your spawn and start a war you're not equipped to win?" He ran his tongue along the edge of his teeth as his grin grew. "Tick tock."

The shaking in her arm increased until she let it fall to her side with a defeated cry of frustration. Anger flared in her tear-filled eyes, as Alex took a step back, looking more smug than seconds before. If that was even possible.

"What is it you want?" Nick demanded.

"You really that dense?" Alex's eyebrows pulled together as he spread his arms wide. "All. Of. This. We've been cast out for so long, restricted from putting down roots in prime hunting grounds like this."

"Do you really think we'll just hand it over willingly?" I interjected, swallowing the anger that continued to bubble in my throat.

This time when he smiled, I noticed his canines were longer. "Wouldn't be any fun for us if you did," he sneered with the barest hint of a growl making its way up his chest. "So, how do you want to play this? Make the right choice, and nobody has to die...make the wrong one, and... well..."

Tyson hissed as the mutt holding him tightened his grip. More blood trickled down his neck and stained the collar of the shirt he wore. One of the hunters cried out, rushing toward the wolf that held Tyson, but he barely made it four feet before one of the strays got in his way, plunging his hand into the hunter's torso and ripping out his heart. The hunter slumped to the ground while the rest of us watched on in disbelief.

Probably satisfied with having shaken some of us up, Alex released a snarl, the rest of his "pack" following suit. The one who had Tyson by the neck tossed him to the ground and kicked him square in the ribs. Unfazed, Tyson was on his feet in seconds, wailing on the werewolf as payback.

Seeing her son out of danger, Ashley's hand tightened around the hilt of her sword, the dying embers of her anger flaring up again before she charged forward. I wasn't able to admire her impressive fighting style for long before a few wolves rushed me and the rest of the pack. I managed to keep them from getting too many hits in, but as soon as I turned to see how Tyson was making out, one of them struck me from behind, knocking me to the ground.

Groaning, I rolled over, looking up to find Alex sneering down at me. My vision was blurred, head throbbing as I struggled to orientate myself so the world stopped spinning. I had just managed to prop myself up when it felt like a weight was pressing down on my chest. It took me longer than I'd care to admit to realize it was Alex's massive biker boot pressing into my sternum and forcing me back down.

He leaned into it, resting his arms onto his thigh as he looked around. I craned my neck to see what he saw and watched my packmates fight his, and hunters trying to fend them off — some successfully, while others were less fortunate. With a smile, Alex gloated. "If it makes you feel better, I don't plan to kill the women. We need to repopulate our bloodline somehow." He paused for dramatic effect before grinning down at me malevolently. "Especially the blonde with the sword. She might not be one of us, but that didn't stop me over two decades ago. Unfortunately the outcome of that union didn't work out the way I'd hoped right away. But I feel like this one could."

"I'll rip your arms off and force feed them to you before you can even lay a finger on any of them," I threatened.

"Is that so?" Alex pondered. "You know, this all could have been avoided. We all could have gotten along..." With a sneer, Alex shrugged. "Oh, who am I kidding, this is way more fun." With a growl that vibrated deep into my bones, Alex lunged forward, teeth bared and aimed right at my throat. I braced myself for the impact, but was surprised when his weight was lifted from my body by an unforeseen force. When I looked up, I saw Alex hovering two feet in the air, seemingly paralyzed. He looked pissed, but something kept him from acting on his emotions.

"I can't hold them back forever!" Alistair shouted from over two yards away, his eyes darker than I'd ever seen them. "Gather the pack and let's get the hell out of here."

One look around, and I could see what he was talking about; Alistair had managed to incapacitate about twenty of the forty strays that were still standing. The others had been killed by hunter and werewolf alike. Nick called out to the pack, and we made our way toward Alistair. I grabbed Ashley by the wrist on my way past, pulling her away from the stray she'd just run through with her blade. Her eyes were filled with the fire of the hunt, and she must not have recognized me at first, because she slashed at me with her sword, the blade grazing my arm and searing the wound.

Recognition flashed in her eyes, and an unspoken apology lingered between us. We had just reached Alistair when Ashley resisted, looking behind us at The Order.

Alistair was already chanting the spell that would take us home, so I knew we didn't have much time. I scanned the area for our son until I found him over ten feet away, walking toward us with purpose, his murderous stare trained on me. It took me all too long to realize it probably looked like I was taking Ashley against her will. He didn't understand what was happening, but before I could explain , Nick came out of nowhere, hit him on the back of the head, and slung his unconscious body over his shoulder as he ran to us.

"Let's go home, Alistair," he commanded.

With a nod, Alistair looked around to make sure everyone was there. As he tucked a battered-looking Roxy into his side and finished his cast, I watched as his eyes turned onyx. The disturbing sight lasted a split second before Alistair transported us all back home. I'd never seen anything like it before, and I had a feeling it had something to do with the magicks he'd just invoked to save our asses.

CHAPTER 25 | ENCORE

"Ash, stop. We're safe."

"Safe? Jax, we're not safe." Ashley paced in front of the cage, wringing her hands nervously. I could feel the waves of anxiety coming off of her, and the smell of her adrenaline filled the small subterranean room. It was both frustrating and intoxicating.

When we first arrived back at the manor, my first instinct was to check on Ellie. After Alex had made threats against our pack, I wanted to make sure she was okay. With Tyson locked up, I was ready to go find her when Ashley's anxiety kept me from leaving her alone until I could find a way to calm her down. While I wanted to believe she wouldn't do anything stupid, the truth was I hadn't known her for fifteen years. I couldn't risk her letting Tyson out should he wake while I was upstairs. I had no doubts he'd kill anyone who got in his way trying to escape the manor.

Unable to take anymore, I stood up from the bottom stair and walked over to her. "We are. Alistair has reinforced the barriers around the manor. If anyone comes onto our property, we'll be alerted before they reach the front door."

Ashley looked up at me, her blue eyes wide with fear. I recognized the look from when we first met. She looked ready to run at a moment's notice. "You think they won't come for me? They will, Jax. They won't let me go that easily." Her eyes drifted to her left, looking at our son asleep on the cot in the cage. "Or him. He's...important to them."

"He's important to me, too." I cradled her face in my hands. Something seemed off about her since we'd been back. She was likely just agitated, but at times, it felt like maybe it was something more. There was an air of uncertainty around her that kept her at a distance. "I won't let them take either of you against your will. Not again."

Ashley closed her eyes, wrapping her hands around my wrists. "Thank you for getting there in time." Her voice was soft, barely audible. "If you hadn't..."

"You don't have to thank me, Ash." Leaning forward, I pressed my forehead to hers and breathed her in. For fifteen long years, I'd missed her scent, and I still couldn't believe she'd been alive all this time. At times, I found myself thinking this was all just a dream that I'd wake up from any minute.

"Get your hands off her, dog."

Ashley and I looked up to find Tyson standing at the bars. His head was lowered, eyes on me, and his hands were balled into fists at his sides. The muscles in his jaw strained beneath the skin when he clenched it. If not for the cage, he'd probably try to kill me.

"Tyson," Ashley said, relieved. She rushed

forward, wrapping her hands around the silver bars. My first instinct was to tell her to be careful, but then I remembered the bars wouldn't hurt her. It had been a while since I'd been around anyone but my own kind. "How do you feel?"

Tyson looked at his mother, not at all comforted by her. In fact, he looked downright murderous toward her. "Like I've been kidnapped and kept prisoner in a wolf's dank dungeon. How the fuck do you think I feel?"

Ashley dropped her hands and took a step back, clearly shocked by the tone he took with her. I wasn't sure why she didn't say anything, but I sure as shit wasn't about to stand for it.

"You watch your mouth, boy. Don't speak to your mother that way."

Tyson's menacing glare came back to me, only this time, he smirked. It was unsettling, but I think because he looked a lot like me at that age. "And just who the hell do you think you are to tell me what I can and cannot say, asshole?"

Anger burned through my veins like lava as I stalked forward, a growl building in my chest. The wolf recognized the look he was giving me as threatening, and it wanted out. Picking up on my anger, Ashley turned around and placed her hands on my chest. I wanted to believe I stopped on my own so I didn't bowl her over, but the truth was, she was holding me back.

It still shocked me how strong she was. It made me realize just how much she must have been holding back when I was human.

"Jackson, stop. He doesn't know any better. He was raised to hate your kind."

I looked down to find her blue eyes pleading

with me. "We need to help him remember what he's lost. The way you helped me."

"Why the hell are you talking about me like I'm not even here?" Tyson demanded. "And why are you talking to him like you're *friends*? His kind is an abomination. Look around, mother, there are weapons everywhere. End him."

"Tyson, enough!" In all the years Ashley and I had been together, I'd never heard her raise her voice like that, and based on the look on Tyson's face, neither had he.

Ashley looked back up to me. "Your shaman… um…?"

"Alistair."

"Get him. It's time."

"Time? Time for what?" The cage rattled as Tyson grabbed the bars and shook with everything he had. "*Time for what?*"

I left Ashley in the pit with Tyson, hearing him lower his voice to plead with her to let him out. Closing the door to the pit behind me, I leaned against it for a minute to gain my bearings. So much had happened in just a few short days, and it was all catching up to me now that the dust had momentarily settled. Anger still filled my veins, the wolf itching to get out, but there was no time for that yet.

Ashley was right; we weren't safe. We wouldn't be safe until the strays were dealt with and The Order was neutralized. Somehow, I didn't think The Order would leave without ridding every last werewolf from the area, though. Especially now that we had two of its most coveted members.

Inhaling one last, steeling breath, I pushed off the bookshelf and headed for the stairs so I could go find Alistair and check in on Ellie. I longed for the silence of the basement the second I hit the main floor and was assaulted with the voices of almost every member of this pack and two wailing babies.

I made my way to the kitchen first where I found Brooke and Nick trying to calm Azura, and Colby and Zach were arguing over near the patio. There were so many conversations going on at once, I couldn't differentiate any of them. I turned to leave so I could search out the shaman, but before I could get very far, Brooke stopped me.

"Oh, thank God." She sounded relieved as she rounded the island and rushed over to me. "Can you take her for a minute. She loves you."

I didn't even get a chance to tell Brooke why I was really up here before she was thrusting Azura into my arms. Once the baby was against my chest, I instinctively swayed back and forth with her, smelling the top of her head until her cries started to slow.

Brooke released a huge sigh of relief. "We literally tried everything to comfort her, but nothing was working."

When I lifted my gaze, I noticed Brooke's eyes for the first time since entering the room. The amber had completely blown out her usual green, and they were glowing bright.

"You need to go for a run."

Brooke shook her head, her breathing a little heavier than usual and her heart hammering. "No. I just…got a little stressed out is all."

I inhaled, picking up on the wolf immediately, and as my eyes scanned her face and neck, I noticed her skin was red and glistening. "Maybe so, but that stress is manifesting. You can feel it, and for whatever reason you're denying it." I looked at Nick, his eyes only a little amber around the outer edges. Chances were, his wolf was only triggered by Brooke's. "Leave Azura with me, and take Brooke outside."

"Jax," Brooke continued to argue.

I shot her a look. "If you don't go, I will dose you, and you know I don't like doing that. Now, go."

Nick was just following Brooke out to the patio when I stopped him. "Hey, you seen Ellie? I haven't seen her since we left earlier, and I want to make sure she's okay after what went down this afternoon."

Nick nodded. "She wanted to go for a walk."

"Okay. Good. As long as she's safe."

Colby and Zach had stopped arguing long enough to catch the tail end of my discussion with their Alpha, and I shot them a look. Feeling like I was on a bit of a roll, I pointed at them. "And you two should…take it outside so you don't wake the kid."

Colby huffed and stormed out of the room. I felt bad for all of thirty seconds before the front door slammed. Zach just glared at me.

"Thanks, asshole."

"I'm not the one pissing her off."

"Everything I do pisses her off anymore."

I wasn't sure when exactly I became the fix-it guy, but I wanted to know who I needed to speak to to resign from this shit. "She's dealing with a lot of shit, man. You can't force her to just get over it. She needs to find her own way to heal."

Zach looked offended. "I'm not trying to force

her to—"

"Maybe not directly, but every time you minimize her grief or push her to do something she doesn't feel like doing because she just wants to be alone, she pulls a little farther away," I explained, knowing firsthand how difficult it was to have people trying to get you to move on when you weren't ready. "Think back to when Brooke went through this. It wasn't too long ago. You saw how we treated her. I know you love Colby and you think this is best, but you need to follow her cues. Everybody grieves differently. She lost her mother, her father, *and* her sister. She's going to need some time."

Zach nodded along, finally understanding. "You're right. Thanks, Jax." Before he left the kitchen, he turned to me. "You always been this insightful? Because I think I prefer it to the asshole persona we've been living with all these years."

I had to fight to keep the smile off my face. "Get the fuck out of here before I kick your ass."

"And he's back," Zach quipped. "You should probably watch your mouth around the baby. Brooke would rip out your vocal chords if she heard that."

I barked a laugh, startling Azura. Thankfully, she only stirred, and my gentle bouncing motion was able to soothe her back to sleep. "Clearly you've never pissed that girl off. She could make a trucker blush."

Seconds later, Zach was gone, and I was left alone in the room, holding a sleeping infant when I knew there was work still to be done. "Shit."

When I heard Vince and Layla's voices down the hall, I went off in search of them, hoping I could leave Azura with them so I could go find Alistair. I didn't want to leave Ashley alone with Tyson like this for long—not because I didn't trust *her*, but because I couldn't entirely trust him yet.

I followed the sound of Vince's voice to the great room. They were both sitting on the floor, with Samuel on the high pile rug between them. Their son was up on his hands and knees, rocking back and forth like he was getting ready to crawl, and they both looked so excited. I hated to break that up.

"Hey."

Vince and Layla both turned to me, big smiles on their face.

"Hey, Jax," Layla greeted in a chipper tone. "What's up?" She noticed Azura immediately, her eyebrows pinching together. "Where's Brooke?"

"I told her to go for a run. She was pretty agitated, and it looked bad. So she and Nick took off about ten minutes ago." I paused, gauging their reactions before I even posed my question. "Here's the thing...I need to go find Alistair so he can work his mojo. And I just got Azura to sleep. She won't stay that way if—"

Layla hopped to her feet. "Say no more. I'll take the little love." Carefully, she scooped Azura into her arms and then sat back on the floor with her, rocking back and forth as she went back to cheering Sammy on.

"You need a hand with anything?" Vince offered.

"Thanks, but there's not even much even I can do but be there for Ashley while Alistair does his thing. It's not easy to watch."

Vince nodded. "Okay, well you let me know if

there's anything I can do to help."

"Thanks, man." I turned to leave when I stopped. "You know where he is, by chance?"

Vince and Layla exchanged a glance. "I think Roxy took him upstairs. You might have to wait."

I honed my hearing, and didn't hear anything coming from upstairs, so I thanked Layla and Vince again and went on my way. As I climbed the stairs, I still didn't hear anything, but the scent of sex definitely lingered in the air. Living in a house with your pack definitely had its perks, but one of the drawbacks was the lack of privacy; we could hear and smell everything, so if you were a particularly private person, this wasn't the lifestyle for you.

I approached Roxy and Alistair's door, and listened before raising my hand to knock. I only had to wait a couple seconds before I heard Roxy's voice, hoarse with sleep. "It's Jax."

"Shit. I didn't mean to fall asleep. They must be ready." There was rustling beyond the door, so I took a step back to give them some semblance of privacy. "I should be done in about an hour. You go back to sleep."

Beyond the door, Roxy hummed, and I heard the mattress shift. "Good luck, babe."

Soon, the door opened, and Alistair was exiting the room, his shirt unbuttoned, hair tousled, and his glasses in his hand. "Sorry about that. She's been craving some alone time."

I held my hands up. "Hey, no need to explain yourself. I get it."

As we walked, Alistair buttoned his shirt and fixed his hair. "I trust he's awake then?"

I nodded. "And belligerent."

Alistair half-shrugged. "He woke up in a cage within a werewolf compound. I'd be more concerned if he was complacent, given his high-ranking positon within The Order."

In the basement, we could hear Tyson shouting at Ashley as we approached the hidden doorway. I disengaged the lock, and swung the bookcase open, pulling it mostly closed behind me, and we walked down in single file.

"Mom, how can you let them keep me in here?" Tyson screamed. "What have they done to you?"

"They haven't done anything to me, Ty. I want to be here."

"With the wolf?" He sounded disgusted. "I can't believe you. Fucking sympathizer. You disgust me. Sleeping with one of those savages..."

Even though he was doing everything he could to push her buttons, Ashley remained composed. I respected her even more for it. "Tyson, it isn't like that... He hasn't always been like this."

"But he's like this now!"

Alistair and I reached the bottom stair, and Tyson's eyes lifted to us. Ashley turned around, her lips curling up into a small smile, but the top half of her face was creased with anguish.

"You'll see, Ty. Very soon, you'll see."

I walked toward Ashley, holding out one of my hands for her, and she took it without pause. Tyson didn't like that, releasing a disgusted scoff. When Alistair approached the cage, Tyson glared at him the way he'd glared at me. "What the fuck do you want, mutt."

"I'm not a werewolf," Alistair told him calmly.

Tyson threw his arms up in the air. "Great. More sympathizers. This is fan-fucking-tastic."

Alistair moved toward the cage door, needing to get in. As soon as he turned the key, Tyson saw this as his opportunity and rushed forward. But Alistair anticipated it, holding out his right hand. *"Recedite."*

Tyson was pushed back by an invisible force, his feet sliding over the concrete floor, until he slammed into the other side of the cage. "A Shaman? You sent a Shaman in here?" He looked pissed, pushing himself off the bars, teeth clenched. "You son of a—"

"Ligabus."

"—bitch." Tyson couldn't move from the shoulders down. Like Ashley before, he was frozen in place like he was bound by some invisible substance.

Alistair closed the cage door behind him, then tossed the key to me through the bars. I caught it and slipped it into my pocket before wrapping a comforting arm around Ashley.

Tyson looked at us again, and if it weren't for the cage and Alistair's binding spell, I might actually be worried. "You can try to fuck with my mind the way you did hers, but it won't work. When I get out of here, I will kill you."

Alistair turned his head. "Up to you, but I can keep him awake for this, or put him out."

I looked to Ashley for an answer since she was the only person I knew who'd been through this before. She nodded toward Alistair. "Put him out. I found it hard to focus, and I worry his defiance might hinder the cast from working."

Alistair returned his focus to Tyson. *"Som-*

nus."

Tyson's head slumped forward, but his body remained restrained by Alistair's cast. It didn't look comfortable, but I knew he wouldn't be out for long.

Unlike last time, Alistair didn't have the old book with him, but he looked confident in what he was about to do, so I put all my faith in him. If he could reunite me with my son the way he had with Ashley, I would owe him the world. He took a breath and rubbed his palms together like last time. As soon as he held them at Tyson's temples, Alistair began his chant. *"Levate vellum."* The same two words quietly left his mouth in quick succession as the energy in the room shifted, the spell rapidly reaching its pinnacle.

Sweat dripped from Tyson's forehead, his blond hair sticking in some spots where it wasn't hanging loose. His body began to tremble slightly, and Alistair's chant increased in speed and volume until Tyson's head flew back with a loud gasp and his eyes opened, glowing a bright blue as the spell sparked something in him.

"Receptui!"

I remembered the way Ashley's body went rigid on the cot when Alistair finished the spell, and the sounds of agony that ripped through her before she went limp had made my blood curdle. It wasn't any easier to watch my son go through the same thing. In fact, it might have been worse. Every muscle in my body tightened, and I could feel the beginning signs of the shift. The only thing keeping me from letting the wolf out was that I knew I had to be present for Ashley.

I kept my arm around her, but I could feel her

breaking down. Her maternal instincts were kicking into high gear as she watched her one and only child suffer. She knew what it felt like, and it was possible she was reliving it. I could smell her fear, her anger, her sadness… All of it mingled together and created this intense aroma that tempted the wolf further.

It wasn't until Tyson's cries ebbed that she finally relaxed against me, her entire body trembling as it struggled to stay upright. I did my best to comfort her as I watched Alistair remove the binding cast and lower Tyson to the cot so he could sleep it off.

I prepared to toss the key back to Alistair, but he said a quick chant and materialized in front of us in a puff of purple smoke. "He'll likely sleep for a bit before he wakes. Keep an eye on him, and call for me if you need something."

"Thank you, Alistair. I don't know how I'll ever repay you," I told him.

Alistair just smiled, clapping a hand down on my shoulder. "No repayment necessary, Jackson. I'm happy to be of use here. It's the least I could do."

Ashley pulled out of my arms and walked toward the cage, gripping the bars and resting her head against the cool metal. "That was…"

"Awful?" I nodded, coming up behind her and lightly placing my hands on her shoulders. "It wasn't any easier the second time around for me."

Ashley turned around quickly, throwing me off a little. "How long will he sleep? How long did I sleep?"

"Alistair doesn't know. I think the body just needs time to recover from the cast as the memories filter back in." Ashley nodded, still looking positively freaked out. I cradled her face in my hands. "He'll be fine, Ash. Just like you were." I leaned down and rested my forehead to hers, my thumbs moving softly over her cheeks. It killed me to see her so broken up, and I just wanted to ease her suffering for just a moment.

Ashley's hands circled my wrists as she tilted her face up to meet mine, and our lips met in a soft, unexpected kiss. Unlike the last kiss we shared, this one was different. While the last one was filled with a passion borne of relief and happiness that my wife hadn't actually died, this one wasn't. This kiss was intended to provide solace and reassurance in the choices we would have to make from here on out...

No matter how difficult.

The kiss lasted no longer than a fraction of a second, but that one moment—a moment that made me realize not what I wanted, but what I *needed*—was obliterated when something crashed to the floor behind me.

Soon it wasn't just Ashley's scent clouding my head, but Ellie's as well, and I registered her confusion before even turning around to see her face. Even though there was nothing impassioned behind the gesture, my guilt solidified before falling to the pit of my stomach like a lead weight.

Slowly, I turned around, noticing the glass plate and the scattered remnants of a sandwich at Ellie's feet. As my eyes travelled up to her face, I noticed she was trembling, her hands rolled into tight balls at her sides. Her eyes were glowing a bright shade of amber, the dark chocolate color completely overrun as they darted between Ashley and me. She was minutes—maybe less—from letting her emotions get the best of her, and if that happened, we'd all be locked in the pit with a volatile werewolf hell-bent on killing.

I took a step toward her, hoping to calm her, but she fled up the stairs before I could even reach her.

CHAPTER 26 | REVEALED

"Ellie, wait!" I called after her, but she didn't stop.

"Who was that?" Ashley asked. "Jax, what's going on?"

"Shit," I muttered, running a hand over my face in frustration. "Shit, shit, shit." How had I fucked this up so royally? Why didn't I just tell Ellie what was going on when it all started happening? Why didn't I tell Ashley? Why did I have to be such a stupid chicken shit?

"Jackson?"

I turned to Ashley, knowing I didn't have a lot of time. Ellie wasn't in a good place emotionally, and if I didn't get to her right away, she'd shift and there was no telling what she'd do in that frame of mind. "Ash, I have to go after her. Stay with Tyson. If something happens and you need someone, call for Alistair. He's probably right upstairs."

Before Ashley could ask me any more questions, I took the stairs two at a time, raced through the basement, and then took the next set of stairs two at a time as well. I followed Ellie's scent toward the front door, finding it open wide.

"Jackson?" Brooke called out, looking confused about the commotion as she came from the great room with Azura in her arms. "What the hell is going on?" She inhaled deeply, recognizing the scent of Ellie's distress. "Never mind. Go. *Now*. Talk later."

Not wanting to waste another second, I raced out the front door, her scent leading me East. Even though she seemed close to shifting back at the house, the scent I was following was mostly still human, so that was good. If I could track her down, I might actually be able to explain myself without her wanting to rip my throat out.

Or try to. There really was no explanation to how shitty I'd been. She deserved better.

I pushed myself to run harder and faster, my lungs and muscles burning, but then I ran too far. Her scent had faded, so I turned back to where I could smell it strongest. I stood in the small clearing, surrounded by full trees and shrubs. She was close, but I couldn't see her. There were too many places for her to hide, which also meant there were too many places for our enemies to hide. I inhaled deeply, making sure it was still just us out there. It was.

"Ellie, sweetheart, I can explain," I called out, scratching the back of my neck before tacking on a quiet, "I think."

There was no response, no movement from the forest. I closed my eyes, hoping to let my other senses give me some kind of indication where she might be. Head fogged up with the combined scents of nature, I had barely just begun to pick up her unique fragrance again when something slammed into my back, knocking me to the ground.

"You son of a bitch," Ellie said. "How could you?"

I rolled over, looking up at her from my seated position on the forest floor. "Ellie, sweetheart..."

"Don't you *sweetheart* me, Jackson Devereux." She sniffled, yellow eyes burning into mine. "What the hell was that back there? *Who* was that?"

I pushed myself to my feet and approached her. Her eyes were still completely amber, and I could tell how tense her muscles were based on how she was standing. But what worried me most was that her claws were engaged, her hands looking inhuman. She'd concentrated the change to a part of her body in her anguish, and I wasn't entirely sure if she even realized it. If she didn't, it might be best not to draw attention to it in case it freaked her out and propelled her further into a tumultuous state. The best thing to do would be to find a way to explain everything without upsetting her further.

I didn't have a lot of faith in myself.

"Look," I began, extending a hand for her to take. "Come back to the manor with me, and I'll tell you everything. We can't stay out here. It isn't safe."

Ellie laughed hysterically. "Are you fucking serious?" She searched my expression for an answer, shaking her head when she didn't get one. "I'm not going anywhere with you. You lied to me and led me on. God, maybe he was right about you."

"I didn't." I argued the first part of her accusation and ignored the last part. I hadn't been around much the last few days, so it didn't actually surprise me that Nick might talk shit about me. "Ellie, I swear I didn't lie... At least, not at first."

Taking a step toward me, Ellie's eyes held mine. "Exactly how long has it been going on, Jackson? The entire time we've known each other?"

Reaching out, I gripped her upper arms. She didn't try to pull away, which seemed like progress in the right direction. "Ellie, it's complicated, and believe me, I never expected for it to happen."

"But it did."

"It did, but...I'm still not sure h—"

"Did you fuck her?"

My mouth snapped shut, unsure how to even approach that question. Her question stumped me. Not because I didn't understand it, but because it was far more complicated than that. "Recently?"

Sometimes I said things without really thinking them through. It was a flaw.

Ellie's jaw clenched, and her amber eyes widened with anger. Pressing her hands to my chest, she shoved me hard, her claws tearing into my shirt, and I faltered back a couple steps. "You're no different than any other asshole out there, you know that?"

"Wait, I didn't mean it like that."

"Oh, no?" She crossed her arms and stared at me. "How exactly did you mean it then? Please, enlighten me, Jackson, because I can't *wait* to hear it."

"She's my wife."

Ellie stood there, unblinking, her expression unchanged. It was obvious she didn't believe me, and that made sense considering what I'd told her shortly after we met. "You said she died. Or is that just something you say to younger women to get them into bed? I mean, who doesn't love a good sympathy lay, right?"

Her accusation felt like a slap across the face. With a baseball bat. Wrapped in barbed wire. "What? No, Ellie. She *was* dead."

I was met with more silence, and I could see that Ellie was trying to work through this new information. Then the laughter started. At first it was a muffled giggle, but soon it exploded into full-on hysterics, laced with an air of disbelief as she dropped her arms to her sides. "Oh, okay. So she just rose from the dead then? Jesus, Jackson. Just how naïve do you think I am?"

"No. Not *just*. She's been alive this whole time, I just…had no idea." I could see the skepticism in her eyes, but her expression did soften a little, so I tried approaching her again. "It's a long, convoluted story. Please, sweetheart. Come back to the house. Let me try to explain."

The amber was finally receding from her eyes, and her hands were back to normal, but she was still clearly upset. And rightfully so. "Can I ask you something?"

I nodded. "Of course. You can ask me anything."

"Did you ever have feelings for me? I mean, it felt pretty real… Did I imagine that?"

"Ellie…" I watched as tears rimmed her eyes, and I pulled her into my arms. "I did…" Ellie's arms wrapped around my body, her fingers curling into my shirt desperately. She held me like maybe it was the last time she'd get to. "I *do*."

With a sniffle, she looked up at me, now clearly confused, which was fitting, because I was right there with her. "Look, Ellie, I can't deny that what you and I have is incredible. I haven't felt this connected to anyone in fifteen years. Since the day we met, there was this instant spark, and as I got to know you, that spark turned into a flame that's still burning. Everything I feel for you is real, but…"

"Your wife."

I nodded again. "My wife. I still don't understand how exactly it happened, and I won't lie to you and tell you that I don't still love her, because I do. She's the mother of my child, and we'd been through a lot."

Ellie pulled back, but I didn't let her get more than six inches away.

"After fifteen years on my own, I'd made peace with the fact that I'd never meet my mate. I threw myself into the mission, always ready to do what needed to be done to protect my own." Reaching out, I cradled her face, my fingers tracing the lines of the back of her neck. "It never occurred to me that one of those missions would bring me face to face with my mate."

Sighing heavily, I leaned forward and rested my forehead to hers, and Ellie licked her lips, drawing my gaze to them. "I'm stuck between a rock and a hard place here, Ellie. The wolf, and a big part of me, wants you — *needs* you — but…I thought she was dead, and I still haven't fully processed her return or what that even means."

Ellie brought her hand up to cover mine, and she leaned into my palm, her big brown eyes looking up into mine through her thick lashes. The

amber ring around her pupil had almost completely disappeared, but what did remain blazed like
embers in the night. Her breathing picked up,
temperature rising as the wolf woke up, and I
smelled the spike in her pheromones immediately.

It didn't take long before my desires matched
hers, and my need for her grew out of control like
a wildfire through dry grass. My skin warmed as
lust exploded through my veins and settled in my
groin. While I knew now wasn't really the best
time, given what was going on back at the house,
the wolf had other plans. The need to be with her
trumped everything else that was weighing on me.

Ellie opened her mouth as though to speak,
but instead exhaled softly. Her warm breath
fanned over my skin, and she tilted her face a fraction of an inch. My other hand slid down her
body, grazing her breast, before coming to rest on
her waist, and my fingers curled into her lower
back as I closed the infinitesimal gap and pressed
my lips to hers.

I knew we shouldn't give in to these desires,
but I was quickly learning that the primal ties between a mated pair were near impossible to ignore, and that our carnal urges often won out over
common sense. Even though I was with Ellie, my
thoughts were pretty evenly split, which then invited my guilt along for the ride. I was just about
to put a stop to the kiss when Ellie pressed her
body even closer to mine, releasing a guttural
moan that vibrated right through my body and
made me hard.

My brain checked out as my insatiable need
for my mate took over, and I gripped Ellie's slender waist, pulling her hips toward me with des-

peration. Slowly, her hands moved up my chest, her nails lightly scratching through the slashes in my shirt, until her arms were wrapped tightly around my neck.

"Oh, God, Jackson," she mumbled against my lips, her fingers threading into my hair. She threw her head back with a sigh, gasping for air, and I kissed a trail down over her neck, inhaling deeply at her carotid and letting the intoxicating aroma of her lust spur me on. "I think I'm falling in love with you."

I froze, lips and nose against Ellie's neck, and let her words sink in. My silence must have been too much for her, because she untwisted her fingers from my hair and stepped out of my grasp. I stood up straight and noticed the disappointment on her face.

"Ellie…"

She shook her head, trying to nervously laugh off what she said. "It's fine, Jackson. I just…got caught up in the moment."

"Sweetheart—"

"Please stop calling me that," she demanded a little harsher than earlier. Bringing her hands up, she pushed them roughly through her hair, gripping it at the base of her neck. "You should go back to the house."

"I'm not leaving you out here," I told her firmly. "It isn't safe."

Ellie scoffed. "It won't be safe if I'm in the same house as her." I wasn't sure if that was her fear or a threat. It sounded like a little of both.

I planned to argue with her further when her expression changed, almost like realization was dawning on her. She lifted her eyes to mine again, bringing one of her hands to her lips and looking at me accusingly. "She's the one who's been trying to kill us — the hunter." Not dropping her gaze, she started walking around me.

"Ellie, listen..." I turned with her, like a pivot point on a compass. While I didn't feel threatened in that moment, Ellie's emotions seemed to be all over the map, and I couldn't be entirely sure if I could trust her.

"Her scent. I recognize it from that night." Ellie circled me as she spoke, her gaze finally drifting as she worked through her memories. "I've been having these...flashes, like little bits of my memory are returning. I've heard that sensory recall is one of the strongest triggers of the memory, but I didn't really put a lot of stock into it until just now."

"She's not a threat," I assured Ellie.

"How do you know that? Maybe she's fucking with you, Jax. Drawing you in and making you all feel like you can trust her, and that's when she'll strike." Ellie rushed toward me, taking my hands in hers, her dark eyes flitting between mine frantically. "Come with me."

I stared at her, not quite understanding what she meant. "What?"

"Let's leave," she clarified, sounding resolved in the decision. Like it wasn't something she thought of on a whim, but had been planning for a while. "Just you and me."

"You make it sound like you've got this all figured out," I said, recognizing the tone of her voice for what it was. My eyebrows pulled together as I tried to read her a little more clearly. "Ellie..."

Likely having sensed my answer from my tone, she grew even more desperate, placing her hands on my chest and tugging on my shirt. "M-my dad," she rushed to say, confusing me, because I was under the impression they had never met. She told me he left her mother shortly after she was born.

"What about him?"

Ellie licked her lips, pushing her hair back before placing them back on my chest. "He...he said we can stay with him." She looked and sounded anxious, and my gut told me it had very little to do with what happened between Ashley and me. "Please, Jax, come with me. He promised to keep us safe."

Confused and concerned, I gripped her upper arms and took a step back, letting her words fully register before I replied. "You talked to your dad about us?" She didn't answer, looking up at me with guilt, and I felt like I failed her by not being around to help her understand Pack Law. Feeling responsible, I tried to remedy the issue gently. "Ellie, humans *can't* know. What have you told him?" Then her last statement hit me, and my confusion turned to dread. I looked around the forest, honed my hearing in the direction of the manor and addressed my concern. "Wait... What do you mean he'll keep us safe, Ellie? Safe from what?"

Her desperation turned to nervousness, and she smiled, trying to brush it off. But I could feel it, I just didn't know why she was so nervous. "You said it yourself, we're mated." While one hand remained over my heart, the other moved up to my face, and she locked eyes with me. "You feel that, right? Because I do, and I don't want to lose you. Not to anyone."

Her fingers moved against my skin, igniting the sparks of attraction I felt for her until they flowed like currants of electricity through my veins. She wasn't wrong; There was an incredibly strong pull between us, not unlike the one the moon had over the wolf, and every time we were apart, I felt her absence like a hole in my chest.

"You know I do." My hands moved back to her waist without my thinking about it, and I tried to stay rational. It wasn't easy. "But, sweetheart, running isn't the answer. We have an obligation to our pack."

"I don't get it," Ellie said, seeming put off by my answer. "What do you have here?"

"My Pack? My family?"

"That's it?"

"It's enough," I told her, pulling away. "You're still so new, you don't yet understand just how important a pack is. How strong that bond can be."

"Oh," a familiar voice said from behind me, "but she does."

As soon as the deep voice registered, my hackles rose and a growl built in my chest, the pressure almost too much to contain. I inwardly scolded myself for having let him get the drop on us. Had I been paying attention instead of letting myself get lost in Ellie, I would have smelled him. I could have gotten us out of there. But now we were face to face with the stray we'd left back near The Order's compound only a few hours ago.

Ellie's eyes never left mine, her eyebrows pulling together and rising a half inch. I could sense her fear, and I needed to assure her she was safe.

Keeping my body in front of Ellie's, I slowly turned around to face Alex, my growl now audible. "You're trespassing, mutt."

"Jackson," Ellie said, sounding surprised.

Alex laughed jovially. "*Mutt? Well if that's not the pot calling the kettle a fucking werewolf, I don't know what is.*" Stepping forward, he trained his eyes on Ellie. "Besides…*trespassing*, Jackson? Come now, I just want to be friends." His confidence grated on my nerves, and I felt the deep desire to rip his arm off and shove it up his nose.

Sure, it wasn't a realistic scenario, but it was always fun to experiment with probability.

"Funny how every time I see you, you're with a different blonde," Alex pointed out with a smirk, nodding his head toward Ellie.

"Stop." Ellie's voice was small and meek. It was unlike her, and I could only assume it was because he made her nervous.

"Stop?" Alex questioned, almost mocking her. He stopped walking, still addressing Ellie, and within seconds, shit went sideways. "What do you mean '*stop*'? You think I like seeing him hurt you, baby girl?"

I wasn't sure I heard him right, but when I looked back at Ellie, all I saw was shame in her eyes. "Ellie…" I glanced back at Alex's smug face. "What the fuck is he talking about? Why is he talking to you like he knows you?"

Ellie tried to speak, but her voice broke, so she cleared her throat and tried again. "Because he does." She stepped out from behind me and walked toward Alex, seeming unafraid yet still a bit hesitant. Once she was by his side, she turned back to me with a shrug. "He's…he's my dad."

CHAPTER 27 | BLOOD

"That's right." His slimy grin growing, Alex threw his arm around Ellie, but she looked uncomfortable with the gesture. I was torn on whether or not I was happy with her unease, given this colossal omission. "I tried to tell you you had something of mine, Jackie-boy. But you just wouldn't listen."

Ellie dropped her eyes to the left, unable to look at me any longer. Her betrayal felt like a thousand shallow cuts all over my body, and the way she couldn't bring herself to look me in the eye added salt in the wound. Even though her tone a moment ago indicated she was being honest, I couldn't bring myself to believe it. There was no way...

"But you were bitten," I pointed out weakly.

Ellie just nodded, finally bringing her eyes up to meet mine. "I was. My mom was human, and I guess I didn't inherit the gene?" She glanced to Alex who nodded like he wanted her to continue with whatever story he'd fed her.

Slowly, my denial and confusion grew into anger, my blood burning in my veins. "So you've been out here yelling at me for lying to you, when you've been lying to me this whole God damn time?" I demanded angrily, taking three giant steps forward. Alex tried to get in my way, but I shoved him hard and grabbed Ellie's arm, yanking her forward.

"Jax," she pleaded, eyes glistening with tears. "I tried to tell you…several times. I swear I did, but you were always running off somewhere."

"More important things than your mate, Jackson?" Alex interjected with a disapproving tone.

I snarled at him before turning back on Ellie. "Do you feel that?" I asked, parroting her earlier words. "Do you feel what your betrayal has done? Like poison, it's seeped into everything we had and is slowly destroying it."

"No, Jax… Please." The first tear slid down her cheek. Seeing her cry made my stomach knot with self-loathing, knowing I was causing it. I hated it, yet couldn't bring myself to apologize or comfort her.

I struggled to wrap my head around this whole fucked up situation, tried to look at it rationally, but I couldn't seem to. "I don't get it, Ellie. So you wanted this? Wanted to invade our territory with this guy's pack of psychotic strays? Right from the beginning?"

When Alex chuckled behind Ellie, I glared up at him. He had his tongue pressed into one of his canines, and the smug look in his eyes sparked a revelation in me until all the pieces fell into place, starting from the night I met Ellie. "You've been using her to recruit," I accused. His silence spoke volumes, so I turned on Ellie finally understanding how she'd accepted this life so easily. It was because she already knew about it, and she played me for a fool every chance she got. How could I have been so stupid? "You were luring innocents out to be attacked. Ellie, how could you do that?"

Eyes wide, Ellie glanced at Alex, who looked back at her with a smarmy grin that I wanted to shred. "What? Jax, no. I didn't even know what was happening until after you told me. I swear it." She must have seen my skepticism, because she rushed toward me again, her panic altering her scent convincingly until I wavered. "Alex...he found me after—that night I took off, remember? When the detective found me?" She paused, waiting for my response. When she never got one, she continued. "After you left, I went for a walk. Brooke wanted to come with me, but I told her I'd rather be alone. I wandered just beyond the grounds when Alex found me.

"I was still so frazzled by everything that had happened. I thought maybe he was one of your pack until he told me who he was and why he was here—and how maybe..." Ellie swallowed nervously, biting her lower lip until the skin blanched. "How maybe I'd be better off with him. Because he was family."

"And I'm just supposed to believe that?"

"Come now, Jax. The two of you clearly have a connection. It would be a shame to take my sweet Ellie's mate from her. Do you know what that does to the other half?" Alex laughed malevolently. "Because I don't, but I imagine it's miserable."

Another growl filled my chest as I glared up under a furrowed brow at Alex, his smile wide and arrogant. There wasn't a doubt in my mind that he was manipulating her and using her against my Pack in an effort to gain intel on them. "So, tell me, Ellie, in all this quality father-daughter time you've been spending with him, why did he tell you he was here?"

"For territory. He told me it isn't fair for those who aren't a part of a pack to have to hop around from place to place, and I have to say I agree with him."

"And do you understand what that means? Do you know what he's been doing?" I asked, my voice rising. Even though I was still pissed about being kept in the dark, I knew I should try to rein in my growing anger; she was still too new to understand all of this, and that was my fault. I should have been forthright from the beginning, and I shouldn't have abandoned her at every turn for my human whims.

Ellie's posture straightened and her confidence swelled. "It means he never would have left my mother—left *me* if he wasn't chased out of town by Marcus' family."

Hearing her condemn any Alpha for doing their due diligence bothered me. I realized she didn't get a chance to know him or understand his reasoning for keeping strays at bay, but how did she not see that Alex was manipulating her? Was I not clear about the threat that had been bearing down on us for months?

Before I got a chance to elaborate on the specifics of Alex's mission, he cut in, probably trying to keep her from learning the truth. It would be a lot harder to manipulate her if she knew he planned on killing most of us and keeping the women around for procreation, after all. "Look,

Jackson. Ellie here has grown quite fond of you over these past few weeks. Even though you're part of a fascist regime, I'd be willing to welcome you into a newer, stronger pack as a sign of my gratitude for having made this transition easier for her."

"Fascist?" I barked a laugh. "Did you miss that day in school?"

Instead of replying right away, Alex glared, a spark of amber igniting in his dark eyes. "Let's see, your Alpha dictates who can and can't stay in the area, often resulting in a violent suppression of the opposition... How is that not the very definition of fascism?"

"Brooke has done no such thing," I argued.

"Hasn't she?" There was something in his eyes that said he'd heard otherwise, but by whom or even *what* he might be referring to, I had no idea. "And Marcus?"

"Marcus is dead," I reminded him. "And even if he weren't, he only killed those who directly threatened his family—the way you plan to do," I corrected him, shooting a quick glance in Ellie's direction. "He had an understanding with the strays who passed through the area, and only used force when needed."

"Really?" Alex said, his tone weighed down with distrust and accusation. "And what about Karl?"

"Karl?" I demanded, feeling a little blindsided. There was no way Ellie could have known about Karl unless Brooke and Nick filled her in, but the confused look on her face told me that wasn't the case.

"That psycho got *exactly* what he deserved. In

fact, I don't know why Marcus didn't have him put down sooner," I fired at Alex, remembering everything Karl put this pack through. Even before Brooke showed up and he attacked her, he'd always been more trouble than he was worth, but Marcus kept him around for reasons I could never understand.

For the first time since I'd met him, Alex's eyes exploded with amber, and he bared his teeth, canines slowly lowering into place. "That *psycho* was my brother!"

Back at the compound, I knew he looked familiar, but it wasn't until that moment that I really saw it. Same hair color, same eyes, same angry expression of a man who seemed to think the world owed him…

"So that's what this is really about, then," I deduced. "The territory is just an added bonus. You want revenge."

"Wouldn't you?" Alex took several menacing steps forward. "That bitch killed him."

"You don't know that," I fired back, knowing the truth behind Karl's death. "It could have been any one of us."

"Maybe she wasn't directly involved…" Alex's eyes shifted to Ellie, who suddenly looked ashamed.

"I'm sorry, I swear I didn't know…" she rushed to say, but I held up a hand to silence her, not sure I had the patience to deal with any more of her betrayals. Accidental or not.

"She's loyal, my daughter," Alex said with a jolly lilt toward the end. He moved around us slowly, eyes always on us. Somewhere beyond us, I heard footsteps before the light breeze carried the scent of several of his pack with it. "Told me all about how the new, inexperienced alpha got a little too cocky..."

"Brooke didn't kill him, and even if she did, she wouldn't brag about it."

"No," he agreed. "But she was there. She watched as her mate snapped his neck."

My head snapped to Ellie, my thoughts turbulent and disorienting. Eyes wide with panic, she thrust her free hand into her light hair and shook her head. "Please, Jax. This isn't how this was supposed to happen! You don't understand. He promised nothing bad was going to happen."

"If I agreed to turn on my own Pack," I deduced, releasing her arm roughly. "You really don't know me, and I clearly don't know you. By siding with him, you've just signed your own death warrant."

"But you do know me, Jax." Ellie's dark eyes widened with fear as she prepared to defend her actions. Before she could utter another word, Alex cut in.

"Now, Jackson, I can't have you threatening my one and only daughter." He stopped circling us, and soon five of his minions were emerging from the woods. "What kind of father would I be if I let that sort of abusive behavior continue?" he glanced at Ellie with raised eyebrows. "I tried to tell you he was no good, Ellie. The Pack's got their claws into him too deep."

"Oh, good," I interjected. "Keep stoking the flames like a typical gaslighting asshole. I can't believe you fell for this shit, Ellie."

"Jackson, I'm sorry. I swear I didn't know. He said..." I could hear the regret in her voice as she trialed off, but more than that, I could also see and feel just how angry she was about being used as a pawn in Alex's sick games as she turned on him. "You promised! You've been using me. Was anything you said true?"

Apparently Alex wasn't a fan of being called out on his bullshit, because he went from cocky to irate in a fraction of a second. With an angry scream that scared the birds from the branches above, he barreled toward me, arms out and claws engaged as though ready to disembowel me.

Pushing Ellie out of the way, I shifted my weight and braced myself for impact. His body hit mine with enough force to wind me, claws slicing through the back of my shirt and tearing into my flesh. Warm blood seeped from the wounds as Alex slammed my back into a tree, igniting the fire beneath my skin that provoked the wolf.

Fury flowed through my veins, pumping with every breath I took. Reaching around Alex, I jammed my own claws into his back, tearing right through his thin leather jacket and shirt. He grunted, pulling us back a few inches before slamming my back into the tree again. When he moved to do it a third time, I brought my arms up before driving them into the tops of his shoulders. While he didn't release me, he did loosen his hold, and I was able to break free on my own.

The two of us continued to fight, our faces and bodies bloodied from fists and claws, feral snarls ripping free of our throats with every swipe. Somewhere beyond our growling, I heard a muffled voice, occasionally pleading for us to stop, but I was no longer in control of my own body. The wolf was defending its territory now.

"Stop! Get your hands off me!" Ellie's voice finally reached me, her panic burrowing its way into my awareness like some kind of parasite. Even after everything that had just been revealed, our bond was apparently still intact, and my need to protect her completely eclipsed my ire with her.

I glanced back to where Ellie was, finding her being held back by two of Alex's goons. They were on either side of her, hands gripping her arms as she struggled against them. Even from several feet away, I picked up on the changes in her as she channeled the wolf and utilized its strength.

It only took that one brief moment of distraction for Alex to gain the upper-hand, forcing me to my knees. With one hand wrapped around my wrist, he pulled my arm back behind me, while his other hand grasped the front of my neck, claws intentionally aligned with my carotid. He had me completely at his mercy. One wrong move, and he could dislocate my shoulder and slash my throat simultaneously.

"She's really something, isn't she?" Alex said, lowering his voice as he leaned down to my level to gloat in my ear.

Before us, Ellie lifted her right leg and kicked one of the men holding her in the sternum. There was a loud crack when her foot connected before he went flying back about five feet, landing in a heap on the forest floor. Then she turned to face her other captor, her usually dark eyes now blazing yellow as she fought against his brute strength. Completely helpless to rush to her aide, I was forced to watch her claws engage before she drove her free hand into the large man's throat, ripping out his windpipe, his blood spraying her face and torso before he dropped to the ground at her feet.

"A chip off the ol' block. She's really come a long way these last few days. You do good work."

Hearing Alex talk about Ellie like she was his protégé in his uprising against my Pack enraged me. Pressure filled my chest, finally escaping as a growl, and I jerked slightly, feeling the telltale pop of my shoulder dislocating and Alex's claws cutting into my flesh.

"Tell me, Jackie-boy, how does it feel to know that I beat you at your own game and got to your mate and flipped her on you all? She was all too willing to tell Daddy everything she learned about each and every one of you."

"Tell me, mutt," I managed to croak under the pressure of his hand tightening around my throat a little more. "Does your ass ever get jealous of the amount of shit that comes pouring out of your mouth?"

His hand tightened again. "You just don't know when to shut up and submit, do you, Jackson? I gave you a chance to make the smart choice. Now, though? Well now I'm not so sure I want to put up with your shit. It's a shame, though. Ellie seemed quite taken with you. I'm sure she'll bounce back, though. I'll make sure I take real good care of her…"

The underlying inflection to his last statement was menacing, and I knew I couldn't let her go with him. Even though Ashley was back, I knew I couldn't lose Ellie. Especially not to this sack of shit.

Chest heaving, Ellie looked down at the stray's body, his blood pooling around her feet. As seconds passed, the realization of her actions sank in, and she dropped the stray's trachea to the ground with a sickening *splat*. Slowly, Ellie turned to us, her eyes widening as she took in the sight before her.

"What are you doing?" She looked directly at Alex.

"I tried telling you he wouldn't side with us, kiddo."

"Ellie, sweetheart, he's been lying to you this entire time. He doesn't just want territory. He wants to take down the Pack—*our* Pack—for what happened to his brother. You have to see that. He's been using you to gather information so he can find our weaknesses."

Ellie's eyes darted between the two of us, and I could tell by the way she looked at me that she believed me. She knew she'd been manipulated, but she wasn't sure how to get us out of this situation.

Seeing this also, and clearly feeling threatened, Alex released my arm and shoved me to the ground, pressing his booted foot into my back to keep me down while he continued to gaslight her. "Ellie, I've been here for you since we found each other again. Helping you understand and learn how to control your new abilities... Where has this guy been?" Alex paused, pushing his foot harder into my spine until I felt it pop. "With his *wife*. A wife he kept hidden from you this entire time."

Ellie shook her head. "Stop," she pleaded.

"Sweetheart," I groaned, exhaling and blowing up a cloud of dirt. I needed to keep her grounded. I needed to use our bond to get through to her. "I told you how that happened. It's not as simple as he's making it out to be."

"Stop," she repeated. Her emotions were all over the place. I could feel her sadness and anger flaring and fighting for dominance.

"He hurt you," Alex proceeded, laying his feigned concern on a little too thick. "What kind of father would I be if I allowed him to do it again. I'll make it quick. He won't even feel a thing."

His heavy foot moved up closer to my neck, and the pressure continued to increase until Ellie ran forward. "No! Stop!" She sounded as desperate as her wide eyes made her look. "Let him live. If…if you kill him, they'll come for you. They'll never hear you out."

"Ellie…" I tried once more to explain that this was never about a peaceful request for territory, but Alex pushed harder, forcing my silence.

"Let him go." Ellie's tone was a little more forceful this time, her fists clenched at her sides. "If you let him go, I'll go with you. Let Jackson go back to his pack and tell them what it is you want."

Before I could attempt another protest, she slipped me a look that told me she was sorry, and there looked like maybe there was something else there, too. My gut told me she was only going along with Alex to ensure my survival so I could rally the Pack.

I could have been way off the mark, though, considering all the new information I'd just learned.

Above me, Alex remained silent, clearly contemplating his biological daughter's request. Finally, he removed his foot, and I coughed, stirring up more dirt as I pushed myself to my feet. Brushing the dirt from my clothes, I watched Alex lead Ellie away. Her shoulders were slumped in defeat as she snuck one final look back at me, lips moving with a silent "I'm sorry."

I debated going after her so I could save her from whatever Alex had planned, but before I could take my first step, Alex spoke. "Deliver my message, Jackie-boy. I'll be stopping by to speak with your...*Alpha* in person soon enough. You tell her to be ready."

Hands balling tightly at my sides, I glared after them. "Oh, I'll deliver your message, you cocky son of a bitch... And we'll be ready for you."

CHAPTER 28 | UNEXPECTED

I wasn't sure how to tell Brooke about Ellie's ties to the strays that were trying to kill us. She had really taken a shine to Ellie, and with her post-partum hormones in full-swing and affecting her wolf side, she was completely unpredictable. There was no telling how she was going to react at this betrayal of her trust. To this intrusion of our privacy.

Chances were it wouldn't be good. She was likely to go off the wall. The whole reason Brooke had me get close to Ellie was to keep this from happening, and I failed in that mission because I'd been too distracted to notice.

The second I walked through the door, Brooke and Nick appeared. Whatever either of them were going to say was sidelined when they took in my limp and my general appearance. While the wounds beneath my clothes had mostly healed, my clothes were still torn and stained with my blood. It had to look alarming.

"I'm fine," I assured them before they could ask.

Then their panic really set in as Brooke

watched me close the front door. "Where's Ellie?"

I laughed dryly. "You're going to want to sit down for this."

We moved into the library, and I had barely made it past the part where Alex showed up and revealed his relationship with Ellie that Brooke cut in. "But she was bitten..."

"That's exactly what I said, but she was born to a human mother. She had a fifty-fifty shot at inheriting the gene." I slumped down into one of the wingback chairs. "Back at the compound, I wondered how that bastard knew so much about us, but I never dreamed it was because he had gotten to her. I can't believe I was so stupid."

"Jax, no," Brooke interjected. "You couldn't possibly have known."

I looked up at her through a furrowed brow. "Yes," I snapped. "I absolutely could have had I not been so damn distracted."

"Jackson, your wife literally came back from the dead... No one can blame you for being distracted."

"Ellie is my mate." I stood up again, my body suddenly feeling on edge; it was the first time I'd affirmed my relationship with Ellie out loud to anyone else, and knowing she was out there somewhere with Alex left me gutted. Even if I was still a little angry with her. "I should have felt something was going on with her, but I kept her at a distance. I made you all deal with teaching her about our ways while I played house with my wife."

When did my life get so damn complicated?

Nick sighed. "Look, man, I know how difficult it is to convince someone what they've become."

My eyes snapped to him, memories of the day I gave him a hard time for not being able to tell Brooke what was happening to her rushing back. I was a dick all those months ago, and I had no right to assume I'd handle the situation better. I owed him an apology. "You were right."

Nick shook his head. "I don't want to be right, and I'm sure as hell not going to start singing the 'I told you sos.' What I am going to do is tell you that I get it." He crossed his arms. "I can only imagine what you've been going through with Ashley being back on top of everything else you've been dealing with. You shouldn't beat yourself up. You did the best you could."

Brooke and I stared at Nick, eyes wide, jaws slightly agape with shock. Nick cleared his throat, looking around the library like maybe he'd said more than he meant to. "Anyway, don't be too hard on yourself. Is that Azura?"

Brooke's lips curled up into a smirk. "I don't hear anything."

"Really?" Nick continued to avoid her eyes. "Because I swear I hear her. I should go check on her."

"Yeah," Brooke replied slyly. "You go do that." Nick was barely out of the room before she tacked on, "You big softie."

Now alone, Brooke leaned on the edge of the desk and focused on me. "Even if it's completely out of character for him, Nick's right. You shouldn't be so hard on yourself about letting certain things slip through the cracks. It would have happened to any one of us. Hell, I spent almost every waking moment with Ellie, and I didn't pick up on anything suspicious..." Brooke looked perturbed. "And I was a detective by trade. If anyone should've seen it coming, it was me."

"Look, we could pass the buck all day," I interjected, knowing we needed to get our shit together and formulate a plan of defense and to see if maybe Alistair had a stronger barrier spell up his sleeve. "He has Ellie."

"He took her?"

I shook my head. "Not exactly. She went willingly, but the look in her eyes as she walked away, not to mention the feeling I got in my gut, was that she was only doing it so he'd spare me long enough to figure out a plan." I paced the length of the library, replaying the entire confrontation in my head. "At first, she seemed to think he was coming in peace to negotiate territory rights, but then he started revealing more and more..." I stopped and looked at her, taking in her inquisitive pinched brows and the frown she wore. "He wants vengeance for his brother, Brooke."

Sensing the shift in my tone, Brooke pushed off the desk and took a step forward. "His brother?"

Nodding, I took a deep breath. "Karl. Karl was his brother."

Brooke's step faltered, her brows shooting up and her mouth dropping open. The night Karl attacked her had shaken the pack to its core and shifted Pack loyalty completely away from one of our own. While Karl had always been a bit of a loose cannon, Marcus always seemed to be able to keep him under control.

"So this has never been about claiming our territory. He's after us because of what happened to Karl?"

"I'd be willing to bet it's a bit of both, but yeah. That's what he said. I'm sure inheriting our territory is just an added bonus."

Brooke took a deep breath and nodded resolutely, her responsibility as Alpha to protect her Pack fast-eclipsing her worry. "Okay. Let him try. We've faced worse threats before and kicked those asses. We'll figure something out."

I had to admire Brooke's optimism, even if I could still smell the lingering remnants of the fear she tried to bury. Allowing myself to smile, I was about to suggest we call a meeting with the Pack when a knock on the library door interrupted us.

I turned around to find Ashley standing in the doorway, looking a little guilty for interrupting us. Then she took in my appearance and her eyes widened with the same concern Brooke had shown earlier.

"I'm fine," I assured her. "What's up?"

"Tyson's awake." Ashley smiled. "He's... asking for you."

With a smile, Brooke placed a hand on my arm. "Go. I'll gather the Pack and call on you when we're ready."

"Thank you."

Placing a hand on Ashley's lower back, I led her from the library. I could feel her eyes on me the entire time we walked toward the basement entrance, and finally she stopped me. "What the hell happened to you out there?"

I sighed, unable to meet her gaze, my guilt bubbling up and threatening to spill over. "We should talk about it later, Ash," I tried to convince her. "It's a long story."

"Jackson…" The firm tone of her voice forced my eyes to hers, and her expression faltered a little as she released a sigh. "She's your mate." It wasn't a question; she knew enough about our kind from hunting them all this time to know with absolute certainty.

"She is," I confirmed. Ashley looked crushed, her heart fluttering nervously as she nodded. I grabbed her hands and pulled them toward me, placing them on my chest. "Ash, I don't know how any of this happened. It's been fifteen years since I lost you. I met Ellie, and it hit me unexpectedly. I was just supposed to gain her trust and bring her into the Pack after she'd been bitten. I never expected — "

"Do you love her?"

I swallowed thickly. "I love *you*, Ashley."

She nodded, placing a hand on my cheek with a whisper of a smile that appeared to be a little sad. "I know you do, but do you love her, too?"

There was no use denying it. She already knew. "I do. But things are complicated now."

"How so?"

I gave Ashley the summarized version of what I'd just learned, and she listened intently. Not once did she interrupt or seem like she was judging me for what felt like indiscretions in the wake of her return. In fact, she looked like she understood.

"Come on," I said, opening the door to the basement. "We should go check on Tyson. We can discuss this later."

It was obvious that something had shifted between us since back at the compound, and while that feeling only amplified in the last few minutes, we didn't have time to focus on that. We had to check on Tyson and see if Alistair's cast was a success.

When we took that final step into the pit, we found Tyson sitting on the cot with his head in his hands. He looked up, the look of hatred gone from his eyes. All that stared back at me was confusion. When his eyes drifted to his mom, his expression changed to show his hurt.

"Are you going to let me out yet?"

Beside me, Ashley shook her head. "Not just yet," she told him. "We need to make sure you're not a threat."

Tyson's gaze shifted back to me. "You mean to him? My father?"

I exhaled with relief, grabbing the key off the table in front of me. Ashley grabbed my arm, stopping me, and when I looked back at Tyson, his eyes were narrowed. Alistair's spell to lift the veil hadn't worked.

"Yeah, I know who you are now," he said, eyes still angry and hurt. "What I don't understand is how my mother could ever be with a monster."

"Tyson, like I told your mother when I found her again, I wasn't always like this. We were happy once…don't you remember?"

Releasing a frustrated groan, Tyson ran his hands over his face, through his hair, and then held the back of his neck as he looked up toward the ceiling. "I'm not sure what I remember—what's real." He looked at Ashley for clarification. "Mom?"

Ashley moved past me, kneeling in front of the cage and gripping the bars. Tyson slid from the cot and mirrored her position. It made me a little nervous, but Ashley didn't seem worried. "You were seven the night we were attacked."

Tyson's eyebrows pulled together. "Vampires?" She nodded once, then he brought his eyes to mine, looking betrayed. "You didn't stop them?"

"I was still human—bitten that night."

Appeased by this answer, his gaze drifted, eyes glazing over. "I remember being so scared. They broke through the windows and pulled me out." Tyson's forehead rested against the bars, eyes clenched closed as though trying to force the memory of that awful night out of his head. I couldn't blame him; I could still hear the sounds of his terrified screams.

"I know, baby," Ashley said, voice cracking with emotion as she reached through the bars and touched the back of his head to comfort him. "I tried to stop them, but I wasn't fast enough. There were too many of them. I should have sensed their presence, but I was out of practice. I wasn't strong enough." Her confession got his full attention, and he looked even more confused than before. "I ran from The Order when I was seventeen, before I met Jackson—your *real* father. He helped me, even though he didn't have to. I never told him about my upbringing in all the years we were together, and before too long, I fell in love with him. He was a good man, Tyson...he *is* a good man."

Shame weighed down on my shoulders like a ton of bricks until it felt like I couldn't breathe; if I was such a good man, how could I hurt both Ashley and Ellie the way I had?

Tyson fell back onto his knees, eyes on me.

"You took me fishing."

I smiled. "As often as I could," I confirmed happily, remembering our boys' camping trips at the lake. We'd return with a cooler full of fish that Ashley would lovingly prepare for dinner.

"But you didn't raise me," he pointed out. "Carson did."

Ashley and I both nodded, and I tamped down the jealousy and rage that started to creep forward. It wasn't his fault I wasn't around; The Order made sure of that. "I know."

Tyson forced himself to his feet. "You're a werewolf. We kill your kind."

"Only when they're a risk to humanity," Ashley corrected him. "Jackson's Pack isn't. They uphold their laws."

"Then why are we here? I don't need to remind you that humans were being attacked, do I?" It was glaringly apparent that Tyson's loyalties still seemed to lie with The Order.

Careful to not take ten giant leaps back in the progress I'd made with him, I stepped forward. "My Pack has been investigating these attacks, and we've found out that a new pack of strays has been building it's numbers by turning innocents in the area. Their leader, Alex, has a grudge against my Alpha for the warranted death of his brother."

"Okay? Isn't that how your kind tend to deal with injustices among animals?" Tyson asked, his tone laced with the same prejudicial inflection as earlier.

I took a deep breath, trying to remind myself that this was my son and not some ignorant hunter. He'd been raised by The Order for fifteen years. These were the memories and habits that were prominent. No Shaman could reverse something that had been that deeply ingrained in him. It was possible the block on Tyson's memories didn't need to be maintained over the years because he was so young when he died. Maybe eventually he just forgot about me.

Having calmed myself down, I addressed his statement. "I assure you Karl's death was justified by Pack Law, but Alex doesn't seem to care about that. He wants revenge and the power and territory that will come with killing our Alpha."

Tyson considered what I'd told him carefully, his eyes continually gauging my expression for any sign of dishonesty. Then he turned to his mother, who'd stood up. "You trust him?"

"With my life."

"You trusted Dad with your life once, too," he pointed out. I wanted to correct him, but decided it wasn't a battle worth fighting considering he'd been raised by the man for the last fifteen years.

"I still trust Carson."

"Then why did you walk out on him?"

Ashley bit her bottom lip. "Because I remembered the truth. I remembered what your grandparents have been doing to me all this time, and I panicked. I never wanted this life for us, Tyson. It's why I left. I never dreamed they'd find us."

"Dad had nothing to do with that."

"I know, but I needed to be away from the lifestyle. I needed to explore these memories of my past and try to figure everything out."

"And have you?"

Ashley nodded, glancing back over her shoulder woefully. "I have."

After releasing a heavy sigh, Tyson's posture

relaxed. "Okay," he said before turning to me. "If I promise not to harm you or your pack, will you let me out?"

Skeptical, I glanced toward Ashley, who gave no indication whether or not I should. I flipped the key over in my hand repeatedly, weighing the pros and cons to his request.

"I swear on my wife's life that no harm will befall this pack."

"You're married?" I inquired, completely flabbergasted.

Tyson smiled. "Five weeks in. Hell of a honeymoon, right? She's back in Tennessee on another mission."

I moved toward the cage door and slipped the key into the lock. I turned it to the right, the room so silent, the sound of the mechanism disengaging echoed off the concrete walls. Tyson reached forward and pushed the door slowly, forcing me back a couple steps to avoid the silver bars.

Tyson's eyes assessed the room, and it was then that I remembered all the weapons on the walls and questioned my decision. I mentally prepared myself for the possibility that I might have to defend myself against my son, drawing on the wolf for an added burst of strength and adrenaline.

Instead of grabbing the nearest broadsword off the wall, though, Tyson outstretched a hand. I stared at it for a minute, unsure what the catch might be, before I took his hand in mine and shook it.

"Jackson!"

My attention flew to the stairs where Colby had just come barreling down, breathless like she'd just run a marathon. I dropped Tyson's hand and walked toward her. "What's going on?"

"Brooke needs you upstairs. Right now." Her bright eyes scanned the room. "All of you."

The three of us let Colby lead the way. I made sure to secure the pit before we headed up to the main floor, and the second we were outside, we stopped in our tracks behind Brooke and the rest of the Pack as they stared out toward the driveway...

...where The Order now stood, shoulder to shoulder in an arc, almost like they were blocking us in.

Suddenly, the center of the arc parted and two older members stepped through before it fluidly merged back together. I recognized them instantly as Ashley's parents. A third person joined them from the right of the army, his hand resting on the hilt of the sword that hung at his side as he glared daggers at me. *Carson.*

Ashley's father was the only one to speak, his eyes not on Brooke, but on me. "I think we need to talk."

CHAPTER 29 | AMBUSH

"What do you want?" Ashley demanded, stepping around me and then in front of the Pack. She stood before her parents and Carson with her arms crossed. Her irritation was felt by everyone.

Above us, the sun had begun to set on another day. Even though the moon was no longer full, its pull on each and every member of the Pack was still strong, and we all felt that surge of energy as it pulsed through our veins.

"Ashley, sweetheart," Carson said, reaching for her. Because I still didn't trust the guy, I growled when he got within a few inches, and he shot a challenging look my way. "You stay out of this, dog."

"Everyone just calm down," Brooke ordered, her tone firm and authoritative. Even the members of The Order listened. She approached Ashley's parents, letting her arms fall to her sides. "Now, you came here for a reason. What do you want?"

Ashley's parents assessed Brooke while Nick tensed in front of me, his body preparing to act if his Alpha—his mate—was in danger. The feeling rippled through the rest of the Pack until my own body followed suit.

Before Ashley's parents could reply to Brooke's question, Tyson took a step forward, moving around his mother until he stood next to a smug-looking Carson.

"Tyson," she said, staring at him with the same disbelief I felt.

"I'm sorry, Mom, but this is my choice. I like my life." He shifted his gaze to me. "Just because I remember one small part of my life, the fact remains, ridding the world of evil is actually pretty noble."

Every member of The Order grinned as Tyson joined them. Especially Ashley's father. "While collecting our own was part of why we tracked you all here, they are not the only reason," he interjected, looking toward his daughter. "When you were taken from us earlier, we lost a lot of good men and women."

"My people had nothing to do with their deaths," Brooke informed him firmly, her posture reading defensive.

Ashley's father looked indignant. "We know your *people* were not responsible for their deaths. But those other animals were. They need to be put down."

"Agreed," Brooke said, relaxing a little. "What are you suggesting?"

Ashley's father inhaled deeply, his face twisting like what he was about to say was going to be painful. "A truce. Once they're dealt with, we can leave you to your business, but you should know The Order will always be aware of your affairs."

"Your attention might be better focused elsewhere. We can handle our own territory," Nick fired back at them, gaining a sneer from Ashley's father.

"Is that why you have a pack of almost a hundred strays rallying against you all now? Because you've *handled* your territory? If you had been paying attention, things never would've gotten to this point." He lowered his gaze back to Brooke. "But I think you probably know that, don't you, little girl?"

"The name's Brooke," she stated.

"Given your tone and placement amongst your kind, I presume you to be the Alpha?" Brooke nodded once, and he held out his hand. "I'm Johnathon. Care to invite us in?"

Brooke looked beyond him at his army, and Johnathon smiled. "I don't think you'll all fit. It's a big place, but not necessarily big enough to accommodate you all."

"Not to worry. They've been ordered to guard the perimeter in case of an attack," Johnathon assured Brooke.

After a moment of contemplation, Brooke nodded. "Come on in, then. I'll put on some coffee."

Brooke turned around and led them toward the house. The Pack parted to let them pass. Johnathon, his wife, Carson, and Tyson followed her, and then Nick and I followed them inside. Ashley stayed close to me the entire time, and Layla and Colby came in last. While they hadn't been ordered to stay outside with The Order, the rest of the Pack did so anyway, closing the gap they'd made in front of the door.

Layla and Colby headed straight upstairs, presumably to watch over the babies, while

Brooke led us into the kitchen where she put on a pot of coffee. She offered up the stools at the island for Johnathon and his wife, and Tyson stood behind them almost protectively while Carson asked for a private moment with Ashley. Even though she was hesitant, Ashley agreed, leading Carson to the couch. I kept a watchful eye on them the entire time, and as the coffee brewed, Brooke set out cups.

"So," Brooke began. "The plan?"

"Beyond coming together in unity, Corrine and I hadn't really considered much. These wolves are definitely less predictable than ones we've encountered before."

"They're new," I offered up, tearing myself away from Carson and Ashley for a moment. No good would come from me eavesdropping. "It makes them more volatile, and they often don't think things through. They act rashly most of the time."

"Yes," Johnathon agreed, his eyes evaluating me. "Jackson, right?" I nodded. "I agree with your assessment."

"You should." I probably sounded more agitated than intended. "I've been around newly bitten wolves a lot over the last fifteen years. Hell, I was one once upon a time."

Johnathon narrowed his eyes and hummed. "Yes. I suppose you were."

Once the coffee was done, Brooke started to fill the mugs, and Ashley and Carson had returned. He looked happy about something, while Ashley still seemed uncertain. While everyone fixed their drinks, Brooke filled them in on what we knew — who the leader was, what he wanted.

Johnathon and Carson didn't have too much to offer on that front, but his hunters had been tracking them and had even taken a few of them out. They were confident we were dealing with close to a hundred strays, give or take a dozen or so.

"So, we have ten," Brooke said before Nick cut in.

"You're not going," he ordered. "You need to be with Azura."

Our guests—if we could safely call them that—watched their exchange curiously, assessing them like a hunter would its target. I didn't like it, but I had to trust that, if we worked well together, this truce would be extended beyond today.

"Nick—"

"And Layla needs to stay with Samuel."

"Nick, I'm the Alpha. I'm not going to stay behind and have them think I'm a coward," Brooke argued. "I agree with Layla staying behind. A hundred percent. I'm sure she wouldn't mind watching over Azura, too. She can keep them back at her place in the safe room or here in the…"

I cleared my throat, not wanting Brooke to say too much until we knew if our truce with The Order could be trusted. "Perhaps we talk logistics later." Brooke nodded in agreement.

"Okay," she carried on. "We have nine strong fighters—one of whom is a very powerful Shaman."

"That explains a lot," Carson muttered, looking at me. When I narrowed my eyes, he shrugged. "My wife and son were perfectly fine before you abducted them and worked your dark magicks on them."

I laughed dryly, advancing on him. "*Fine*? You people brainwashed them after bringing them back from the *dead*. You want to discuss the dark arts, perhaps we should start there…"

"Jackson," Brooke scolded at the same time Tyson said, "Dad, please."

My gaze shot to my son, only to find him looking at Carson. My hope for a relationship with him plummeted, and Ashley sensed this, placing her hand on my forearm as a show of support.

"Now isn't the time," she told me quietly.

"Our numbers are higher than yours," Carson said, directing the conversation back to our common problem. "But we'd still be outnumbered. We lost a few good fighters in that last battle."

"We are all proficient with casting, however," Corrine offered up. "And our weapons are all laced with silver for those who are negatively affected by it, and our training is unparalleled."

"No shit," I muttered, remembering how Ashley's blade felt on my skin when we'd first run into each other. It felt like ages ago with everything that had happened, but it had really only been days.

"Do you think we stand a chance?" Brooke asked.

Johnathon's lips curled up into a sinister grin. "I don't allow my people go into a fight thinking they don't."

Brooke exhaled. "Then let's spread the word. The sooner we—"

There was a loud crash to our right as the patio door shattered. We all looked toward it, Maggie and Johnathon shooting off their chairs. The hunters all had weapons in their hands already.

Even Ashley had grabbed a large knife from the block on the counter near her.

There was a groan from the floor as a body pushed itself to its feet, shards of glass falling from him as he stood. It was Zach.

"Little pigs, little pigs, let…me…in!" Alex bellowed from the yard, punctuating the final three words. One look outside and we could see that, along with the night, Alex and his army had descended on us. Several hunters were panting, blood on their blades, but they were in a holding formation as Alex stood at the head of his pyramid of werewolves.

I spotted Ellie immediately as she was positioned directly behind him and to his left. The look on her face wasn't one of compliance toward Alex. She looked troubled and scared. I took a step forward, my growl rumbling low in my chest as my claws engaged. Ashley grabbed my wrist and stopped me.

"You're upset."

"Of course I'm upset," I barked. "He just threw one of mine through a damn window and he's got her…"

Ashley swallowed thickly, keeping her expression as neutral as possible. But I sensed the twinge of pain she felt. "But if you go out there half-cocked and let your anger control you, you'll get yourself killed." She kept her tone even and calm, maybe hoping it would affect me in kind. Sure, what she said made a lot of sense, but I couldn't seem to think clearly knowing Ellie was out there with a known psychopath when she didn't necessarily want to be.

"Listen to her, Jax," Brooke said. "You know

she's right—you've told me the same thing a time or two before."

Closing my eyes, I took a deep, calming breath. The wolf stepped forward at a steady pace instead of rushing into the fray, and I felt its strength aligning with my own. "Okay," I finally said. "Let's not keep our company waiting."

Setting the knife on the counter, Ashley rushed from the room and grabbed her sword from where she left it by the front door. She unsheathed it, and we all walked out onto the back patio, checking on Zach, whose cuts were already healing. He joined us, and we moved through the members of The Order who'd formed a wall of bodies between Alex and the manor.

Brooke led the way, Nick and I flanking her the way we should. Ashley and her parents followed us, Tyson and Carson not too far behind. Even though we were supposed to be adversaries, we moved in on our common enemy and his team of goons like we'd been allies for more than just a few hours.

Alex's lips slid into a sneer, his tongue peeking out to press against a canine as he eyed Brooke up and down like a piece of meat. "You're a pretty little thing, aren't you?" He paced back and forth in front of Brooke, assessing her like she was property. "No wonder my brother had a thing for you." Next to me, Nick growled protectively, gaining Alex's undivided attention. "Problem?"

When Nick didn't answer, Alex shifted his focus to me, then around us. The Order and the Pack had gathered around us, our numbers pretty close to Alex's. "Impressive turnout," he said. "Too bad it isn't going to help."

"You're in breach of Pack Law," Brooke stated, her tone steady and commanding. Alex looked amused. "Not only are you trespassing and hunting on another Pack's territory without permission, but you've been attacking and turning humans with the intent to build an army against the governing pack."

Still grinning, Alex watched her. It was obvious by the look on his face that he wasn't taking her seriously. "Yeah?" He laughed. "And what, *exactly*, are you going to do about it little girl?" He leaned forward. Nick and I both took a step toward him, but Alex gave zero shits, getting right in Brooke's face.

She didn't flinch, though. Didn't even blink. In fact, the longer she stood there, reactionless, the more agitated Alex became. His temper flared, glowing yellow eyes holding hers as his chest heaved angrily. He was trying to intimidate her, but she held her ground.

I was so intently focused on Alex and Brooke that I wasn't paying much attention to anyone else, until movement to Alex's left caught my eye. I glanced up to find Ellie staring at me. Her expression had changed from earlier, eyes darting around like she was trying to tell me something.

One quick glance around told me that we weren't even looking at Alex's entire army. How had we missed that when we first came out here? I honed my hearing, surveying the grounds carefully, and that was when I spotted movement from the brush around us. I didn't know how many there were, but it was obviously Alex's intention to lull us into a false sense of security—make us think we might stand a chance—and then he would signal his ambush.

He was smarter than he looked.

"You know," Alex said, his already sinister voice laced with a growl, "I was going to rip you right up the middle for what you did to my brother, but I think maybe I'll have a little fun with you first."

Nick looked like he was ready to lunge forward, but I shook my head, nodding toward the outskirts of the yard. He saw what I saw and knew Alex was trying to bait us so he could signal his pack.

When I looked back at Alex and Brooke, I saw she was smiling. "Want to know what happened to the last son of a bitch who tried to have a little *fun* with me?" In a move too quick for any of us to see, Brooke reached out and grabbed the collar of Alex's jacket and yanked him forward, her sneer showing off her elongated canines. "I fucking killed him." She brought her knee up swiftly, hitting him right in the groin and forcing him to his knees.

Even though he'd been momentarily incapacitated, he shouted, and waves of transformed wolves rushed from the trees that lined the property. It only took seconds for the fight to break out, Order and Pack members fighting side by side against Alex's pack.

With a ferocious growl, Alex charged Brooke. It became obvious very fast just how predictable and unskilled his fighting style was. He relied on his size and brute strength, whereas Brooke had been trained to use speed and agility to avoid these attacks before finding the right moment to use her opponents size against him. It wasn't often I admitted to it, but she'd bested me more than once.

Several of Alex's goons tried rushing Brooks as she landed a perfect roundhouse kick to Alex's jaw. Blood dripped from a cut in his lip as he righted himself. Before any of them could reach her, Nick and I dealt with them. They were new and inexperienced, so they were easy enough to terminate.

Like any narcissistic psychopath, Alex didn't give up. He landed a punch to the side of Brooke's face, setting her off balance for a second. Nick saw red. With a feral growl, he rushed Alex, but before he got within two feet of him, the man I pegged as Alex's beta tackled him. They fought several yards away, three more strays joining in. They had Nick surrounded for all of ten seconds before Nick had everything under control, two of them dead before I could even make a move. He was a very skilled fighter.

While I dealt with a couple more of the mutts that were trying to get to Brooke and Alex, I noticed Alex had Brooke in a choke hold. She struggled against his grip on her, and her erratic movements forced his step to falter. He staggered backward as Brooke's eyes searched frantically for something.

I was already on my way to help her when she swung her body hard in his arms, her face turning red from lack of oxygen. This forced Alex to shift to the left and gave Brooke the opportunity to use the tree near her as leverage.

With an impressive use of her core strength, Brooke brought her legs up, planting her feet firmly against the trunk of the thick trunk of the maple tree before flipping up and over Alex's head. This caught him by surprise, and forced him to release his hold on Brooke. She landed in a crouching position behind him before using her full strength to grab him around the waist and slam him into the tree trunk.

Relieved that Brooke seemed to have Alex handled, I returned to the task of disposing of the rest of the strays. After snapping the neck of one of the human soldiers, a large black wolf crashed into me, sending me to the ground. It's huge paws pressed down on my chest, his jaw snapping at my face against my hold on his neck. Saliva dripped on my face as he fought against my strength, getting so close his cold nose grazed my cheek. I tightened my hold on his neck, digging my fingers in as tightly as I could, and I gave one sharp jerk to the left, reveling in the satisfying *snap* of his spine breaking.

I stood up, looking around at the carnage. Quite a few of Alex's horde had fallen, and while I counted every single member of the Pack still standing, none of them were at a hundred percent. Regardless, they fought through their injuries and created their own pile of bodies. Next I looked for Ashley, panicking when I didn't see her on my first pass, then I spotted her about thirty feet away and felt a little more at ease.

Much like the first time we fought, I admired her skill and precision, the way the blade she held was an extension of her arm versus a weapon she merely wielded. This time, however, Ashley wasn't fighting alone; Carson was with her. They stood back to back, moving as though they shared the same body, fighting with such incredible teamwork, you'd think the entire thing had been choreographed to precision. It was the most amazing — and the most maddening — thing I'd ever seen.

"Jackson!"

I turned toward the voice — toward Ellie as she fought her way through the fray — and I found one of Alex's men trying to come up on me from behind. We fought, but it was short-lived. He dropped to the ground at my feet within seconds, and his heart joined him from my hand directly after. When I returned my eyes to Ellie, I found her fighting, but she wasn't fighting anyone from The Order or the Pack; she was fighting off one of the shifted members of Alex's pack. She may have only known about being a wolf for a few days, but the way she drew on the wolf in her time of need told me she was meant for this life. She reveled in the strength the wolf gave her, and she never looked more beautiful.

I felt better knowing she was on our side, and I moved to go help her, but was grabbed from behind. Whoever it was turned my body around to face them with such force it threw off my equilibrium, so I never even saw the fist before it connected with my face. Before my vision could return, Alex's scent wrapped itself around me — most prominently, his blood — and when my vision finally cleared, I saw him. He stood before me, blood dripping from a deep gash above his right eyebrow, his bottom lip cut to shit, and his dark hair disheveled and sticking to his sweaty face.

"That Alpha of yours is scrappy."

Worried that maybe she had been hurt and

that was why Alex was in front of me, I whipped around, only to find her fighting alongside Colby and an Order member against four of our attackers. There were bodies everywhere. I had no idea how we were going to explain this away.

Relieved, I returned my attention to Alex. "Looks like you were wrong about us being no match for you. Seems we outnumber you now."

Ellie called for me again, but I knew if I let her distract me, Alex would use it to his advantage. So I kept my eyes trained on Alex, watching as he wiped the blood from his head on the back of his hand and spit the blood from his mouth onto the ground at his feet. "You know, I was really hoping she'd be easier. But then you had to go and bond with the little whore."

The wolf didn't like hearing him talk about Ellie like that—neither did the human, for that matter. My lips curled back, a snarl escaping and building until it was a full-blown growl. I could feel the tips of my fingers split as my claws engaged. Alex seemed to feed off my reaction, his eyes turning amber.

"I figured it would be easier to get to her," he continued, his voice deepening with a growl. "Especially after I killed that human she associated with and left him for her to find."

"*You* killed Nate?" I demanded, shocked at this revelation, considering I'd found Ellie with her fur covered in his blood.

Alex smirked. "I had no idea you'd brought her out here that night, and I was looking for a way to lure her back into the city. I still had an army to build, after all." Alex moved to the right, and I mirrored him, not about to let him get the drop on me again. "He'd been skulking around, and he reeked of her. Figured they had a deep and meaningful human relationship. I had no idea she'd gone and gotten herself a mate so soon. Guess I'll have to remedy that. Maybe with you out gone, she'll be a little more...compliant."

Alex rushed toward me. The feral look on his face was completely inhuman, fangs bared and claws engaged, as he closed in on me faster than I'd anticipated. I braced myself for the impact, but before I could act, I was shoved from the left. Because I wasn't expecting the hit, I fell to the ground, rendered momentarily helpless as I watched Alex's claws tear into Ellie's neck, her blood spraying his face before she collapsed at his feet.

CHAPTER 30 | RECKONING

It was like the world stopped around me as the horror unfolded. Ellie's body crumbled to the ground in slow motion, and the smell of her blood soaking into the soil filled my head. Rage coursed through my veins, igniting the pain of watching her fall like an accelerant until I was completely consumed by the flames of vengeance.

Alex looked pleased by my reaction and not at all upset over his fallen daughter, widening his stance and inviting me to come at him like the cocky son of a bitch he was with open arms. Even though I knew I shouldn't let my emotions fuel my attack, I was too blinded by fury to think rationally. It wasn't until my body collided with his that I realized the howl of sorrow I heard was coming from me.

Using everything I had in me, I propelled us forward until I slammed his back into the pillar that held the eaves above the patio. The plaster cracked under the force of our bodies, the joints groaning as the integrity of the structure was compromised. We exchanged blows, Alex doing everything he could to try and flip the balance of power. I opened up my mind, inviting the wolf forward without giving it complete control, and I let its grief over losing Ellie drive us both toward retribution.

Heat flared all over Alex's body as we fought. Like me, he was losing control of his humanity. Even though we were both still in our human bodies, we fought like animals, claws engaged and tearing at flesh, elongated canines snapping in each other's faces, and feral snarls and growls competing for dominance over the rush of blood in our ears.

I wrapped my hands around Alex's neck, squeezing until I felt his quickened pulse against my palms. Pain ripped through my ribs as Alex slid his claws into my flesh, right down to the bone, in a final act of desperation. My body instinctively wanted to pull away from the violent intrusion, but I leaned into it instead, my anguish drowning out the burning sensation of dirt in my fresh wounds.

Even though his life was literally in my hands, he didn't look worried. His fingers continued to dig in, twisting and pulling at the tissue around them. I winced, and he smiled triumphantly, blood seeping from between his teeth and out the corners of his mouth. I could feel my flesh tearing as he used his strength to slowly drag his fingers up my sides, blood flowing freely down over my skin. The higher he went, the harder I squeezed until I felt a thick snap and his neck collapsed in my hands.

Alex's expression went blank, the amber in his eyes fading as the life left him, and I released him, letting him fall to the ground, his fingers leaving my body on his descent. Chest heaving, I looked down at him with disgust before nudging him with my boot. I spit the blood that filled my mouth onto the ground and turned around slowly, taking in the silence around me. The sight that greeted me was unexpected.

The fighting had stopped. Fifty bodies—maybe more—littered the ground, hunter and stray alike. Every member of the Pack still stood, though barely for some. Ashley, Carson, and Tyson were alive, staring at the ground. Carson had his arms around Ashley as she wept, Tyson laid a supportive hand on her shoulder, and her parents were dead at their feet. All other eyes were on me and my kill, the army of strays looking horrified and unsure what they should do now that their leader had fallen. Some looked ready for a fight, while others looked like they were about to piss their pants.

Brooke stepped forward, around Nick's protective stance, and she approached me. She knelt next to Alex and felt for a pulse. With a satisfied smirk, she stood up and patted my upper arm, visually assessing my injuries before she found Ellie lying six feet away from us. She masked her own heartache at the loss of a packmate she'd accepted, and turned to everyone.

"Your leader is dead," she declared strongly. "Your numbers have dwindled significantly. You have a choice: you can stay and we can continue on until every last one of you has met the same fate as them, or you can pick up your fallen and get the hell off Pack territory." The strays all looked to one another like they were silently weighing their options or waiting for an order.

Slowly, the strays moved through the carnage, gathering their own and leaving our land. Only a few fallen hunters remained and one of ours.

While Brooke and Nick assessed the injuries to our people, I sank to my knees next to Ellie, reaching out and stroking my fingers over her cheek, pushing her blonde hair back off her face. "Ellie, I'm sorry," I whispered to her. "I should have been there. I never should have let you go with —"

With a gasp, Ellie's eyes flew open. A fresh wave of blood flowed from her wounds and a little trickled from the side of her mouth. Alarmed, I called for help, ripping my own shirt from my body to apply pressure to her wound with the cleanest part of it I could find. Ellie was gasping for air, her eyes wide with alarm and confusion as she tried to figure out what was happening.

"You're okay, sweetheart," I assured her.

"I'm...s-sorry," she croaked around her injuries.

Forcing a smile to mask my panic, I gently shushed her. "Don't move or try to talk. We're going to get you help."

Brooke was by my side in an instant, taking Ellie's hand while Nick and Vince came over to assist as well. "We need to get her inside. Layla is locked down in the pit with the kids. We need to get her up here to help," Brooke started to order.

"I'll go get Layla," Colby said from behind me. I hadn't even realized she'd joined us, and she was gone just as quickly, hopping the low partition between the yard and patio and running through the broken patio door.

Vince and Nick worked together to lift Ellie

while I held the shirt to her neck as we carefully maneuvered toward the house. Before disappearing inside, I got the feeling I was being watched, and when I looked, I saw Ashley had pulled away from Carson and was looking at me with sympathy. I nodded my appreciation as we slipped through the door.

Once we had Ellie comfortable in her bed, Layla arrived with Miranda's medical bag full of supplies. She ushered us all from the room, save for Brooke, and we all stood, helpless and a little stunned in the hall. Nick and Vince left me alone so they could go back outside to help assist The Order with their dead. I don't know how long I stood in that spot, waiting for that door to open, but when it did, I sucked in a deep breath and held it, unsure what to make of the looks on Layla and Brooke's faces.

They were both covered in blood, and the coppery scent was so potent in the air beyond them, I could actually taste it. I only caught a glimpse of Ellie before Layla pulled the door closed, wiping her hands on a towel.

"She's stable, Jax," Layla said, laying a hand on my forearm to draw my focus. "For now. The next twenty-four hours are critical. We'll need to be vigilant."

I nodded, not sure I really heard anything beyond "she's stable."

"The cuts were deep," Brooke tacked on. "She's lucky to be alive. But she's a fighter. She's strong."

Before they excused themselves, Layla smiled. "I'm going to call Alistair up. I'm sure he can do something for her pain. Keep her comfortable until she's ready to wake up."

Nodding, I finally exhaled. "Can I see her?"

Brooke looked at Layla, who nodded her ascent. "Yes, but be careful. She's stable, but not out of the woods."

Once they were gone, I opened the door to Ellie's room and slipped inside. She had been changed into clean clothes and was beneath a fresh set of blankets and sheets. Her neck was heavily bandaged, but I could still smell the blood and the medication used to help prevent infection. Her breathing seemed shallow, and her heartbeat faint as it produced and pumped fresh, new blood through her veins.

I pulled the chair from Colby's old desk up beside the bed and sat in it, sandwiching Ellie's hand between mine and kissing her fingertips. Her skin was cold, which for a werewolf wasn't normal, and her complexion was even more pale than usual, her flawless ivory hue now ashen from extreme blood loss. She probably should have died, but her accelerated healing must have been what kept her alive.

As I pushed her hair off her clammy forehead, I noticed it was slightly furrowed, her brows pinched tight in the middle. It was obvious she was uncomfortable, even while unconscious.

"You'll be okay," I told her with a shaky voice. "You have to be. You're a good person, Ellie, and I'm so sorry for how I treated you earlier. " I pressed my forehead against our joined hands and took a deep, calming breath, trying to control my racing heart. "If you can hear me, Ellie, you should know you weren't responsible for Nate. I know you still carry a lot of that guilt, but it was

Alex. He killed him and left him for you, knowing you'd shift. It wasn't you."

A throat cleared behind me, and I turn, startled, to find Alistair. "Layla said I should come up and try to keep her comfortable?"

I nodded. "Please. Whatever you can do."

Releasing her hand, I stepped back toward the door, giving him room to do his thing. I watched as Alistair moved his hands inches above Ellie's unconscious body, and as I watched, I swore I could see the second his cast worked. It was like all the tension left as her body relaxed into the mattress, and the pain was erased along with the creases in her forehead.

Alistair emerged with a smile. "I've lessened the pain. From what I gathered during the cast, her energy is strong. She's fighting to stay alive."

"Thank you."

With a nod, he clapped a hand down on my shoulder. "If she doesn't wake up in the next eight hours, call me. We may have to do the cast again to keep her comfortable, but her accelerated healing seems to be taking care of most of it."

Alistair moved out of my line of sight and headed for the stairs, revealing a familiar face. He gave Ashley a curt nod before descending back to the main level, and she continued toward me. We embraced, and I inhaled deeply. The smell of her relief was mingled with fear and something else I couldn't quite place, but holding her in my arms was still comforting.

"How is she?" Ashley asked.

"Stable." I pulled back, bringing a hand up to cradle her face. "How are you? Your parents…"

Ashley's eyes dropped, sadness tugging at the

outer corners of her mouth, and she shrugged. "They fought valiantly, like they always have."

"Ash?"

She sniffled, looking up to me with glistening eyes. "They might not have been perfect—far from it—but they died protecting me. They protected me when I've been nothing but awful to them since I found you again."

"They loved you, that much is obvious. They only wanted what they thought was right for you."

Ashley turned away from me, waves of that one emotion I couldn't quite nail down radiating off her. It was unsettling, leaving a sour taste in my mouth and turning my stomach. "I get that now," she said softly. "Too little, too late, I suppose."

I placed both of my hands on her shoulders and kissed the back of her head. "It's never too late, Ash."

We stood like that for a moment, staring into Ellie's room, and Ashley sighed. "We had a whole life ahead of us." She brought a hand up to cover one of mine, squeezing it gently.

"But it was taken from us..."

Inhaling deeply, Ashley nodded. "It was, and in that time, I've come to realize what The Order does is necessary. The mission is important."

"You're right."

Ashley turned around, her eyes slowly locking on mine. "We're both in very different places now, Jax."

"Because we were forced apart."

"We live in different worlds. You're *mated* now." She held my stare, looking more resolute by the second. "I'm fully aware of how deep that bond runs in your biology. It's woven into every part of your physiology. It's primal. Beyond what you and I shared once upon a time."

"Ashley—"

"I need to go back," she interjected. "I didn't think I wanted this life, but now that my parents are gone, I'm in charge. Carson and I have the chance to change the way The Order does things." Bringing her hands up between us, she laid them on my chest. "Maybe us coming together after all this time was the universe's way of bringing us closure after the attack. Of uniting wolf and hunter."

Even though I knew she was right about everything, I desperately took her hands in mine and gripped them, hoping to hold onto my past a little longer. "Closure? Ashley, I don't want closure. You're my wife."

"When you were human," she said softly. "Before I died and you were mated. We live in two completely different worlds now. And you have Ellie now."

I turned to look at Ellie, still unconscious, and every part of me felt that pull to be by her side as she healed. "I…"

"Every single cell in your body calls for her, and hers for you. You can't deny that."

My head snapped back to Ashley. "But I love you."

"And I will always love you, Jackson, but this—us—can't work…not with the way things are. Deep down, I think you know this."

With a sigh of defeat, I dropped my forehead to hers. "I can't believe I'm losing you again."

"No, Jax," Ashley was quick to refute. "If any-thing, this time together has done so much good for us—the Pack and The Order. We've proven that we can overcome our differences and work together, regardless of what we've been told in the past. Look at what we accomplished tonight."

I sat with everything she'd told me, my hu-man half still in denial that I was about to willing-ly let her walk out of my life. Thinking about it like that made me nauseous. She made a lot of sense, though, but that didn't mean I had to like it. I glanced back toward Ellie, felt that familiar tug I'd been feeling since the moment I met her, and I nodded.

"How am I supposed to let you go? I just got you back."

Ashley smiled, bringing her hands up to run them along my jaw. "You're not letting me go, you're just moving on with the life you've worked so hard to build. Just like I'm going to do."

I could feel myself losing grip on my emo-tions. I wasn't normally one to cry, but I could feel my eyes beginning to burn with tears. "Why does this feel harder than last time?"

Ashley opened her bright blue eyes and looked up at me through her thick black lashes. "It doesn't have to be," she whispered. "I can...I can take the memories if you want."

I'd like to say I didn't consider the idea for even a second, but the truth of the matter was, I did. It might have been easier to go back to think-ing she was dead, it might have been better. But then I thought back to my struggle to let people get close to me due to the paralyzing fear I had of losing them again, and I shook my head.

"No. I don't want to do that…do you?"

Ashley grinned. "I don't."

"Mom?" Ashley and I looked toward the deep voice, finding Tyson at the top of the stairs looking a little uncomfortable. "Dad's…that is, uh…" He struggled with his words given he still barely knew me. "We're ready to go."

Ashley dropped her hands to her sides and nodded. "Of course. Glancing back up at me, she licked her bottom lip before stepping up onto her toes and kissing me softly. "Goodbye, Jackson."

"Bye, Ash," I murmured. "I'll see you around."

Ashley approached Tyson and stepped down onto the first step before addressing our son. "You coming?"

He nodded. "Yeah, just…can you give me a minute?"

Ashley shot me a smile, tucking her blonde hair behind her hear, and she nodded. "You bet."

Tyson waited until his mother was out of sight before he took a few steps toward me. "Look, I'm sorry about earlier — all the shit I said."

"Don't worry about it," I assured him. "I get it."

Tyson didn't accept my response so easily. "No, I was an ass, and I shouldn't have been. You're…my father, and I'm mostly angry about the relationship we never got to have. It wasn't fair, and it wasn't right, what my grandparents did, but The Order isn't all bad. We do a lot of good."

"I know you do, son," I told him, proud of the man he'd become, even if I barely knew him.

"What I'm trying to say is, even though we've

340

lost the last fifteen years, I'd like to get to know you. I think we're owed that."

I couldn't contain the smile that spread across my face as I took several long strides toward him, holding out my hand. He took it without hesitation, pulling me forward and hugging me with his other arm. I returned the gesture happily before we said our goodbyes, and I watched him descend the stairs and exit the house to be with his mother.

While the day might have started out shitty and progressively gotten worse, it had definitely turned itself around and given me hope for a future I'd never anticipated. And just when I thought it couldn't get any better...

"Jackson?" I turned toward the strained voice to see Ellie was trying to sit up.

Relieved, I rushed to her side and eased her back onto the pillows. "Take it easy, sweetheart. You need to rest."

"What happened?" Her voice was scratchy from the wounds she'd sustained, and she reached up to touch her bandages.

I only had to remind her of the first few minutes of Alex's raid on the manor before she remembered everything. "He's dead," I told her, taking her hands in mine. "He won't be bothering us again."

Her dark eyes implored mine. "Us?"

With a smile, I nodded. "You're my mate, Ellie. I've been so confused about what I thought I needed in my life, and I'm sorry for putting you through that, but what we have can't be fought. I see that now. Our bond is unbreakable."

Ellie looked wary, a smile trying to tug at the corners of her mouth. "So you're choosing me?"

I shook my head. "It was never a choice," I told her. "I just wasn't looking deep enough. I've never felt this way before, so I didn't understand what was happening between us. I pushed you away out of fear, and I cannot apologize enough for my behavior." I picked up her hand and kissed her knuckles. "But I'll spend the rest of our lives trying to find a way to do just that."

Ellie's smile grew into a genuine one as she weakly tugged me forward. I complied, not wanting her to overexert herself, and I pressed my lips to hers. "I love you, Ellie."

"I love you, too," she replied, her happiness quickly turning to worry. "And I'm sorry about everything I did — the lies, the omissions, the betrayal..."

I shook my head. "Don't worry about that right now. You need to rest. We'll address all that when you're well again."

Ellie nodded, her eyes drooping as exhaustion set in again. Even these few minutes had drained her.

Leaning forward I kissed her forehead. "You should sleep. The more rest you get, the quicker you'll heal." I stood to leave so she could sleep, but before I even turned away, Ellie grabbed my wrist.

"Stay with me," she rasped. "Lay with me?"

Just the idea of lying next to her invited waves of my own fatigue to wash over me. I couldn't even remember the last time I'd had a full night's sleep since all of this began, so I happily sidled up next to Ellie, wrapping my arms around her and holding her close.

And for the first time in fifteen years, I was

completely at peace as I drifted off to the beat of Ellie's heart against my chest, lulling me to sleep.

EPİLOGUE | VOLUNTEER

Months had passed since the threat to the Pack had been neutralized. Ellie had settled into her new role within the pack nicely. She was nervous at first, given how she'd been feeding Alex information on us all, but they were very forgiving — just as I told her they would be.

Brooke and Ellie had grown closer over the months, and while Brooke was still learning, she had taken Ellie under her wing and was teaching her everything she knew. Ellie loved every minute of it.

I think there was a part of her that missed Alex. Not that it was *him* she missed. I truly believed it was the idea of having a father she craved. She'd gone her entire life not knowing he was out there, and then he came back into her life at a tumultuous time, and for the worst possible reason. It was easy to see how she was so blind to his manipulation.

But she was adjusting. It took a little time, but she soon realized what kind of man he was and that his motives for coming back into her life when he did were purely selfish. According to a few of his betas, who'd come to us seeking asylum in exchange for information and loyalty, Alex had plans of purifying his bloodline. The idea turned my stomach, and Ellie was stunned. While it wasn't something I or anyone else in the Pack would have chosen, it wasn't uncommon for purebloods to want to breed selectively like that.

Things between Ellie and I were going well, too. While I still struggled with losing Ashley again, I was comforted by the fact that she was out there somewhere, living her life and making a difference. Even if that life wasn't something she ever wanted for herself when she was younger. It helped that Ellie was extremely understanding about everything; it definitely alleviated a lot of the guilt that crept up when I started to think about my estranged wife.

"Hey." Small hands run along my sides as slender arms wrap around my waist, and Ellie stands on her toes to prop her head on my shoulder.

I was standing in the great room, staring out the large picture windows at the mountains, enjoying a hot cup of coffee when she snuck up on me. "All done?" I asked, turning my head to kiss the tip of her nose.

"Yeah. Brooke says we can pick up tomorrow. Azura was getting fussy, and Nick couldn't get her to settle."

For the last few weeks, as soon as Ellie was feeling well enough, Brooke started showing her a lot of our history in the library. She started with the journal of Marcus' great grandfather, and then the dossiers the Pack had been keeping ever since. It was a lot to take in, but Ellie seemed fascinated by it all and eager to learn.

"So what do you want to do with the rest of your afternoon?" I turned in her arms and pulled her close, pressing my nose into her neck and inhaling deeply. With the full moon set to rise in a few hours, her scent had changed, and her rising pheromones complimented it nicely.

The amber ring pulsed around her pupil, the wolf preparing for the sun to set. We'd been practicing more and more with every full moon, but Ellie still hadn't fully mastered her transformations. While she was definitely getting better on days where the moon wasn't full, she still struggled for total control when it was.

Ellie hummed, biting her bottom lip and looking up at the ceiling innocently, her irises glowing brighter. I could tell there was more than just the wolf behind it, because I felt it too. It was a combination of lust and the need for release. "We could...go for a run? Shift early? I'm getting better."

"We could," I agreed, ensnaring her hips and pulling her toward me so she could feel my arousal and know what we both really wanted. "Or we could head upstairs and —"

Before I could finish convincing her to go upstairs for a little pre-shift sex — which was usually the most intense and passionate — the doorbell rang. A little annoyed, I kissed her. "Just...hold that thought, sweetheart."

Ellie followed me through the house and toward the front door, turning for the stairs as I grabbed the knob. "How about I meet you upstairs and get a head start?"

Smiling, I turned the knob. "That better not be

a joke." I pulled the door open and was surprised by our company. "Detective Matthews."

I heard Ellie's footsteps stop, then I heard them get closer as she descended the stairs again and stood beside me. She seemed just as surprised as me to see him standing on our front steps. It had been a while since we'd seen him—not since the day he had Ellie in custody and then came to talk to Brooke, actually.

"Please, call me Tom," he replied with a strained smile. Now, I didn't know him to be a particularly cheery individual, but something about the way his smile didn't quite reach his eyes told me something was really wrong.

"Of course," I replied, standing back and holding an arm out. "You want to come in?"

Detective Matthews stepped through the front door, saying hello to Ellie. I noticed the yellow folder in his hand as I closed the door behind him. Tucking it under his arm, he turned to me. "Brooke and Nick home?"

"Tom," Brooke said, appearing at the top of the stairs with Azura in her arms. She was smiling like his visit was a happy surprise, but her smile faded when she took in his somber expression. "I thought I heard you down here."

"Brooke." Tom nodded, watching her as she joined us on the main floor. "You guys have a minute? I know I'm cutting it pretty close to sunset, but, uh...I've got a situation I'd like to discuss with you."

Brooke looked at Azura like she was debating taking her back upstairs, but Ellie stepped in. "I'll take her for a bit. You should go talk to the detective."

"You're sure?"

Ellie nodded. "Yeah. We'll be fine."

Brooke handed Azura over. "Thanks. Come find me if she's too much trouble, okay?"

Before leaving us, Ellie came over and kissed me. "To be continued."

Seeing Ellie interact with Azura these last couple months had been...interesting, to say the least. At forty-three, I didn't think I'd want more kids, but Ellie was still only twenty-five, and the way she looked at Azura and Samuel often gave away her unspoken desire to one day have a family. And I was shocked to realize I wouldn't exactly be opposed to the idea, should she bring it up.

Nick showed up a couple minutes later, and Brooke suggested moving the conversation to the library so the rest of the Pack could move about as they pleased. Once we were all settled, Brooke invited Tom to take the floor.

"I'm assuming you're all aware of the recent murders in the city?" he began.

We all nodded along while Brooke said, "The two teenage girls, right?"

"Yeah." Closing his eyes, Tom shook his head. "We haven't been cleared to release many details to the media yet, but I think we might be in over our heads here."

I pinched my brows together, confused and curious. "Are you suspecting wolves? Because we haven't heard of anyone on our territory in weeks unless they were cleared to pass through, and we have eyes everywhere."

Tom shook his head again, looking up at me. "No. It's not wolves. There are no signs of animal attack. The wounds are clean cuts." He took the folder and handed it to Brooke.

Nick and I moved to stand beside her as she opened the folder and leafed through the large color photos inside. The images were shocking, and not because we were strangers to seeing dead bodies, but for another reason entirely.

"These are sacrificial markings," I said, looking up at Tom. "Runes."

He inhaled deeply. "That's what I was afraid of."

"Are there any connections between the two girls that you're aware of?" Brooke inquired, her past as a Detective for the Scottsdale Police Department taking over.

"They were both sixteen and attended the same high school," he answered. "But that's about it. There's no other connection that we've been able to uncover."

Brooke closed the file, but the red pagan marks carved into pale flesh were burned into my mind like a light when you look at it for too long. "Tom, we've never dealt with this sort of thing before," I told him regretfully.

"But Alistair might have?" He was grasping, and I couldn't blame him. "Brooke, you said he was some sort of…Shaman?"

"He is," she confirmed. "We can definitely ask him. He's usually pretty informative, but I don't know what he can do to help us find the killer. If they go to the same school, then maybe that's where we start."

"Yeah, we're investigating."

Nick looked at Brooke, then at Tom. "Teens don't even talk to their parents," he said, "so I doubt they're going to open up to a bunch of cops.

You almost need someone on the inside... Some-one their age."

Tom's eyes widened with interest, his head bobbing affirmatively. He seemed extremely receptive to Nick's idea. "That's not a terrible idea."

"It would have to be someone young if you want the kids to open up," Brooke interjected. "Nick's right. Teenagers will be reluctant to open up to adults—especially new faces. But they're all too willing to gossip amongst their peers."

Tom looked perplexed. "I don't know if we have anyone who looks young enough to pass as a student, so that could be a problem."

We all thought about that for a minute, each of us probably trying to find a solution, when we were interrupted.

"Send me."

The four of us turned to the open library door to find Colby standing in the hall. Her dark hair was pulled off her face and into a ponytail, and her eyes looked more rested than they had in almost a year. Still looking a little unsure of herself, she took a tentative step forward, not allowing her feet to cross the threshold, her eyes purposefully avoiding the spot where we found her father's body.

"I want to help," she clarified, standing tall and looking resolute as she projected with a confident tone. "Send me."